The Offer

A Novel

KARINA HALLE

First edition published by
Metal Blonde Books June 2015

Publisher's Note: This is a work of fiction. Names, characters, places, and incidents either are the product of the author's imagination or are used fictitiously. Any resemblance to actual events, locales, or persons, living or dead, is entirely coincidental.

Cover design by Hang Le Designs
Metal Blonde Books
P.O. Box 845
Point Roberts, WA
98281 USA
Manufactured in the USA
For more information about the series and author visit:
http://authorkarinahalle.com/

ISBN: 151436526X
ISBN-13: 9781514365267

For those who think they're lost in the struggle,
whatever that struggle may be.
You're not alone.
Keep on keeping on.

Also by Karina Halle

The Experiment in Terror Series

Darkhouse (EIT #1)

Red Fox (EIT #2)

The Benson (EIT #2.5)

Dead Sky Morning (EIT #3)

Lying Season (EIT #4)

On Demon Wings (EIT #5)

Old Blood (EIT #5.5)

The Dex-Files (EIT #5.7)

Into the Hollow (EIT #6)

And With Madness Comes the Light (EIT #6.5)

Come Alive (EIT #7)

Ashes to Ashes (EIT #8)

Dust to Dust (EIT #9)

Novels by Karina Halle

The Devil's Metal (Devils #1)

The Devil's Reprise (Devils #2)

Sins and Needles (The Artists Trilogy #1)

On Every Street (An Artists Trilogy Novella #0.5)

Shooting Scars (The Artists Trilogy #2)

Bold Tricks (The Artists Trilogy #3)

Donners of the Dead

Dirty Angels

Dirty Deeds

Love, in English

Love, in Spanish

Where Sea Meets Sky (from Atria Books)

Coming Soon

Dirty Promises

Racing the Sun (from Atria Books)

Table of Contents

Prologue

Six Months Earlier

"Live with no regrets."

"What was that, sweetheart?"

I slowly raised my gaze from the blank spot on the grass I'd been staring at for the last five minutes and saw the tall silhouette of a man as he crossed in front of the floodlights, coming toward me. I blinked a few times then looked back to the ground. His face was in shadows but I knew who he was. His Scottish accent told me everything I needed to know.

I cleared my throat and finished off the glass of wine in my hand. The raucous sounds of the wedding were dying down and I was surprised that Bram McGregor was still here. He was the best man while I was the maid of honor, but I never pegged him to be the type to stick around for very long, even at his own brother's wedding. Bram's eyebrows had been wagging at every female that walked within a five-meter distance, myself included, and he'd seemed so bored during the ceremony that it looked like he was trying to stifle a permanent yawn.

"Sorry," I said, clearing my throat. "Talking to myself."

"I can see that," he said, sitting down beside me on the stone bench and bringing with him a whiff of cigars and sandalwood.

We were around the side of the Tiburon Yacht Club's lawn where the wedding had taken place. I had stumbled upon the bench and the garden, with the lights of the city across San Francisco Bay twinkling in the background. I was ready to call it a night and just wanted to be alone before I headed back to my apartment to relieve the babysitter. Even though my best friend Stephanie was getting married to a great guy, Bram's brother Linden—and don't get me wrong, I couldn't be happier for her—it was a wedding, I was single and feeling worse about it every minute that passed.

"So, live with no regrets," he repeated, casually leaning forward on his knees and lacing his fingers together. If I was sober I would have felt a bit embarrassed that he had caught me talking to myself, but as it was I couldn't care less. What Bram thought of me was the least of my problems.

I shrugged. "It's my motto."

He snorted and I immediately glared at him.

"Hey," I said, my face growing hot. "Most people have mottos."

The corner of his lips twitched up into a smile. He was a handsome man, I had to give him that. But after my ex fucked me over so loyally after I was pregnant, leaving me alone to raise our daughter, playboys were on my hit list and Bram McGregor was definitely a playboy. Which meant he was public enemy number one and nothing but a whole lot of trouble and hot air.

I'd made it my goal in life to avoid trouble. I wasn't about to start now, just because of his Scottish brogue, grey eyes, dimpled smile and built physique. And, you know, other terrible attributes.

"I don't," he informed me, as his eyes slid to mine, mouth lifting up. "But does it count if other people have mottos about you?"

I didn't want to ask him what he meant by that, yet somehow my mouth was opening and I was taking the bait.

"People have mottos about you?" I asked.

His smirk deepened. "Women do."

"I see," I said, trying to think of something clever that would take him down a peg. "Once you go Bram…"

"You won't give a damn," he filled. He looked up at the dark sky and tilted his head, considering. "Or I've heard one night in my bed and your legs are forever spread."

My lip curled in mild disgust. "That's terrible."

He shrugged. "Don't knock it till you try it, sweetheart." He paused. "I guess that's another motto for you."

He eyed the empty glass in my hands, then me, and blinked as if seeing me for the first time tonight. For a hot second I was glad that Stephanie had picked out the most flattering cocktail-type bridesmaids dress from Anthropologie. Then I had to remind myself, once again, that I didn't care what he thought of me.

"What?" I asked, my skin prickling at the fact that his gaze was skirting over my body for just a little too long.

"Why are you out here alone and sober?"

I twirled the stem of the wine glass between my fingers. "I'm not sober."

"I suppose you're not alone either," he said. "Can I get you another drink?"

"You're offering?" I don't know why that surprised me but it did.

He stared at for me for a moment, his dark brows knit together. Then he relaxed, his grin widening lazily. It reminded me of a cat stretching after a nap.

"I never let a beautiful woman pay for a drink," he said.

Though part of me (a small part) thrilled at the fact that he called me beautiful, especially after how rough my dating life had been lately and how the only person that called me beautiful lately was Ava (okay, and Steph before the wedding, once I was magically transformed through hair and makeup), I wasn't about to let his slick words charm me.

I gave him a steady look. "Do you really think I'm going to fall for that pick-up line?"

He let out a laugh, eyes twinkling in the dark. "Pick-up line? The best man can't get the best woman a drink? You know, I heard you were no fun, I just didn't believe it. Not with that body."

I was stunned. My face flushed hot and somehow I found my words. "Who told you I was no fun?"

His smile was softer now but it still looked like he was having the time of his life toying with me. "It doesn't matter. I gave you the benefit of the doubt, but I guess they were right after all."

"Was it Linden?" I asked, feeling nauseous. I liked Linden a lot, and though his own personal opinion of me didn't really matter, I hated the idea that I was known for something negative, especially if it was something I feared. I used to be fun at some point, I swear to God, but when life gets hard, fun becomes something that gets swept under the rug along with manicures, one-night stands and eating at nice restaurants.

Bram didn't say anything to that, so I knew it was his brother.

"It's hard to tell, is your face going red?" he asked, peering at me closely. The mellow scent of cigars wafted to me again.

"I am fun," I told him, inching myself away from him. It was pointless but I still had to defend myself.

"And that's why you're out here alone with an empty drink?"

"Just because I'm not getting shitfaced and spreading my legs in your bed, doesn't make me a square."

Oh geez, a square? Now I was talking like I was from the 50's.

"No," he said slowly and leaned in closer. "But that does sound like fun, doesn't it?" His breath was hot on my cheek and I resisted the urge to turn and look at him. There was something about his eyes that felt vaguely X-Ray-ish, like he could see right through you. Already, I knew he was probably imagining what I looked like naked under this dress. I didn't need him to look any deeper and see what kind of no-fun mess I really was.

"I like it when you look embarrassed," he said, voice lower, that accent roughing up each syllable. "I bet you look the same when you're about to come. Caught off-guard and exposed."

And again, I was speechless. My eyes bugged out and I almost slapped him in the face and ran away, because that's what I've been taught to do with men like him. Deflect them. Let them know what they'll never have, what they'll never deserve.

But I didn't do that. Because against everything I hold dear, his words did this slinky thing in my brain, sliding down into my heart and between my legs. It made me want to clench my thighs together to keep the heat building even though it had nowhere to go.

It revved an engine inside that I tried my hardest not to think about.

I swallowed hard and kept my eyes focused on the shrubs in front of me. The wedding sounded even further away, as if it were leaving in order to get us alone.

Bram gently placed two fingers underneath my chin and slowly turned my head, so I had no choice but to look at him. "If I tell you you're beautiful again," he said, whispering, "will you blush? Or will you believe it?"

Damn. Damn, damn, damn. I'd be a fool for falling for this swarmy little act, but boy did I want to believe it.

At least I didn't blush. There wasn't any time to.

Before I knew what was happening, Bram leaned in a millimeter and kissed me. His lips were soft and wet, tasting like rich tobacco and mint. I sucked in a breath, my body frozen and caught-off guard, exactly what he wanted. The back of my brain screamed, "The best man and maid of honor, hooking up at a wedding, what a cliché!" and "He's a player and he's playing you" while my lips, spurred by alcohol and a deep-rooted ache for *something*, kissed him back.

It all went in slow motion. The voices in my head quieted down, turning to a hazy hush, and all that was left was this stoked fire burning deep inside. His hands went to the sides of my face and he held me there with strong, warm fingers. It steadied me as his tongue slipped against mine and our mouths danced with each other in perfect rhythm. If I could have formed any thoughts, I would have considered that this wasn't at all what I thought kissing Bram McGregor would be like. This was soft, sensual and, dare I say it, meaningful.

Just as I found myself relaxing into his body, though, wanting more from his hands, wanting to slip my own underneath the tuxedo jacket and feel the hardness of his chest, he pulled back, eyes closed and breath ragged.

"You're beautiful," he said, clearing his throat. His eyes opened, gazing at me lazily through long, dark lashes, lashes I would kill for. "You're still blushing, though. Actually, you seem a little more than flushed." He raised a brow, his face still inches from mine. "Did I turn you on?"

My God, this guy was forward. I know that Linden had always been rather lewd and definitely very vocal with Steph, but Bram was taking it to another level.

My mouth parted while I tried to think of words and he ran his thumb over my bottom lip. "Such a beautiful mouth. What else can you do with it?"

Finally I blinked, clueing in that he was being rather crude. I flinched and brought my head away.

He frowned. "Ah, don't get your knickers in a twist," he said, his hand slipping down to my arm. "I've been watching you all night, you know."

"Well, that's not hard to do when we're part of the wedding party," I said, my voice suddenly parched, like kissing him had taken a lot out of me. I suppose it had at least taken my sanity.

"You have a hard time taking compliments," he commented.

That, I knew was true. I wasn't ugly or even plain by any means, but motherhood – and being ditched by my ex – had taken its toll on my self-esteem. There was a time when I used to walk into the room and own it, or at least believe in what I was offering, but I hadn't felt that confidence in a long time.

Even the attention of Bram, a wealthy, eligible Scotsman, wasn't helping. Probably because I knew his reputation as a lady-killer and, even though he wasn't drinking at this exact moment, I could taste the Scotch on his lips.

Oh, those damn lips. I quickly tore my eyes off of them, trying to forget their feel, their sweet, captivating taste.

"Did that surfer dude say anything you believed?"

Surfer dude? I had to take a moment to realize what he was talking about.

"Aaron?" I asked. "That's Stephanie's ex-boyfriend."

His shoulder raised in a lazy shrug. "She's a married woman now, I'm sure he's up for grabs. He was hitting on you all night."

That I knew, though Aaron had such a casual, dopey way of doing it, it hadn't bothered me. "You really were watching me."

He smiled softly. "Most beautiful woman at the wedding." He paused. "Aside from the bride, of course, but I have to say that." He put his hand behind my head and I tried not to flinch at the thought of him messing up my updo. "How about you and I ditch this scene? I think Stephanie and Linden left a while ago and the night is still young."

Things were happening way too fast. As much as his words seemed to unravel the tight binds inside me, the ones that kept me sane and respectable, as much as the rough gravel of his voice made my hairs stand on end, I had responsibilities and they didn't involve having a one-night stand with Bram McGregor. Even though that little voice, the one that did like "fun" and was so often buried, was pinching my insides, demanding I live a little, I couldn't. Besides, it's not like this could ever be more than a fling, not with someone like him.

He leaned in close again and very gently brushed his lips against mine, shooting heat into my veins. "Come on," he murmured. "I know there's a wild child somewhere deep inside you. I can tell. Let her loose. Let me help."

Oh God. If only he could.

"I can't," I said quietly. "I have to go home."

He smiled against my mouth. It felt wonderful. "Bring me home with you. I promise to behave myself." He kissed me softly, long and lingering before slowly, achingly, pulling away. "Actually, I promise to misbehave," he said huskily. "But I know you'll like it."

I took the moment to put an inch of distance between our faces. "You don't understand. I have to pay the babysitter. She'll want to leave soon."

I didn't expect him to freeze like he did, only because I had assumed he knew I had a child. But from the way his brows came together, I could tell this was news to him.

"Babysitter?" he said, clearing his throat. "You have a kid?"

I nodded, feeling my defenses go up bit by bit like I was rebuilding a wall that had momentarily come down. "Ava. She's five."

"I didn't know that about you," he said, blinking a few times. Why did men always have to freak out when they found out I was a single mom? You'd think in this so-called progressive day and age men would at least be a little more open-minded about, if not exposed to the situation more often. Besides, I was thirty-one, not a teenager.

I couldn't help but flash him an acidic smile. "There's a lot you don't know about me." When I thought about it, I guess I had only met him a couple of times before and they were usually in social situations where the most I got was a handshake or a nod and that was it. I don't think I had talked to him alone until tonight.

He looked at the watch on his wrist, something I had noticed for the first time. It gleamed silver in the outdoor lights. "Well, I guess you better be on your way then, Cinderella."

"Is it almost midnight?" I asked, feeling awkward now about everything. I slowly got to my feet and they screamed in pain from the Ross Atwood sandals that Steph had gifted me for the wedding. Sexy they were, comfortable they weren't.

He stood up beside me and even in my heels, which added four inches to my five-foot-seven body, he was still a lot taller than I was. I tried not to take in how devilishly handsome he looked in his tux, how close I was to feeling what I knew had to be the very hard lines of his body. All the things I tried to ignore about him earlier were now all I could see, flashing like a neon sign that screamed, "*Hot fuck, one night only*."

"Aye," he said in his brogue. "Can I call you a cab?"

I shook my head. "I'm going to Uber it."

He stared at me for a moment as if thinking then he nodded. "Too bad I can't convince you to let your hair down, if just for the night."

I gave him a look, my fingers clenching the empty wine glass. "Letting your hair down isn't always an option for a single mom."

"Right," he said. "Let me at least take you back to the party." He held out his arm for me, and after a moment's hesitation, I took it. I have to say it felt nice as he led me out of the garden and into the reception area as if he were my date for the night.

But as soon as we got close to people, he dropped his arm and gave me a quick smile. "Get home safe, sweetheart."

So, that was it.

I watched as he slid into the crowd of lingering people and headed for the bar. The party was still going, though he was right that Stephanie and Linden must have left because I didn't see them anywhere. I did see the fathers and mothers of both bride and groom, as well as Aaron, Kayla, Penny, James and a few other of our mutual friends. Most were dancing and having a fun time, drunk as hell, while in the background the boats in the marina swayed lightly with the waves.

Sometimes being Cinderella really sucked.

Sighing, I fished out my phone and ordered an Uber cab. It was a busy Saturday night, so the driver was fifteen minutes away. I headed toward the gates to the yacht club and sat on an iron bench beside a marble anchor, giving my feet another rest. I tried to keep watching the road to see if my Uber was pulling up, but when I heard a loud giggle, I had to turn my head back to the reception.

There, in the distance, was Bram with his arm around some skinny blonde chick I'd seen earlier. I think one of Steph's distant cousins. She looked way young, way drunk and way into Bram.

Unfortunately, he looked to be the same way about her. While her heel caught in the grass and she nearly went stumbling, he caught her and brought her to him. She laughed and kissed him and he eagerly kissed her back, pressing her lithe body and slinky dress to him. Her hand slipped down to his crotch and pressed it against what must have been quite the erection.

He grinned at her, that stupid, wicked grin, and took her toward the garden area we had just come from, disappearing behind the rose bushes. Her giggles floated through the air and I couldn't help but picture him stripping her naked, bending her over the bench, and unzipping his pants.

I watched the bushes for a moment, seeing them rustle, feeling both sick and strangely turned-on.

That could have been me.

But it wasn't. And when I started hearing her breathy moans, I snapped out of it. Jesus, he was fast to move on after he figured out he wasn't going to get lucky with me.

By the time the car pulled up for me, all my feelings had swirled into a cauldron of shame and anger. What a fucking pig! I was lucky as hell I didn't end up throwing caution – or my panties – to the wind and sleeping with that slimy Scottish jackass. I had been right all along. He was trouble, danger, and I needed to stay away from men like him. Only now I wished I hadn't even kissed him back, let alone exchanged words with him at all.

While I stewed in the back of the Uber car as we crossed over the Golden Gate Bridge, I thought back to my motto. Live with no regrets? I was definitely regretting that I let him even think he could have slept with me that night.

I also had another motto: Fool me once, shame on me. You won't fool me twice. My pride will never, ever let me fall for something again.

If Bram McGregor wasn't on my hit list before, he definitely was now.

Chapter One

NICOLA

"Nicola Price, you're fired," my boss says to me in his most Donald Trump-like expression. Only he's not smiling like it's a joke and his coif is so shellacked with hair goop that it would put Mr. Trump to shame.

Also, I'm pretty sure he actually said, "Nicola, we're so sorry to tell you this, but we're going to have to let you go." But what's the difference when they pretty much mean the same thing? In one damn second I've lost my job. My income. My stability.

My future.

It's a wonder I don't have a meltdown like the ones Ava throws when she can't find her favorite plush toy, Snuffy. Or even leak a single tear. Instead, I just sit there like an idiot, a frozen, slack-jawed failure, while my boss, Ross (ex-boss now, I guess), prattles on about how sorry he is and how he wished they could have kept me but the company is downsizing and they're removing one of the stores and yadda, yadda, yadda.

But none of that matters whatsoever since I know I'm one week shy of having worked for them for three months.

In one week, I would have finished my probationary period and my health insurance would have rolled in. I would have gotten a raise. I would have gotten peace of mind and a career in the field I've been striving for.

And now I'm angry because I realize these assholes knew they'd never offer me a permanent position, they just wanted the cheap fucking labor. This had been their plan all along, to string me along under false pretences and then kick me to the curb before it became serious.

Sounds a lot like my love life, come to think about it.

"Is there anything we can do for you?" he asks, peering at me with concern, perhaps watching my face for signs of an imminent explosion.

Ava, it always comes back to my daughter. If it weren't for her, I probably would have just nodded at the dismissal. Take it graciously like I try to do with everything life throws my way, like I'd been taught at a young age. Never let them see you cry; never let them see you as anything but perfectly appropriate. Suck it up and carry on, a vision of cool.

But my life at the moment isn't cool and there isn't a single appropriate thing about it. My rent at my shitty apartment recently increased. My car needs a part I can't afford, so it just sits on the curb collecting rust from San Francisco's eternal mist, and Ava has been increasingly sick lately. Nothing to worry about, the doctor says, just lethargic on some days but I've got an endless supply of worry for my kiddo and not always enough money to pay for a doctor's visit. Not to mention a pretty useless doctor at that. I was counting on that goddamn medical insurance for her, not for me.

And so, like Bruce Banner when he turns into the Hulk – minus the shirt-ripping – I let it all unleash on my unsuspecting ex-boss. For three months I have been prim and proper and yes sir, no sir, running around all the stores like an overworked slave, all while keeping a big smile on my face. Never let them see you sweat. Always keep your cool.

Fuck that.

I'm not even sure what to say. It's like I go into some deep, black pit of pent-up resentment. I think I even blackout for a moment. All I know is that when I realize what I'm doing, I'm standing up, my finger jabbing in the air towards my ex-boss, and I'm spewing a load of obscenities.

"You know if you had just fucked me over sideways, that would have been fine. But you're hurting my daughter by doing this. How dare you just toss me aside a week before my health insurance kicked in!" I yell at him. "Don't you have a damn heart?"

But from the way Ross calmly picks up his phone and asks his assistant, Meredith, to come in the room as if I need to be escorted out, I can see he doesn't have a heart at all.

Meredith has never liked me and the last thing I need is her gloating, so I hightail it out of his office before she can get a glimpse of my red and distraught face. I quickly gather my purse from my cubby in the staffroom, grateful for once that while I was the company's visual stylist for the past three months, I never had a desk of my own. What a pain that would be to clean out.

I don't even say goodbye to Priscilla, the buyer whom I'd become somewhat close with, or Tabby, the regional merchandiser, someone whose job I hoped to have one day.

I'm just too ashamed to tell them what just happened and I feel worse when I suspect maybe they knew all along.

When I first got the job for the popular yoga clothing chain, Rusk, I thought I'd finally made it. I'd spent enough time taking two steps forward and one step backward. The city doesn't always make it easy on you, no matter what industry you're in. And fashion is definitely one of the more challenging ones.

I went to college with Stephanie at the Art Institute in downtown San Francisco, connecting with her after being decades apart. I grew up near Steph in Petaluma, a town north of the city, and I knew her in grade school until my parents got divorced and I moved with my mom to the Pacific Heights in San Francisco to live with her terribly rich new husband. Long story short, after spending high school with the rich kids – and being one of the rich kids – I enrolled myself in college, wanting to do something with my passion for fashion. After all, the garments I designed and made in my spare time, ones with screen-printed graphics and kooky phrases, would never grant me an income or a career. They were good but not "that good" (as my ex-stepfather had pointed out). So, I thought a career in fashion merchandising would be the next best thing.

And it was. I mean, school was amazing. I finally felt in my element, surrounded by people who understood my passion, who "got" me. But finding jobs after school wasn't so easy. And even though I managed to snag a few internships in some pretty important places (Banana Republic being one of them), I struggled to find a job that was related to my field and paid enough to give Ava everything she needed.

That's usually what it came down to, my daughter. Her arrival was a curveball to my perfectly crafted life but I took it in stride, determined to love her. And I do, with all my heart. I never regretted keeping her for a second. But it was Phil, my baby daddy's leaving that really undid me. And after that, everything just kind of kept falling apart. Me and Ava against the world.

One day, though, while I was still with Phil, I thought my prayers had been answered. I had gotten a job at an online jewelry store as the copywriter and buyer. It was actually pretty amazing. The pay was excellent and all signs pointed to a long and promising career. But online retail is a cutthroat and fickle industry, so after a couple of years the site went bankrupt. I was out of a job. Then I was out of a boyfriend. Then my mother cheated on her new husband and, thanks to the indemnity clause, I was out of any extra financial support as I bounced around the city from a nice apartment to a so-so studio to a run-down in the sketchy Tenderloin district trying to find work again in the industry.

Finally, after a yearlong maternity leave stint as a sales clerk in the Nordstrom shoe department (not at all what I wanted to do but it paid the bills), I came across the position at Rusk. I thought I found something that would kindle my passion while providing the financial support I wanted for Ava. It's not that she asked for anything, but I wanted to be able to give her whatever she desired. I'd do anything for her including working my ass off just so she could have all of life's opportunities.

Rusk promised a great career in visual merchandising and an amazing paycheck with fabulous benefits. Even though my probationary salary was barely above minimum wage, I was fueled by their beautiful promises. I quit Nordstrom and jumped at the chance. I really thought everything would change.

And it did. For the worst. Now...now I'm hurrying past the people on Sutter Street on the verge of a panic attack. Every person's face is a blank blur and my vision occasionally clouds over as tears swarm my eyes, hot and potent. They never fall, though. That has to mean something. That I'm a trooper. That I will get past this.

I will find another job. I will find another chance.

Sometimes I feel life is just one episode after another of trying to find another way. I wonder what happens when you discover there is no other way this time.

I make my way down Leavenworth as the streets become a little less clean and the people a little less friendly. Or too friendly, depending on how you look at it. The same man with his toothless smile asks me for change outside a liquor store, but today I don't spare him a cent. I just keep my head down and brush through the riff raff of the neighborhood, a place I've resented ever since it became my only option in this high-priced city until I'm unlocking the door into the lobby of the apartment building.

Pausing, I stare at the door just as I'm about to close it behind me. The door is glass and there are long vertical bars on the windows, indicative of the neighborhood. I remember when Phil moved out and I lost my job at the online retailer, how I could no longer afford to live in Noe Valley, a gorgeous neighborhood next to the Castro. That apartment was everything to me but there was no way I could afford to live there on my own while supporting Ava. The two of us bounced from apartment to apartment, the standards of living slipping each time, until I found myself staring up at the bruised façade of this building, both hoping I could get an apartment and promising myself I'd move us out of there the first chance I got.

It looked like that chance wasn't going to happen for quite some time.

I sigh, my heart a stone in my chest, and make my way up to the second floor. My mom usually babysits during the day on Thursdays and Fridays and I pay Lisa, my usual sitter, to watch Ava the rest of the time. I've been trying to get her into some affordable daycare but that shit is hard to come by in the city. The waiting lists are epic and you really have to be wary of where you put your kid. Before I had Ava, I had no idea how difficult it could be to keep your child secure and safe. I thought daycare and babysitters and education and healthcare would be easy, maybe because I had it easy growing up (or maybe as a child, you just don't pay attention to those things). But now I know better.

No one is looking out for you or your child but you.

I slip my keys in the door and quietly open it just in case Ava is down for a nap. The apartment is a one-bedroom but only about 550 square feet. I made it as beautiful as possible, though, and in my opinion it looks just as good as my fancier place in Noe Valley did. To be honest, it's pretty much an Anthropologie showroom. I couldn't afford to shop there anymore so I held onto my old stuff like it was gold, gluing back coffee cups if the handles fell off or sewing curtains back together if Ava tugged on them too hard (which has happened more than once).

Ava and Lisa are playing with dolls on the shag carpet and the moment I step in, Ava smiles that big, gorgeous bright smile of hers and gets up, running over to me. She wraps her arms around my leg and before I can even shut the door behind me, I crouch down to her level and envelope her in a giant hug. Just being around my daughter elevates my mood and increases my heart rate. It makes things both hard and easy at the same time, something I have a hard time figuring out myself. I think sometimes when you love something too much, you're that much more aware of how much you have to lose. Holding my little girl in my arms brings me peace but makes me realize that I'm going to have to do everything in my power to make sure she's okay in the end.

When I pull away, Ava looks at my face with open curiosity. "Mommy, why are you crying?"

I hadn't even noticed. I quickly wipe my tears on my shoulders and give her a shaky smile. "I'm fine, angel," I tell her.

Lisa is standing up, wiping her hands on her jeans. I get to my own feet, close the door behind me and put my hand on Ava's ash-blonde head. Normally my hair is long and dark brown, many shades darker than Ava's, but Steph recently chopped it off to shoulder-length and put lots of highlights in it. I tell her when she's done with running her own business she should become a hairdresser instead.

"Everything okay?" Lisa asks, peering at me through her glasses. Tall, reed-thin and sporting an ever-present ponytail, Lisa's a whip-smart student who seems wise beyond her age, sometimes more mature than me. She's been looking after Ava for two years now, whenever she can fit it into her schedule. I don't want to let her go and I have no idea how I'm going to even broach the subject, but the fact is I don't see how I can possibly afford her while I'm out of work.

Shit, if I ended it a bit better there's a chance I could have at least worked the last week and gotten more money. I doubt I can even put Rusk on my résumé now after the way I yelled at Ross. No one wants to hire a crazy person.

I give Lisa a small shake of my head and tell Ava to go into our shared bedroom and put her doll to bed. She runs off and I collapse onto the couch with a hard exhale.

"What is it?" Lisa asks, sitting on the arm of the couch.

I chew on my lip for a moment, avoiding her gaze. "I got fired today."

She breathes in sharply. "What, are you serious? Why?"

I shrug. "They told me a whole bunch of bullshit about closing down some of their stores, but they weren't the stores I worked at anyway. I think they just wanted cheap labor."

"Dude, that sucks," she says. "What are you going to do?"

I eye her apologetically. "Look for another job. But until I find one, I'm afraid I can't afford to pay you anymore. Money is going to be really tight around here."

Her face scrunches up for a moment but it quickly becomes sympathetic. I forget that she may have depended on me the same way I depended on her. "I understand. And I'm sure you'll find something really fast."

"I hope so," I tell her. "I kind of have to."

She gives my shoulder a light pat. "Well, I better get going. I guess you don't want me to sit tomorrow night?"

I give her a quizzical look and then quickly remember. "Shit," I swear loudly while hoping Ava doesn't hear me. Linden's birthday is tomorrow night and he's celebrating it on a Tuesday instead of the weekend like any normal human being. I eye Lisa. "No, I guess not. It's best I stay home."

She nods and picks up her purse from the counter. For a moment she looks like *she's* going to cry.

"I'll text you as soon as I've got something lined up," I tell her and she gives me a quick smile before she walks out the door and closes it behind her.

The apartment is silent for a few moments and I can't even hear Ava playing in the bedroom. Then comes her small voice, "Mommy?"

I get up, feeling extremely old all of a sudden, and shuffle over to the bedroom. I lean against the doorway and see Ava putting her doll in her bed. She looks up at me, full-cheeked and proud.

"See, I take care of her. Like you take care of me."

It takes all that I have not to break down in front of her.

...

I spent last night in a daze, cuddling with Ava on the couch watching her favorite shows and trying not to think about anything except Dora the Explorer's terrible haircut and fashion sense. After Ava went to bed, I finished half a bottle of wine, flipped through *Vogue* and *Harper's Bazaar* and avoided texts from Steph and Kayla, also letting a call from my mom go to voice mail. They didn't know anything and I wanted to keep it that way for as long as possible.

My father, before my mom left him and he jetted across the world to India to do charity work (wish I could have done that after Phil ditched me) used to tease me about my pride. My mom and I both suffer from it, never admitting our faults, never asking for help.

But now in the cold, grey light of day, as I'm able to sleep in for a bit and explain to Ava that her mother will be home with her for the next while, I know I have to face the music. I need to get my life on track as best I can. If I can do it without anyone's help or anyone feeling sorry for me, then all the better.

I spend the morning going through Craigslist and a bunch of other job sites before the anxiety becomes too much and I take Ava to a playground in Little Saigon. After, we get Pho and I keep checking my phone, hoping to hear back about something already. It's maddening applying for jobs. Each time I read a job description that I fall in love with, I become obsessed with it. All my hopes go riding on it as if the job will make my life a million times better, as if I even have a chance. Not being able to put Rusk on my résumé really put my career a step back, too.

After the fifth text gets ignored, Steph finally calls me just as I'm putting Ava down for a nap. I close the door to the room, take in a deep breath and answer the phone.

"Hey," I say brightly. "You never call."

"Because you usually answer your texts," she says quickly. "Where have you been?"

"Here," I tell her.

"Like in California, or somewhere more specific?"

"Just…here."

"Are you okay?"

This is why I didn't want to talk to Steph. She usually has a sixth sense about things.

"Mmmm." A non-committal answer is best.

"You're still coming out tonight, right?"

"Well..."

"Nicola!" she says. "I haven't seen you for weeks."

That's true, though that's more on her end. She's been super busy with her new online business. She used to run her store, Fog and Cloth, in a bricks and mortar location but went online to go with the times. But, as it was for the company I used to work for, it hasn't been easy. It's very competitive and she's a two-woman show so far, having only one person working for her in the warehouse. I rarely see her, especially coming into the summer season.

"Look," I say, pushing my hair behind my ears and eyeing the bottle of wine on the kitchen counter. I'd give my left boob to have a glass right now but I wouldn't dare with Ava under my care. "Something's come up and I don't have Lisa to sit right now."

"What happened?"

"I don't want to talk about it."

"But I want to know."

I roll my eyes. "Well, you always want to know." I take in a deep breath. "Okay, promise not to make a big deal about it?"

"Yeah..."

"Actually promise you won't talk about it? At all."

Silence. "Maybe."

"Then I'm not telling."

"Oh, come the fuck on."

"Whoa, language, angry lady. Your husband is rubbing off on you."

At that she giggles and I have to roll my eyes again. I believe that even if the person can't see you roll your eyes, they can tell.

"Never mind," I quickly say, "you pervert."

"Seriously," she says. "I won't talk about it. Just tell me."

And so I launch into it. To her credit, she doesn't say a word until I've caught her up to speed, breathless and angry all over again.

"Wow," she says. "That...well, I won't talk about it. But...seriously?"

"Stephanie," I warn.

She groans. "Okay, fine. But you have to come out tonight. You can't be there alone."

"Maybe you didn't hear the part about me not having a babysitter."

"Bring Ava along!"

I almost laugh. "Yeah, right. To a bar?"

"Well, maybe not the bar, but we're meeting at our place first for an hour or two, for pre-drinks. At least you can come to that."

"I can't even afford a cab and my car is still messed up."

"Don't worry about it," she says. "I'll take care of you."

"I don't need anyone to take care of me," I tell her, feeling my hackles go up.

"I know, but still. I've got you, okay? That's what friends are for. I'll get a car to you and you'll come here and we'll have a nice time with friends and we won't discuss anything you don't want to. Please. Don't make me beg."

"But I like it when you beg."

"So does Linden."

"Okay, TMI, I'm hanging up now."

She giggles again. "Sorry. All righty, be ready at 6pm. We'll have appies here so don't worry about dinner either and I'll fix something up for Ava. And by that, I mean Linden will since he's the only one who knows how to cook. See you soon and hang in there. You're going to be okay."

I hang up the phone not at all wanting to be around people, even if they are my friends. But I also don't want to have a staring contest with that half-drunk bottle of wine either and spend the evening wallowing in feelings of panic and inadequacy.

Luckily as I take a quick shower and get ready for the evening, I feel my spirit perk up a bit. It's probably because I haven't gone out in a really long time and there's something about dressing up that makes me feel like I'm in my element. I bring out the waves in my hair, squeeze myself into a pair of skinny jeans and a white fluttery, off-the-shoulder top, add a pop of red lipstick and I've got this sultry señorita look going on, even though with the freckles on my nose and my English rose skin, I'm the furthest thing from it.

Ava is beyond excited to go to an "adult party." She seems to copy my lead by spending a lot of time picking out an outfit, even though in the end she wants to wear her SpongeBob pillowcase. I put her in a purple dress instead and we head downstairs to wait for the cab to show up, booster seat in tow.

When I see a navy blue Mercedes pull to the curb, I wonder if Stephanie ordered the priciest Uber in town.

The car parks and I hold Ava's hand, remaining at the door to my building until I know for sure they're there for us. When the driver's side opens and a tall gentleman in a suit gets out, I know it can't be for me. No Uber driver dresses that well.

That is, until I see his face.

Bram. Fucking. McGregor.

I blink. My cheeks grow hot and I'm wishing this is all a huge mistake. Bram can't be here for me, can he? I mean, the last time I saw Bram was at Steph and Linden's wedding and even though we shared a hot make-out session, it wasn't long before he found another pair of lips to hook up with. And by "not long," I mean minutes.

"Nicola," he says in his Scottish accent, looking incredibly dapper as he leans across his spiffy car. "Are you ready?"

Oh, fuck. He *is* here for me.

I nearly drop the booster seat.

I squeeze Ava's hand and take in a deep breath. I want to kill Stephanie, even though I never told her I made out with her brother-in-law, so there's no way she could possibly know that I hate Bram with a passion.

Remember what I said about pride and how it's something I've got in spades? Well, Bram bruised that far more than he could possibly know.

And now I have to get in a car with him, with my daughter, when I'm at one of the lowest moments of my life.

He eyes the heavy seat in my hands. "Do you need a hand?"

I'm this close to telling him, "Thanks, but no thanks," and that I've changed my mind all together about the party. But Ava pulls me forward toward the car, as if I've never taught her to be aware of strangers, and says, "Come, mommy. His car is shiny."

She's going to get herself in a whole load of trouble when she's older.

My eyes briefly meet Bram's and it brings out one hell of a jackass smile from him, a smile that boils my blood.

I guess I'm going to the party with Bram McGregor.

Shit.

Chapter Two

NICOLA

I steady myself, throw my shoulders back and hold my head up just like I used to do in high school when I was the new girl in the halls and not accepted yet into the throngs of mean girls with inflated self-entitlement. I flash Bram a confident, albeit hella fake, smile and walk over to his car, all prepared to handle the situation with ease.

But he's fast and he comes around the hood and right up to me, quickly taking the booster seat out of my hands. I'm prepared for him to smell like cigars and mint again, but this time it's just something fresh and earthy like the woods after it rains.

"I can handle it," I tell him. I can't help but snipe at him, aware that I'm being a bit of a bitch.

He doesn't seem to notice and before I can ask him if he knows what he's doing, he's opening the back door to the vehicle and strapping the seat in like a pro.

I'm almost impressed. "You always give rides to moms?"

He raises his brow. "None as beautiful as you." He looks at Ava and crouches down to her level. "What's your name, little one?"

"I'm not, little one," she says, frowning. "I'm Ava. And I'm a big girl."

He nods, his face sincere. Now looking at him in the waning daylight, he looks different than I remember six months ago. Older, I guess, though I know he has to be around thirty-five. Maybe the suit and the way it cuts to his body perfectly is making him look more mature. Maybe it's the car. Maybe it's the few strands of grey I can see at the temple of his thick head of dark hair. Maybe it's because I'm sober and so is he. At least, I hope so.

"So, are you the designated driver for the night?" I ask him, picking up Ava and placing her in the booster seat. "Or did you lose a bet?"

"I never lose bets," he says smoothly as he stands behind me. I quickly look over my shoulder and catch him checking out my ass.

"Get a good look?" I straighten up and turn around.

"Of your arse?" he asks, sticking his hands into his pockets in a boyish gesture. "Yes. But only because I know it bugs you so much. You know, anything that's remotely sexual."

My eyes widen and I look down at Ava. She's completely oblivious and I carefully shut the door. "Look," I quickly say, pointing at him. "You may think you know me from our little…meeting, but you don't."

He reaches out and grasps my finger in his hand. His skin is warm and surprisingly soft, but then again, even though he may have the body for it, I'm sure Bram didn't get his money from chopping trees all day or doing hard labor.

"Hey," he says, voice gruff, still holding onto my finger. "I know we don't really know each other and when we last, erm, talked, well, I may have been a few sheets to the wind. But how about we start again? I'm Bram McGregor."

He turns my hand over so that he's now holding it in a handshake. I'm not sure I can do this as easily as he can, but I find myself saying, "Okay. I'm Nicola. Price."

"Pleasure to meet you, Nicola Price. Can I give you a ride?"

I nod. "That would be nice." I know my voice sounds stiff, but I guess it's a start. The problem with my pride, though, is that it rarely lets me forget when it's been burned.

Luckily Bram is completely genial during the drive to Linden's apartment in Nob Hill. He spends most of it talking to Ava in the rear-view mirror, asking her questions and treating her like she's an adult. I can tell Ava adores it and by the time we're close to Steph and Linden's, she's all googly-eyed over him. This is not good. Can't she be like her mom and be suspicious of the men who smile too brightly and say all the right things?

Though I guess with Bram, he has a habit of saying all the wrong things.

"So, Nicola," he says slowly as we wind through traffic. "You know, I don't know much about you. Linden says you work in fashion like Stephanie."

I did, I think bitterly but I manage to say, "Uh-huh."

"So what's your job?"

"What's your job?" I ask, deflecting it back to him. Besides, I'm curious. In the past, Linden only described Bram as a playboy (or "bloody manwhore" I believe were his exact words) who didn't do much but party it up in New York City. He moved to San Francisco a year ago, I guess to be close to Linden who had a frightful helicopter crash at the time, but I don't know what he really does except flash those perfect teeth at people.

"I'm an apartment manager," he says and when he sees the disbelieving look in my eyes, he goes on. "I'm serious. Well, to be more correct, I own an apartment complex in SOMA. Folsom and twelfth beside a Thai restaurant."

He's looking at me like I'll know, like most newbies to the Bay Area do, like we know every Thai restaurant in town and every person called Dan.

"That couldn't be cheap," I say, looking back out the window as we crawl past the cars. There are so many gorgeous buildings in this city, places to die for, and over and over again I can't help but wonder who can afford to live here. I once met an Uber driver who used to drive trucks across the country, who grew up in the city. He said back then, San Francisco was full of children. Now, you rarely see them. Sometimes I wonder if it would be better for Ava, and for me, to just move to a small town where she can have a different kind of life. Then I think about my dreams for my future, my career, and wonder if it's okay for me to give up on them. I know it's selfish of me not to, but I still can't quite let go.

"Nothing in life is cheap," Bram says but I barely hear him. I have to bring myself back into the moment and stop my head and my worries from running away on me. I came out tonight to put those on the backburner. God knows I'll have more than enough time to worry after this.

"Am I boring you?" he asks and I turn my head to look at him.

"No. Sorry, I was just thinking."

"About what?"

My brows lift up. "I don't think we're at that 'let's tell each other what we're thinking' stage."

"Not yet."

Not ever, I think. But I don't want to answer any more questions about myself, so I ask him to tell me more about the apartment and I force myself to listen. The more he talks about it, though, the more I see this is something he's actually stressing a bit over. I mean, it's hard to tell if Bram is stressed or not because he always has that charmer expression on his face like he's always trying to get in someone's pants, male or female. But there's a harder glint to his eyes when he talks about the rent of the building and how much he has to charge in order to make his mortgage.

"So why did you buy it?" I ask.

He shrugs. "I needed to do something."

"Well, I wouldn't worry about it," I tell him. "Rent is phenomenal in the city even in SOMA. Everyone predicted it would be the next place to become the *it* place. Hell, I bet the Tenderloin will turn that way soon too. Hanging with crack addicts will become the cool thing to do and hipsters will take over the street corners. And my rent will go up once again." He shoots me a quick glance at the hardness that crept up in my voice. I try to sound breezier. "Anyway, I'm sure you bought at the right time."

"Maybe," he says, running his long fingers over his dark stubble. He's got a very manly-looking chin, but I quickly chide myself for noticing. "But when I bought the place, I was hoping to...well, doesn't matter does it? What's done is done."

And luckily before he has any chance to ask me about my non-existent job, we pull up in front of Steph and Linden's building. Just as I'm lifting Ava out of the car, the doors open and Steph comes out, wobbling a bit in her strappy heels and carrying two glasses of wine.

Married life looks good on her. She's gained some weight, but it's all gone to her boobs, so that's not really fair. Her hair is dyed mermaid blue (or baby blue, to be more specific) and she always looks happy and flushed like she's just had some good sex. It's a wonder I don't hate her.

"Nic!" she yelps and comes speed-walking over as fast as she can without spilling the wine. She hands me a glass of red and says, "Here, drink this. We've got you." She looks me deep in the eyes and I feel momentarily calmed.

And that's why I could never hate her. She's pretty much the best friend a girl could have.

She glances over at Bram and gives him a quick smile before beaming down at Ava.

"Ava, you look like a princess!"

"I am a princess," she says. "You're just a mermaid."

Steph lifts her head in mock supremacy. "No one is *just* a mermaid."

Ava seems to consider that for a moment then eyes the glass of wine in my hand. "Can I have some? I'm thirsty."

"You're always thirsty," I tell her. "This is mommy's *adult* drink. I'll get you some juice when we're inside, okay?"

She nods and licks her lips. She's always been a thirsty child, but seems so even more lately. That and she gets just about as hungry as I do when I haven't eaten. I don't know where she puts all the food either. She definitely didn't inherit her mom's curvy calves and thighs. She's all chicken legs and twig arms, something my doctor said is totally normal for a girl her age.

I turn, about to thank Bram for the ride. After all, he didn't have to come get me, but he's back in his car and driving away, the sleek façade of the Mercedes disappearing down the hill.

"Where's he going?" I ask Steph. "My booster seat is still in the back."

She takes a lengthy sip of wine. "To pick up his girlfriend of the week from her job. He'll be back."

"Right," I say slowly. "Let me guess, supermodel?"

She shrugs. "Dunno. Probably. Haven't met her yet. What's the point when they never last very long?"

"I thought you were sending me an Uber."

"He volunteered, actually," she says, turning back toward the building. "He's tonight's designated driver."

I can't help but snort. "Why would he do that?"

"He's changed a lot since he's moved here. He's a lot closer with Linden and since it's his birthday, I guess he's just trying to be a good brother and make up for lost time." She shoots me a wry look over her shoulder. "Why all the questions?"

Was I asking questions? "No reason."

"You don't like Bram much, do you?" she notes as she swipes her key card and the door buzzes open.

"I like Bam," Ava says, mispronouncing his name. I don't bother to correct her.

"No you don't," I say. "You just like shiny things, like his car."

"I *like* Bam," she says again, this time more forceful.

I look at Steph who is watching me with interest. "What?"

"I don't know. It's just after the wedding, every time his name comes up, I can literally see you shudder. Did something happen?"

I shake my head, trying to keep a straight face.

"Because," she goes on in a conspirator tone and peers at me closer, "Kayla says she saw you and Bram come out from behind the bushes. You were holding onto his arm."

"Is Kayla here?" Because I'm going to kill her.

"She'll be at the bar later," she says. "So, was that true?"

"That was like, six months ago. I don't remember. We may have talked but that's it, I swear." *And way to wait that long to bring it up with me, Steph*, I add in my head.

She raises her eyebrows. Most people aren't usually very good at reading me. I guess I don't give them enough to go on. But Steph has always been succinct at getting through my layers and it takes a lot not to look away.

"Just talked," she muses and jabs the button for the elevator. "All right then. Well, I'm glad you *just talked* because you know he's bad news."

"You were just going on about how much he's changed!"

"Yeah, and he has. But I still wouldn't let any of my friends date him. Well, Kayla maybe, but not you."

"Well you don't have to worry about that. He's definitely not my favorite person. And you know how I feel about guys like him."

"I do know," she says. "But I have to watch out for you, that's all. Remember when you had a crush on your gynecologist? You would have said something to him if I hadn't made you promise."

My cheeks grow warm at the memory. "He was such a nice guy. And so mature."

"He was mature about your vagina and that's because he had to be."

Moments later, we step into her apartment and I'm glad for the change of subject. Music thumps from the speakers and we find Linden, his best friend James and his girlfriend Penny in the kitchen drinking beer and laughing.

"God, it's loud!" Steph screeches and runs over to the stereo to turn it down. She shoots me an apologetic look and the rest of them a scathing one. It tickles me to see how overprotective of Ava she can be sometimes.

"Sorry!" Linden yells and then when he sees me, gives me a wolf whistle, looking me up and down. For a second there I think he's a lot like his brother – the same cheeky smile with dimples, the same dark brows, thick hair and masculine jawline. But when he comes over and pulls me into a hug, I feel no judgement or ulterior motives. So, no, nothing like Bram at all.

He pulls away and holds me at arm's length. "You're looking pretty spiffy, lady."

"Spiffy?" I repeat. "Never heard that one before."

"I've always been original," he says with a wink.

He then says hi to Ava who smiles at him shyly like she always does. Ever since she learned he can fly in the sky, albeit in a helicopter, she's been bashful around him like he's some kind of superhero.

I say hi James and Penny, complimenting Penny on her new cherry red and rhinestone glasses. The two have always been a bit more alternative than I'm used to and I always feel a bit uncool around them with their tattoos, piercings and fun lives. James runs our "local" bar, The Burgundy Lion, and Penny apparently now works in web design for porn sites. Luckily, they're hella nice.

I quickly get Ava a cup of orange juice cut with water (I don't like her to have much sugar) and spend the next half hour sipping my wine slowly and listening to people's conversations. When someone starts talking about work, Steph deftly switches the subject, knowing I'm not ready to talk about what happened.

While Linden makes my hungry monkey pasta with cheese and I scarf down the sliders and prawn rolls he prepared for the rest of us, my mind keeps wondering when Bram is coming back. It's just that I want to know that I'll get my booster seat at the end of the night (those things ain't cheap), unless he's also volunteered to drive me home. I'm not sure how his new girlfriend, or whoever she is, will feel about that but I guess it's sort of a given when you're dealing with someone like him.

As if he's heard my thoughts, suddenly the front door opens and in parades Bram, all smiles, with a lean chick dressed in a silver sequined dress, giant silver hoops in her ears and her blonde hair piled high above her head, fastened with silver clips. If she walks under the lights in the middle of the room, she'll go off like a damn disco ball.

I make my usual snap judgement in two seconds. Her boobs are fake. Her lips are fake and her teeth are fake. *She's fake, period*, I think, then I wonder when I became so bitter.

I roll my shoulders as if to physically shed the unwanted feelings from me, and attempt to play nice as Bram introduces her to the room as Astrid. Astrid says hi, we say hi, and then the two of them disappear into the kitchen.

So, as it is, I'm the only single person here. I can't even bug Ava because she's scarfing down more food that Linden prepared. Steph makes sure to occupy most of my time, though, chatting about purses and shoes even though I know she's secretly dying to talk about the real issues in my life. Still, she stays true to her word and doesn't bring it up.

Eventually it starts getting late. Ava sort of stumbles toward me in an apparent food coma and tugs on my jeans.

"Mommy, I can't find my bed," she says.

"That's because you're not at home," I tell her. Just then Steph announces to everyone that they're moving the party to a bar in the lower Haight. Perfect timing.

"I'll give you a ride," Bram says, seeming to appear from out of nowhere. He looks at Steph. "It's on the way. I'll take whoever."

I can't help but glance at Astrid to see what she thinks of this but she's still smiling. For a moment I'm envious. Not of her toned body and glossy limbs, but because she doesn't seem like the jealous type and Lord knows I am.

"Mommy, who are these people?" Ava asks. My heart skips for a minute, then I remember how confusing these kind of gatherings must be for a child.

"Mommy's friends," I explain. "We're going home now, okay? Bram is going to drive us home in his shiny car, remember? Bam?"

She doesn't nod, just stares at me with a dull expression. Poor kiddo must be so tuckered out. So am I. When a party is over, there is nothing you want more than your bed, making the time between getting from where you are to getting under your covers seem to stretch for eternity. It's a physical ache.

Thankfully it's not long before we're in Bram's car. Astrid is in the passenger seat and Ava, me and Steph are squished in the back. It's not exactly meant for three people back there, let alone a booster seat, so Steph is half-sitting on me and giggling.

It's been about five minutes into our drive as Bram takes the sports car up and down the hills when Ava makes a gagging sound. The distinctive smell of fruit fills the air and I look over to see Ava has thrown up on herself.

"Jesus," I say, "Ava, are you okay?"

I try to turn in my seat and put my hand on her forehead. It feels hot and clammy at the same time and her eyes are wild as she takes in short, sharp breaths.

Everything inside me freezes, wanting to take me hostage in a panic-induced horror, but it doesn't last. I push it aside. I function.

"What is it?" Steph yells in my ear and Bram immediately turns off the radio and starts pulling over to the side of the road.

"I don't know," I say, my voice trembling. I keep brushing Ava's hair back from her face and once we're parked, Bram flips the light on in the car.

Now I can see better and I'm absolutely horrified. Vomit covers the front of her dress and she's pale as anything. Her chin keeps dipping down and when she looks up, she's looking at me like she doesn't know who I am.

I don't think I have ever been so scared.

"Mommy?" she finally asks, sounding breathless.

I grab her hand and squeeze it. "It's okay, angel, mommy's here."

"Do you have a doctor?" Bram asks. "Or should we go to the hospital?"

I don't want to admit right now that I don't have insurance. "Let me try my doctor," I say, trying to fish my phone out of my bag but I drop it, my hands are shaking so much.

Steph picks it up and says, "Let's take her to the emergency room."

I shake my head. "No. Just…"

But I know if I try my doctor, he won't answer. I don't have his home line and the clinic is closed.

"Nicola, it's okay," Steph says, squeezing my leg. "Let's take her to the hospital. Just in case. This could be an allergy."

"She's not allergic to anything."

"But they pop up all the time when you're a kid, right?"

"That's right," Bram says and I finally look over at him. He's trying to be casual but I can see the concern threaded through his brow. "When I was a wee one, I suddenly developed an allergy to strawberries. I threw up in class in front of everyone including Mrs. Haversham, whom I had a mad crush on."

I can't even smile at that admission. I just nod, knowing I have to do what's best for Ava, even if it's going to cost me an arm and a leg.

"Let's go," I tell him. "Any hospital, it doesn't matter. Whatever is closest."

He nods and we speed off down the street. Bram is driving like an absolute maniac, or like he's trying to recreate scenes from "Bullet." I'm not paying much attention, though. I'm listening to Ava breathe, trying to keep her focused and calm even though I'm not.

Soon, we're zooming up to the ER and I'm flying out of the car trying to get Ava out of her seat. I lift her into my arms and run inside to the hospital. The smells of rubbing alcohol and plastic and blood fill my nostrils. Suddenly the cost is the last thing on my mind. All I want is to see a doctor and to see one fast. My mind spins a million different ways and all of them are bad.

What's wrong with her? Did I do something wrong? Is she going to die? Is she going to be okay? What could I have done differently?

I wish Phil was here.

I don't often think that. But he was there for the first year of her life and it's hard to forget that I used to have someone who cared just as much about Ava as I did. Then again, if he cared, he never would have left. Sometimes I think it would have been better if he had just skipped town when he first found out I was pregnant, instead of being there for that first year. He had a chance to know her – how come he didn't love her the way I did? I understand why he left me. I neglected him, I became that doting, obsessed mother I swore I would never become. But how the hell could he leave *her*?

I swallow down the hard lump in my throat as razor-sharp memories threaten to undo me. I have to be strong. Always so damn strong.

Because the ER is packed, it takes what seems like forever to get the doctor to see us. Steph yells at the receptionist a bunch of times and I think Bram and Astrid are still milling around, even though I'm not really aware of anything except my daughter in my arms. Ava is still having trouble breathing and it's only when she vomits again that a nurse takes pity on us and leads us away from the moaning, bandaged, sick people in the waiting room.

It's all going by in a blur. The doctor comes in, but all I can hear is my own heartbeat, not his name. His face is a blank smudge. Steph holds my arm but all I feel is Ava.

He gets Ava on the bed and examines her. Takes blood. Asks me questions.

"What did she eat?"

Steph tells him pasta and cheese, I fill in that she normally has that and has never had a reaction.

"What did she drink?"

I tell him I gave her orange juice with water.

Then Steph tells him Linden gave her some caffeine-free Coke.

This was news to me and now Steph is looking sheepish. I try my hardest to have Ava eating as healthy as possible. Coke is the enemy, as is any soft drink, diet or not. But I also can't see how Coke could have caused this. It's not like she's never had any in her whole life.

The doctor nods at that and then quizzes me more about her dietary habits and other issues.

"She's totally healthy," I tell him defensively. Then I remember the last few trips to the doctor. "She's been really lethargic lately. Tired. Irritable."

"How long has this been going on?"

"A few months. But the doctor, her doctor, said she's fine."

"Has she always been this thin?"

"She's got more gangly since January," I explain. "I brought it up with the doctor and he said it was normal."

"It can be," the doctor says. "But I think this is something else. Has your daughter been excessively thirsty?"

That question hits me hard. I remember being a thirsty child growing up, always opting to drink something rather than eat, so it never struck me as unusual that Ava is the same.

"Yes," I say carefully, looking over at Steph. She nods.

"Mrs—"

"Miss," I quickly inform him. "There is no Mr. in the picture."

His stoney blank face attempts a look of sympathy. "Okay, Ms. Price. We'll have to see what the tests say, but it looks like your daughter might have Type 1 diabetes."

I gasp. I can't help it. Steph holds my hand tight, but I'm already going numb.

He goes on, "And what she's going through right now could be diabetic ketoacidosis. Do you know what ketones are, Ms. Price?"

"The stuff your body produces too much of when you're on the Atkins Diet," Steph fills in.

He raises a brow. "Yes. We're going to have to take a urine test to look at her levels and for now we've got the IV full of electrolytes to rehydrate and stabilize her. But we may need to give her an insulin injection. And if we do, you're going to have to give her injections every day for the rest of her life."

I can't breathe. Diabetes? "But no one in my family has it," I blurt out. "She's always eaten so well. There must be some mistake."

"We'll know for sure soon," he says. "But type 1 has nothing to do with diet or history, not always. Her pancreas just doesn't produce enough insulin. Just sit tight and I'll be back."

I don't know how long he's gone for. Ava is still breathing hard, though her eyes are closed. I keep talking to her to make sure she's awake but she's just too tired. The nurse assures me that her vitals are doing a bit better and she's not in danger anymore, that we brought her in right on time. But still, panic and guilt weighs down on me like a damp, dark cloud.

Somewhere in the back of my head, I'm aware that Steph is here with me, dolled up to the nines and she's missing her husband's birthday party. But I'm also afraid to tell her she should go, afraid that she will, that I'll be alone.

So I don't say anything and she stays right by my side.

The night stretches on and on. The doctor comes back.

It's bad news.

Chapter Three

NICOLA

Ava has Type 1 juvenile diabetes. It takes a moment to sink in and even though there is some relief that there is a name for what's wrong with her, I realize that this damn name – diabetes – has a world of connotations.

A disease.

No cure.

My little girl.

Suddenly I'm filled with so much rage with my current doctor that he never suspected, that he never had her tested.

"She's quite young," the doctor says, catching the fire on my face. "Usually it happens from around eight to ten years old. She's going to be fine and live a long healthy life as long as she gets her shots."

"And how much do those cost?" I can't believe I'm blurting that out.

He rubs his forehead. "If you aren't insured, it's about $300 for a month's supply. That's for the insulin. You'll also need needles, an insulin pen when you're on the go, and a blood sugar monitor."

I can't even fathom what the hospital bill is going to cost me, let alone $300 a month to keep Ava alive. Obviously there is no alternative – I'll pay it. But I don't know how, and that, that scares me more than anything.

Steph has her arm around me and she's saying words of comfort, telling me she'll help, but I could never let her do that. I can't even comprehend anything right now.

The doctor injects Ava with insulin on her stomach, showing me how to do it. I force myself to concentrate, to break through the fog and pay attention. Ava doesn't seem to notice, she just squirms a little but still appears to be asleep. Steph pays attention too, telling me she might have to do it one day if I can't.

And then, maybe out of the kindness of his jaded heart, the doctor puts a vial of insulin and a package of needles into my hands and tells me this will do her well for a month. He also writes Ava a prescription and tells me I still need a monitor but he quickly shows me with the one he has how to use it to make sure her levels are normal. He adds that I can have a nurse or a diabetes educator to show me again how to do it all when we're later settled at home, plus help with overhauling her diet.

It's a lot to take in and I'm not sure how much that I do. I know I have to see Ava's doctor and give him a piece of my mind and hope that he can explain again just what the hell I have to do.

Ava is kept under observation for a few more hours. Time goes slow under the night sky and especially under the glow of a hospital's fluorescent lights.

Ava is starting to look like her healthy self, though. She's still sleeping but her skin is a normal color and her breathing is normal. The nurse tells me she can go home with me in another hour.

I look at Steph who seems almost white with fatigue.

"Please go home," I tell her. "I love you so much for being here, but I've got it now."

She gives me a soft smile. "Okay. But only with your honest blessing."

"It's honest," I tell her. "And tell Linden I'm sorry."

"It's not your fault," she says, getting up from the chair and stretching her arms above her head. "And tell Linden yourself. He's been here for hours."

"What?"

"In the waiting room with Bram." She frowns. "I told you but I guess you didn't hear me…or notice where I've been going every five minutes."

I shake my head. "And Bram is still here? With that blonde Swedish thing?"

"Ha," she says. "She lasted two minutes and made Bram drive her to her friend's place. Not that I blame her. I am surprised Bram came back, though. I'm going to see if he can drive me and Linden home and then come back for you guys."

"No," I say quickly, not wanting to have anyone else do anything special for me. "That's okay, I'll cab it."

"Nicola," she warns, pausing at the door. "Money spent on cab is better spent on your daughter. Besides, he has your car seat. I'm sure it will be fine. Call me in the morning, okay, sweetie, and send Ava my love. I'll come by and bring her something nice and the two of us can go over the medication again. I'll take you to Target. I'm sure they have good deals at their pharmacy. If they don't, we can at least pick up some cheap beer."

After the door closes behind her, I feel the coldness of the room and fragility of the night. I'm eternally grateful that Steph was here, but now that I'm alone with Ava, I feel like I can finally be myself and feel the feelings I buried deep during the night.

Only the tears don't come. Nothing does. I'm either in shock or just too tired to take in the enormity and futility of the situation—this damn, horrible situation.

It's around 3am when the nurse comes in, checks on Ava and with a big smile, tells me it's time to go home. She unhooks her from the IV and I put her back in her clothes, her dress already cleaned by the kind nurse.

I gather Ava in my arms, holding her up and in a slumber state she wraps her own little arms around my neck. I take a long moment to just breathe and let my heart swell.

When I step out and walk down the halls, I'm shocked to see Bram sitting in the waiting room. He's sleeping in his chair, but he's there when he has no reason to be.

I take a moment to stare at him. His legs are stretched in front of him, still in that same slick suit from earlier, though now I notice he has the world's ugliest socks on. It actually throws me off a little – they are brown and yellow with what looks like the Loch Ness monster on them and totally don't jive with his expensive suit (Armani, by the looks of it) or the fact that he's in his mid-thirties. His head is back, his thick throat exposed, his eyes closed. He looks like he'd be in the throes of ecstasy if it weren't for the fact that I can hear him snoring lightly.

I go over to him and peer down at his face. I've never really stared at him like this before since I never wanted him to catch me looking – his ego might chalk it up to something more than it is.

Though, I guess, he has a right to be impressed with himself. It's a good face. Dark, arched brows, that firm and wide jawline, perfect lips that stretch into the perfect grin, sly grey eyes that always seem on the verge of telling you a secret but don't just to toy with you. He's like a big cat, a very, *very* big one.

But big cats are dangerous and so are playboys. I straighten up and clear my throat.

His eyes snap open and he blinks a few times at me. "What time is it?" He looks at Ava. "She's okay?"

My mouth twists. "She's okay for the moment." I pause. "I'm sorry you had to wait. I was happy taking a cab."

"Hey, my sister-in-law asked me to drive you home and I'd do anything for family," he says, getting to his feet. "I'm glad your little one is okay, though."

I nod, unable to say more. We leave the ER and go to his car in one of the lots. Once Ava is all strapped in and we're on the road, I want to thank him for the ride but everything is caught in my throat.

"Are you okay?" Bram asks as I repeatedly clear my throat.

"Thank you for driving me," I manage to say, my voice nothing more than a whisper.

"No worries," he says. His expression turns grave in the passing lights. "But are you okay?"

I nod again, trying to give him a reassuring smile, but the pressure behind my eyes and nose builds and I feel everything crumbling down from the inside out. I look out the window, and for the second time in two days, I know I'm going to completely lose it.

The tears come first, then the sobs that squeeze the breath out of my lungs. I want to cry just for the fact that I'm crying in front of Bram of all people, someone I barely know. But I'm really crying for the hopelessness, the frustration, that never-ending feeling of why me? A pity party, I know. I have them all the time. Except now I feel fear for myself, for Ava, more than pity. Fear that I won't be able to get through it without majorly overhauling my life.

Bram doesn't say anything, which I guess is good. He just ignores me and I hope he can pretend I'm not there. He keeps driving.

And then I start talking. The moment I open my mouth, I know it's a mistake, but there's nothing I can do to stop it.

"I got fired yesterday," I say in between sobs. "A week away from my health insurance kicking in. My rent went up in my shitty, fucking apartment. My car doesn't work. Now Ava's sick. She's really sick, and I have no idea how I'm going to pay for anything, how I'm going to help her get better, how I'm going to be a good mom. A good mom would have her life together but I don't have anything. I'm just...useless. I can't keep a job. I got an education in something passionate, not practical. I have nothing going for me but her and I don't know how I'll even keep her alive. I mean, I didn't ask for this responsibility, I didn't ask for it. But I promised I would take care of her and it's like the world is testing me every moment it gets." I pause and try to think of something positive to stop the tears, but there is nothing. "The insulin will cost me $300 a month. How can I pay for that when I could barely pay my rent before, let alone now without a job?"

The car is silent except for my shaky breath. A few moments pass, then Bram says, "What about your parents?"

It figures he would say that since he coasted by on his parents' money for so long.

I swallow and shake my head. "No. No, my mom helps out doing what she can. She watches Ava twice a week. But she's a fucking maid. I mean, if you knew her, if you knew me growing up, you'd never believe it. What she's become. But she made a bunch of mistakes and now she's lost it all and…she's no better off than me."

"I get it. And your father?"

"He's a good guy." I wipe my tears away with the palm of my hand. "But I talk to him once a month. He does a lot of charity work out in India and South East Asia. Whatever money he has, he gives."

"So he could give to you."

"It's not the same," I say. "He helps those in real need."

"It sounds like you're in need."

I can feel his eyes boring into me. I stare down at my hands. "I wouldn't ask him. I don't want him to think I'm anything but okay." I can see Bram nod out of the corner of my eye and the car is silent again and I'm feeling worse than before.

It's not long before we've pulled up in front of my apartment building. Through the stream of tears I can see the usual crack bums and derelicts milling outside. They always get worse at night.

"I'm going to take you inside," Bram says to me and his deep, rich voice tells me I'm not to argue. "I can't believe you live here. You shouldn't live here."

I should feel insulted by that but I'm not. "I can't believe it either," I whisper. I step out of the car and with Bram standing watchfully between me and the junkies, I get Ava out of the seat. He quickly scoops up the booster, locks his car with a flashy display of his fancy alarm system, and we go inside.

Once in the lobby I reach for the seat to take it out of his hands but he holds firm. For once, the arrogant smirk is all gone and he's damn serious.

"I'm taking you to your apartment," he says. "I don't trust this neighborhood, and believe me, I went to school in Glasgow. I'm going to make sure you're safe."

"You don't need to do that," I say, still holding onto the seat.

"I don't need to do anything," he says. "I want to. I'm going to."

"Your car…"

He glances out the glass door to the street. "My car is fine. I got a good look at them all and they know it. The alarm is loud. They wouldn't dare."

Reluctantly I let go of the seat and go up the stairs to the second floor. Outside my apartment I stop and take out my keys. I really don't want him to see it or to come inside. It's weird, but I feel like he'll think he knows me if I do that, as if he could garner a glimpse of my soul from my furniture, art and framed photos. Though I guess after everything I just bawled to him in the car, he probably knows me enough by now.

"This is me," I tell him, giving him a stiff smile and the unfriendly stare I do when I want someone to leave me alone.

He licks his lips and nods. "Okay." He puts down the seat against the door. "I better get back home. But…listen." He leans with one arm against the door and stares so deeply into my eyes I'm forced to listen. Hell, I'm practically hypnotized. "I know I'm probably not your favorite person and that's okay. But I honestly think I can help you."

"Help me?" I say, just a bit too loudly. Ava stirs her head on my shoulder.

He takes a business card out of his wallet and hands it to me. "Call me. Tomorrow. And we'll talk. I have a solution." He looks at Ava's sleeping body and then at me. "She has a good mum." Then he walks down the hall and down the stairs.

He goes before I can thank him again.

Chapter Four

BRAM

"Let me just wank off on your tits, babe," I tell Astrid in a begging voice that I'm not too proud of.

She stares up at me, my cock in her hand, drool and precum at the corners of her wet lips. She's too fucking gorgeous, even though that vapid stare of hers can be right creepy at times. I'm not keeping her around for her intelligence, that's for sure. But considering how hard I'm trying to step away from my past, I hope for her sake she's not into coke.

"Am I not good at sucking your dick?" she asks in a hurt little girl voice before wrapping her tongue around my throbbing head.

She is good. Bloody good. I have no doubts how she got that way either. Things I don't want to think about, just like she'd rather not think about how my lips and tongue can get her coming faster than she can scream my name. But when I texted her this afternoon to come over and make me come, I was counting on fucking her on the floor. Or on the bed. Or anywhere, really.

But she's got her period, and so, this will have to do. Now, I honestly don't mind sex when a lady is on the rag. It's messy and kind of hot. But she, like most girls, can't fathom the idea. And it's not like I'm not enjoying my BJ – again, she's good. But the position, her on her knees, causes my mind to wander.

I don't want it to do that. It's been doing that a bit too much lately. About things I've tried to keep buried, things that keep surfacing in different ways.

Thankfully, I'm almost ready to come, so I pull out of her mouth and flip her around, pushing down on her shoulders so she's on the ground. Then I stroke myself off and come all over her neck and shoulders, glad to have it over with.

"You're a bit rough," she says with a breathy giggle.

Why does everything have to be so fucking funny?

"Only because you love it," I tell her. She pretty much loves everything I do and I think it's for more reasons than just what I can do in bed. Money speaks louder than a lot of things. "Stay put."

I go and get a dishtowel from the kitchen and quickly wipe the cum off her back. I wonder what's the easiest way to get rid of her. In hindsight I shouldn't have even invited her over but I needed something to get my mind off of Nicola.

The thing is, when I give a girl my phone number, I expect her to call me. They always do. And I wasn't even giving it her on the pretence of fucking her or anything like that. I genuinely can help her out. I want to. And she needs it. It's rare that I have all three of those.

But it's two in the afternoon and she hasn't called. Wasn't she curious? Isn't she desperate?

Does she really hate me that much?

I can tell when women "hate" me. You know, as a precursor to getting naked, a fun way to make our interactions more exciting. And then there's women who *hate* me, as in they wish I would die. I've gotten that impression from Nicola ever since I first met her at a bar early last year, right after I moved here. At the time I would have just blamed it on her being an uptight snob, but she was so nice to everyone else and so snide with me, that I couldn't help but take it personally. And, of course, be challenged by it.

It's bothered me ever since. I saw her twice more after that and it was the same. The cold nod, the death glare, like I had wronged her in a past life. When I saw her at my brother's wedding, I thought maybe she'd come around. I kissed her when I shouldn't have, but I just had to see. And for a split second I thought maybe I could win her over. I saw something in her eyes that was wild and free and I just wanted to let it loose like that damn tight-arse hairdo she had going on.

That didn't happen. My dick got the better of me.

Now I think she really hates my guts. I'm pretty sure she saw me take that chick into the bushes and I'm pretty sure I pissed her off to a point she'll never come back from.

Still, when I said last night that I could help her, I wasn't just trying to make her like me, to make up for past misdoings. All right, maybe that last part a wee bit but really I'm coming from a good place.

But if she doesn't call me, she won't ever see that. Now I've got Astrid naked from the waist up and on the floor of my apartment, wiping the remains of my cum off of her and I don't know how to get her out the door.

I zip up my pants and give her an exaggerated yawn. "You know what, I think I'm going to take a nap. I have a lot of work to do this evening."

She gets to her feet, her tiny, perky breasts bobbing in front of me. For once she doesn't look vapid, but annoyed. It's a nice change. "So, you invite me over for this and now you're throwing me out?"

"I'm not throwing you out," I tell her as I grab her shirt and chuck it at her. "You may want to put that on, though."

She scowls out me. "You're a pig," she says, quickly slipping it on through a huff of anger.

"More like a hog," I correct her. "They tend to be bigger."

"First you invite me out to a party and you end up spending it in the hospital."

I frown at her. "Hey, no one asked for that to happen."

"Well, it did," she says, going for the door. "And I've had enough. Don't call me."

The door slams behind her.

No worries on the calling part. Most girls don't last more than a week with me before they've also had enough. They may act all dumb and easy-going, but I know they all have their limit and I'm pretty good at dragging them to it every time. Some might call that a sad way to get through life, but when it's just *your* life, you learn to accept it.

I pick up my phone off the counter and stare at it. No missed calls, no texts. I don't even have her number, so I can't call her.

I can call my brother, though. If he's not out flying the chopper for the chartering company, that is.

He answers on the third ring, but the connection is a bit fuzzy.

"Aye, what do you want?" Linden shouts.

"Don't tell me you're in the air and answering your phone all willy nilly."

"Just about to take off. What's up?"

I clear my throat, wondering how to phrase this without him getting the wrong idea. "How is the girl? The wee one?"

"Like the child, Ava?" he asks, his voice rising above the rotors I can hear starting. "She's okay. Diabetes they said, like some kind of shock. You were there."

"I know I was there. I mean, how is she now? And how is her mum?"

"I guess she's fine as she can be, I don't know. I know Steph is at her place right now, helping out. She's worried as hell. You know how she can dote on people."

That I do know. Steph's like the mother we never had. I don't tell Linden that or he'll balk at the Freudian implications.

"Do you have her phone number?"

"Nicola's?" he asks. "Not on my phone. I have her Facebook. Why?"

"No matter," I say, then pause. "Tell me something about her."

"What, why? Wait. No, Bram. No," he commands, like I'm some rangy pooch.

"No, I'm not asking because of that."

"Right, you're not asking because you don't want to stick your dick in her."

"I honestly don't," I tell him. "I think she'd cry if she saw a dick in real life."

"Nice," he says dryly. "Anyway, she's off-limits to you. She's gone through enough. She doesn't need my arsehole brother fucking up her life anymore."

"Arsehole?"

"Yes, Bram," he says, tiredly. "Look I have to go."

He hangs up and I mutter a swear at the phone.

There's only one thing to do.

Soon I'm parking the car in an above-ground garage near Union Square and walking several blocks over into the heart of the manky Tenderloin neighborhood. Other than good music venues, the place is crawling with crazies. It's not that bad during the daytime. I mean, it ain't pretty but the people just really annoy you to death with their begging and aren't dangerous. But if I were Nicola's parents, or even friends, I wouldn't want her living there. The thought of fuckheads outside her apartment at night makes me strangely pissed off.

By the time I reach her place, I've been asked for change by eight different people and was told I "smell like crunchy toast" by a random running down the road with a severed parking meter under his arm. I'm not sure if I do smell like toast, but it is hot out. I've been warned how San Francisco's seasons don't follow any rhyme or reason.

I take off my suit jacket, run a hand through my hair in an effort to look respectable, and buzz her apartment number having remembered it from last night. Borderline stalker-ish, I know.

"Hello?" I eventually hear her voice come through the crackly intercom.

"Nicola, it's Bram."

More crackle. Silence. Maybe she's hung up.

"From last night," I go on. "And other times."

"Uh, hi..."

"Can I come up?"

I can sort of hear Steph in the background, "Who is it?"

"Tell her it's her brother-in-law!" I yell and then I'm disconnected.

I stare at the door wondering if I'm being told to fuck off when it buzzes and I go on up.

The funny thing about Nicola, the thing I've gathered from what little I know about her, is that if there's anyone that shouldn't be living in a place like this – bars on the doors, mildew on the stairwell walls, stains on the carpet – it's her. Maybe some hipsters could make it work, or James and Penny, Linden's friends on the alternative side who might call this type of living as "being real." But Nicola seems too stiff, prim and proper for this place, like she should have been born in a palace instead. From the way she was talking, well blubbering, in my car, I have a feeling she might have been.

Just before I'm about to knock on the door, it opens and Stephanie is staring at me with a suspicious twist to her lips.

"What are you doing here?" she asks, blocking the door.

"What are you, her guard dog?"

"Well, I am a bitch sometimes," she says. "Woof, woof."

"Can I come in?"

She shakes her head, her skull earrings rattling. "Why?"

"I want to know if they're okay."

A line slowly forms between her brows. "They're going to be okay," she says in a drawn-out tone. "Sorry, Bram, not used to you caring about people."

I guess I deserved that. "Can I talk to Nicola? Alone?"

Steph flinches. "What?"

I look over her shoulder and see Nicola appear just beyond the door. She looks like shit. Her hair is greasy and pulled back, her face sallow, her eyes puffy and red. Other than sad, though, I can't really read her face and tell if she's happy to see me, or pissed off, or indifferent. I'm betting it's the latter.

"Hey," I say to her. "I just wanted to check up on you. You never called," I add.

Steph looks between the two of us. "He gave you his number?"

"Business card, actually," Nicola says wryly.

Steph folds her arms across her chest and I try my damndest not to stare at her cleavage. Damn, Linden is a lucky guy. Good thing I think of her more as the mother type. "What did I tell you?" Steph whispers harshly to her.

I raise a brow. "What *did* you tell her?"

"Never mind," she says quickly, fixing her eyes back on me. She's like mother hen with teeth in that beak. "I'm watching you," she says to me.

I raise my arms out to the side. "Watch all you want, babe, I'm used to it."

Nicola gives out a small sigh of resignation. "It's fine. Bram, you can come in. Just be quiet, Ava's sleeping."

Victory. I step inside and take a quick intake of my surroundings. It looks like some trendy grandmother's cottage in here. The type who puts ruffles and doilies on everything but also listens to the Rolling Stones on vinyl to remember the days when she'd get so bloody high.

Nicola walks over to her tiny kitchen, which is cluttered with bright cups and plates. "Want coffee? Or tea?"

Do I admit I drink tea over coffee? Hell. "I'd love a cup of tea, please. Do you have orange pekoe or Earl gray? With cream?"

I can't see her face but I know she's not looking too impressed. "I have chai."

"That's fine," I say, aware that Stephanie is staring at me. "What?" I say to her.

She just narrows her eyes, points her finger at me as if she's about to say something, then picks up her purse. "Okay, Nic," she calls to her. "I'm going to go. Call me later, okay? Please?" Now I'm not sure if that please is because of Ava's situation or the fact that I'm here.

"I will," Nicola says. "Thanks for everything."

"Love ya!" And then Steph is out the door and I'm alone with Nicola.

It's suddenly very awkward. While the kettle is boiling, I sit down on her sofa. It's like sinking into a marshmallow. I'm afraid I won't be able to get up.

She's not talking, so I attempt to fill in the gaps.

"Nice apartment," I comment.

"Thanks," she says, still puttering around in the kitchen.

"Did you inherit all your furniture from your grandmum or something?"

She shoots me a killer look over her shoulder. "It's from Anthropologie."

I shrug and run my hands over the couch cushions. I can feel all the rough threads where she tried to sew together any rips and tears. I don't think she's hanging onto it out of love, but out of necessity.

"How's your little one?" I ask.

She doesn't say anything for a moment. Her voice turns quiet. "I think I'm having a harder time than she is."

I hear her pour the water and the clank of a spoon against porcelain and she comes over, placing a cup of tea on the coffee table in front of me, making sure to use a coaster. It's black.

"Sorry," she says, cradling her own cup of tea and sitting at the opposite end of the sofa, legs curled up, as far away from me as possible. "I don't have any milk in the house. I'm lactose intolerant."

Though she's curled in the corner, she doesn't look all that comfortable. Her head is up high, chin out and her mouth is set in a firm line. I can't read her eyes at all, so I stop trying.

"Did you get the medicine okay?" I ask.

She nods and takes a sip. "Thanks to Steph's insistence on paying, yes. The doctor at the hospital gave me a month's supply of insulin, but Steph paid for everything else. The pharmacist at Target gave us both a crash course on injecting Ava again, so I don't have to go and pay for my doctor either." She exhales heavily. "I really needed that reminder. Last night just seemed like a horrible nightmare." She looks at me and maybe I see her face softening. "Thanks again for driving me around. I kind of ruined everyone's night."

"Shit happens," I tell her with a wave of my hand. "It's no big deal."

"I bet your girlfriend was upset."

"Aye," I nod. "But she's not my girlfriend. Especially not now." I don't say anything else.

"So, what did you want me to talk to you about?" she says, sounding tired. I realize talking to me is probably the last thing she wants to do.

"You look like you need a nap," I tell her. Her eyes look sad and I realize it's a jerk thing for me to say. No one wants to hear they look tired. "I mean, you're still pretty hot but you look tired as hell." And now I'm just making it worse.

"I don't dare sleep," she says. She seems to shrink down before my eyes. "Not now, not when something can happen to her."

"You could," I say. "Right now. Just have a nap. I'll stay here. I'll be up, make sure that everything's okay."

She looks at me like I'm crazy. Maybe I am. I have no idea why I just volunteered to do that – maybe because it's the right thing to do – but it makes me sound like the world's biggest creeper.

"No thanks," she says, looking a wee bit disgusted. "So." She sounds impatient now. "What is it that you want from me, Bram?"

I lean forward on my elbows and twirl the watch on my wrist over and over again.

"I have a proposition for you."

She watches me for so long I have to look up. She doesn't look curious, she looks worried.

"Is this going to be like 'Indecent Proposal?'" she asks. "Because Robert Redford loses at the end."

"A) I'm surprised you're old enough to remember that movie," I say. "And B) no, it's nothing like that. I know my reputation precedes me –"

"That is does." She takes a quick sip of her tea.

"But, this offer is coming from a good place. An honest place." I pause. "I think you should move in with me."

She nearly drops her mug.

Chapter Five

NICOLA

Did I just hear him right? My hand starts to shake and I put the mug of hot tea down before I scald myself.

"I'm sorry, what?" I ask Bram, bewildered. "Did you just ask me to move in with you?"

He gives me a placating smile. "Not exactly. What I mean is, the apartment next to mine is vacant. The tenant moved out at the start of the month. I think you should take it. You can live there rent free, just until you get a good job and your feet back on the ground. What do you say?"

What do I say? I have no fucking idea. Why on earth would Bram McGregor offer me a place to live for free? It doesn't make any damn sense and I don't want any part of it.

"You can think about it..." he goes on.

"No," I say and he looks shocked. "Sorry, but...no. Move into your empty apartment? Why? Why would you do that? Why not rent it out for thousands of dollars a month, which is what I'm sure the rent is."

"But I don't want the rent to be that high," he says.

"It doesn't matter what you want," I tell him. "You have a mortgage on that place and I know it costs a pretty penny." And it doesn't really jive with everything I've known about Bram. He's grown up with money. He spends it like a gambler who thinks he has nothing to lose. Everything about Bram screams, "I'm here to make money and spend money!" Letting Ava and I live in his complex for free would completely mess up those plans.

It doesn't make any sense and I sure as hell don't like it.

"You let me worry about matters of money," he says, rolling up the sleeves of his dress shirt. I notice his perpetual tan, his skin a nice honey bronze that I don't think is fake and makes me wonder where on earth he's gotten color like that. His forearms are large, muscular and toned. Forearms are my weakness. As are hands. He's got good hands too, big and strong.

He catches me staring and smiles, just a little. "Please, this isn't anything weird."

"Like hell it isn't." I scoff, tearing my eyes away. "This is an insanely generous offer and I have a hard time believing you aren't coming from a despicable place."

He flinches. "Wow. Just how poorly do you think of me?"

"I don't think of you at all," I fire back.

He mouths, "Ouch." For a moment I feel bad but then I remember him pulling that chick into the bushes and how humiliated I felt, and I don't feel so bad anymore.

"What do you want, really?" I ask him. "Just be honest."

He throws his hands up. "I am being honest. I want to help you and your little one. Sometimes people do things because they can help and because they want to."

I ain't buying it. My eyes narrow at him. "What do you want in exchange?"

"Nothing," he says, sounding strangely sincere.

"Right. As if I'm not supposed to be your sex slave or something and, like, suck you off anytime you want. Nothing is for free." Boy did I know that.

He grins. "Sweetheart, you wouldn't know what to do with my dick even if you tried."

"I most certainly would!" I blurt out, unable to help myself. I regret my words immediately.

There's one hell of a long, mortifying second as he slowly raises his dark brow, a twinkle in his eye. "Oh really?" he muses, smile dancing on his lips.

Shit.

I cross my arms. "You know what I mean."

"Not really. But you could show me."

"You aren't selling me on this at all, you know."

He rolls his eyes and gets up. In another lifetime, a naïve one full of meaningless sex and yellow-brick roads, I would have been completely enamored with how damn handsome this man is. Because, really, he is. But in this lifetime, the short stick I've been handed (I haven't had a long stick in a long time, if you know what I mean), his good looks and hot bod and slick suits mean nothing to me.

"Look," he says. "I'll be honest with you. I'm not just trying to be a nice guy."

And the truth comes out. I breathe a sigh of relief that we're finally getting somewhere.

"If I take in a low-income resident," he explains, "someone who can't find affordable housing in the city, then I get a big tax break from the government."

"Well, why didn't you just tell me that to begin with?"

He gives me a lazy shrug. "Thought I could earn some extra brownie points with you."

"And why would you want to do that?"

"I don't want to live next door to a bitch, I guess."

I actually laugh at that. "Fair enough."

He sticks his hands in his pockets and peers down at me. "So, what do you say? Do you think you and Ava will be comfortable in a nice building, south of Market? Rent free, take the time to get a job, get a handle on things?"

It sounds too good to be true. I hesitate.

"Can I think about it?"

"Of course," he says. He looks at his watch. "I better be on my way. You do have my card right? You didn't spit on it and throw it out?"

"I still have it."

"Good. Because if I don't hear from you over the next few days, I will have to find someone else. I don't want to have to show up here unannounced again. And I'm guessing you're not about to give me your phone number either."

"I'll call you," I tell him and this time I know I will.

I just don't know what I'm going to say.

...

After Bram leaves, I take my time to think about it. Actually, I don't take that much time at all. Ava wakes up from her nap and though she's lively and happy as ever – as if last night never even happened – she also asks if she'll have to get the needle tomorrow. I can't lie to her. I tell her the needle has medicine that will keep her strong and healthy, so she can turn into a big girl. She seems to understand but…it's still something I can't wrap my head around.

Giving her the injection earlier was also a challenge and if Steph wasn't with me, I don't think I could have done it. It doesn't seem right putting your child in pain, even though it's the only way from now on, even if it's what will help her in the end.

But as proud as I am, as much as I want to turn down Bram's offer, I honestly can't. For Ava's sake, I can't. My pride must be swallowed if she's going to have a shot at life. Living rent-free would save me $1000 a month. If I put that money into food and medicine, we could get by. It wouldn't be fun, but I could do it. And that's before I even get a job. I know I can't afford to be too picky about that either, but I decided to give it another week just to see if I really can shoot for something that pays well and in my field. It's a longshot, but I have to try.

I make us both some sliced avocado on whole-grain bread (the doctor said the way I'd been feeding her – low in sugar – was excellent and to keep it up. It's nice to know that at least I didn't bring it upon her). We sit down on the couch and I read a picture book to Ava between bites. Somewhere in the building I can hear a couple arguing loudly. The neighbor above me has a shower – the pipes rattle the walls. To think I could be out of this place, one foot out of the mess, one foot toward my future.

I just really hope there's nothing else that is owed for this. That Bram doesn't expect anything from me. I hadn't really thought I'd be his sex slave. I just wanted to poke fun at his manwhore ways, but even so I have a hard time believing that I won't be in debt to him in the end. The thought of owing something, anything, to a man like that is a scary one.

And I hate that I find it kind of exciting as well.

I stare at my phone on the coffee table. I could call Steph and get her opinion, but in the end, it's not going to change anything. I know already what has to be done.

I fish out the card, pick up my phone and dial.

"Hello, Bram?"

...

"I can't believe you're doing this," Steph says to me as she walks into my near empty apartment and hands me a giant cup of coffee she just picked up from Bluebottle. I slurp it back, even though it burns my lips and throat as we survey the place.

It's Saturday morning and just over a week after I told Bram I accepted his offer to move into his apartment complex. My landlord was angry at my short notice but he was angry to begin with, so that didn't make much difference. With Steph, Kayla, and sometimes Linden, we were able to pack up my apartment really fast. Even though it's a small place, I was surprised how much junk I'd collected over the years. I think there's a sentimental hoarder somewhere inside me but it was very freeing to give a lot of it away. Clean slate.

Ava is off with my mom in Livermore for the day, which is wonderful, although I'm extremely nervous about her giving the insulin shots correctly. I know I shouldn't doubt my mom – I showed her how and she has a neighbor with diabetes just in case she needs help but I think my worry meter has been pushed to eleven for the rest of my life.

Steph, Kayla, Linden and Bram are all helping me this moving day. Bram said he would gladly pay for the cost of a moving company, but I don't want any more of his charity, and to be honest, I wanted to see him sweat a little. We've been up since 6am and working like maniacs to get everything packed up. With a few final boxes we were back in the apartment, probably – hopefully – for the last time.

I mull over what Steph just said. "In a good way or a bad way?"

"In a good way," she says, drinking her own coffee for a second, her bright magenta lipstick leaving clean marks on the lid. "I mean, this is amazing. I just hope Bram stays true to his word."

"Well, I'm a charity case, remember?"

"I gotta say that surprises me too. Because I never knew he was big on charity, even when tax breaks were involved." She smiles at me. "But you know what? Charity or tax breaks or whatever, this is awesome for you."

"Almost done?" Kayla asks, appearing at the doorway. Her pale skin is flushed with sweat, her long black hair pulled back into a ponytail underneath a pink baseball cap. She's not wearing any makeup and as usual she looks fantastic. Her Japanese mother passed onto her perpetually flawless skin.

"Almost," I tell her. "There's a box for you." I nod at a huge one in the corner.

"Oh, great," she says sarcastically and goes over, bending down to lift it. "Don't tell me all your hardcover books are in here."

"Pillows and cushions," I tell her just as she lifts it up with ease.

She comes over with it and looks around at the empty walls. It doesn't even look like I lived here at all. "Wow. I know you made this place real cute, Nicola, but I think we all need to have some champagne tonight to celebrate the fact that I don't have to come back to this damn neighborhood and get asked by Hustlin' Joe outside for change and a BJ every time I visit."

"Hustlin' Joe?" I repeat.

She shrugs. "His words, not mine. Okay, ladies, are you done taking in the water-stained ceiling and the peeling linoleum? Because the men want to get this show on the road. Remember unpacking is just as bad as packing."

I take in a deep breath. I'm ready.

We go outside and I see my landlord – soon to be ex – Mr. Stanley, standing by the building with his short arms crossed over his portly stomach, smoking a cigarette and glaring at the moving van. That was one thing I let Bram hire for the day.

"Mr. Stanley," I say to him, coming over, cradling my box that I've labeled "Kitchen Crap." In a second, Linden comes and wordlessly takes the box out of my hands and puts it in the van.

"Don't expect to get a good reference from me," Mr. Stanley says to me, cigarette puffing out the sides of his fat mouth. He frowns so much he looks like he has a unibrow.

"Well, that's not exactly fair," I tell him calmly, though what I really want to do is give him a piece of my mind. "I would have given you a month's notice but it just didn't end up that way. Wouldn't you have rather had this than me not paying rent and having to evict me?"

"But I enjoy evicting people," he says with smile. "And this way, you don't get your security deposit back."

Shit. Shit. Shit! I completely forgot about that deposit. $500 is a hell of a lot of money for me right now.

"Is there a problem here?"

Suddenly Bram is at my side and he's putting one hand on my shoulder. It's warm and steady in the cool, grey morning. It feels good. That's probably why I want to shrug it off.

But I don't dare in front of Mr. Stanley. Besides, Bram is putting up a pretty intimidating front. For once he's not in a suit, but dark jeans and a white t-shirt that fits every contour of his body and shows off his muscles. I'd been trying not to notice during the move – not the tan of his skin or the way his arms flex when he lifts something or the damp spot of sweat on his back. But now I'm grateful that his bulk is on display because I don't for a second want Mr. Stanley to think he can get away with being an asshole.

"No problem," Mr. Stanley says through a sneer. He rips his cigarette out from his mouth and glares up at Bram who towers over him and pretty much everyone else. "Just informing the girl here on how to be a good tenant. You leave like a good tenant. She hasn't."

"The girl," Bram drawls out in his brogue, "is leaving because she and her daughter don't want to live in a rat-infested hell-hole. You don't think I haven't been inside your building and seen how many building code violations you're breaking, let alone any of the ones that would get you fired from being a building manager?"

Mr. Stanley's face falters for a moment. I don't think I've ever seen his eyebrows come apart.

"I've also been moving shit out of her apartment all day," Bram goes on and takes out his phone, waving it at him. "I have pictures of the damaged between-floor barriers designed to prevent the spread of fire, a broken dry sprinkler system, a fire alarm system control panel flashing 'trouble' and an out-of-date fire safety plan, as well as rat droppings in the hallways, an elevator that doesn't work, forcing all people, even the elderly, to take the stairs, and carpenter ant damage in the lobby. I'm going to assume its spread throughout the rest of the building."

My mouth drops open. Bram noticed all that?

Mr. Stanley is pale. The cigarette is shaking in his hand.

"One call to the fire department and you'll be fined at least $20,000," Bram tells him, head high. "You'll probably lose your job too. Or you could give the girl her security deposit back and we'll be on our way."

"Wow," I hear Kayla say from behind me. "Bram's the man."

Bram looks at me briefly and winks. "There's another motto for ya." Then he fixes a steady gaze back on Mr. Stanley. "So, what's it going to be?"

Mr. Stanley doesn't have to think twice. He rips out his check book from his back pocket and writes me a check for $500. He hands it to me, unable to look me in the eye now then quickly heads back to the building.

"And no worries about being her reference," Bram calls after him. "She's got me for that."

He nudges me in the side with his elbow. "Come on, let's get the fuck out of here."

We walk to the van where Steph, Kayla and Linden are watching us. I quickly give Bram a sidelong glance. "You really want me to like you, don't you?"

He smiles, dimples and everything. "Oh, you like me. You just don't know it yet." He nods at Linden. "Come, brother, let's go."

I walk over to Steph who will drive me and Kayla in her car.

Kayla calls out at Bram. "Did you really notice all those violations?"

Bram nods. "I've learned something as a building manager. And believe me, next week, I am putting a call into the fire department."

The three of us stand on the curb and watch as he gets in the van and it starts with a rumble.

"Damn," Kayla says as they drive off. "That was some hot shit." She looks at me. "You're lucky you're moving in next to that guy." She pauses, lips pursing. "Are you going to move into his bed too?"

I roll my eyes. "Hell no. I mean, maybe he's a bit nicer than I thought at first," Kayla raises her brows, "okay, a lot nicer, but he's still a jackass."

"Jackass is a strong word for you, miss manners," she teases. "Does this have anything to do with what happened at the wedding?" she asks.

"No," I say, glaring at her before I walk over to Steph's car. "And you didn't see anything, so don't go thinking something happened between us. It didn't. It really didn't."

I can feel Steph and Kayla exchanging a look behind my back.

Later in the car as we drive down Van Ness, Kayla taps me on the shoulder from the backseat. "Why do you think he's a jackass?"

I blow a piece of hair that came loose from my bun. "Because…he's a manwhore."

"That doesn't make him a jackass. That makes him fun."

Which makes me "no fun," I think, remembering what he'd said to me at the wedding.

"I just don't trust guys like that," I tell her after a moment.

"But you're not dating him," she says. "So you don't have to worry about that, do you?"

I shake my head. "You're right. I don't." And really, I shouldn't. But that night plays over and over in my head, the sweet feel of his lips, the sharp sting of rejection. It probably doesn't help that the last man I kissed, the last person who turned me on and made me feeling something, instead of nothing, was Bram.

Once you go Bram, you won't give a damn. But I did.

"Why all the questions Kayla?" Steph asks, her tone cautious as she eyes her in the rear-view mirror.

"I can ask questions," Kayla says.

"Mmm hmm. But you've got that look in your eyes."

"What look? I'm Asian, you racist."

"Shut up," Steph says. "You know the look. The one you get when you find your next lay."

Oh? I turn in my seat and look at Kayla. Yup, she's got that look.

"Are you interested in Bram?" I ask her. Kayla had broken off her engagement with her ex-boyfriend a couple of years ago and now was always perpetually single but not for lack of trying. Any hot bod and she's all over it. She even had a fling with Linden for a few weeks back in the day when Steph and him were just good friends. I'm not sure how Steph dealt with that but she doesn't hold a grudge like I do.

Kayla shrugs casually but I can see right through her. "I don't know. He's just really hot, that's all. And he's got money. And he's got that bad boy appeal but like the ante is upped because he's a man, not a boy. I mean, now that's a man. Like if you hooked up, he'd probably ruin your vagina for everyone after."

I scrunch up my nose. "Way to be classy."

"Yeah, Kayla, that's my brother-in-law you're talking about," Steph admonishes her.

"So," she says. "You're not blood relatives. You told me you thought his brother was hot."

"I did. But he's not Linden."

Kayla rolls her eyes and flops back into her seat. "Of course he's not Linden. How dare anyone be even close to Linden?" she says mockingly. "You know, Steph, just because you're married doesn't make you blind."

"Sure, but I don't try and think of Bram as hot. Still, you're right. He is. And if you don't mind being played, then go right ahead and have your fun," she says. "But don't come crying to me if it doesn't work out and don't you dare fuck anything up with the nice relationship everyone has at the moment. You know you've done that once before," she adds under her breath.

Ah, so Steph hasn't forgotten the whole Linden and Kayla hookup.

Kayla grows quiet. We drive for a bit then she says, "Fine. I guess one McGregor brother was enough for me."

I snap my head back at her and find Kayla grinning wickedly. Steph's hands are growing white on the steering wheel. I feel like we're seconds away from a catfight and I start wondering what I'll do to try and break them apart. I've got strong arms from lifting Ava and booster seats.

But Kayla bursts out laughing and smacks Steph on the shoulder. "I'm fucking kidding! Jeez, can't we joke about the past anymore?"

Steph gives her a dirty look. "Things change when you get married."

"And that's why I cancelled my wedding," Kayla says. "I wasn't ready for that. But you and Linden are. And don't worry, I'm not going to go near Bram." She looks at me. "He's all yours."

"Mine?" First of all, Bram isn't anything of mine except for a landlord now, and second of all…I dunno. I don't exactly appreciate being told I can have something as if I wouldn't have had a chance with Bram if Kayla went after him.

I can feel Steph's eyes dart between me and the road. "Nuh uh," Steph says. "Nicola needs a nice guy. And while Bram is generous – I mean, he's really stepped up his game lately as we all know – he'd chew her up and spit her out."

"Might be fun to be chewed up, though," Kayla says.

I wish that thought hadn't already crossed my mind.

Finally we arrive at the apartment building and everything is so surreal. I realize it has in no way sunk in that I've moved to this place. I mean, the building isn't anything special. It's two stories with bump-out windows typical of the city and this pinkish taupe color that Bram says he's going to have painted cobalt blue in a few weeks. But even though it's on the old side, it's clean and renovated. The small lobby has art deco-style tiles. There are no bars on the doors. People have doormats outside their doors and there are vivid watercolor paintings of the city in the halls.

My apartment is even better. It's on the second floor and it's a two-bedroom. Both of the bedrooms are barely big enough for a bed, but still, it means Ava can have her own space, something I know would make her really excited. I can't wait until later tonight when my mom drops her off and she gets to see the place. We hadn't had the time to check it out until now.

The kitchen is darling as well with white subway tiles and gleaming appliances and a window over the sink that looks down into the palm trees in the backyard that runs the length of the property. The city skyline stretches in the background, from the Transamerica Pyramid to the Top of the Mark. There are hardwood floors in all the rooms and crown moldings on the walls. It's absolutely gorgeous and perfectly me.

However, the moving in and unpacking seems to take longer than moving out, maybe because now that I'm here I am so damn excited that I can't wait to start decorating and get everything in its perfect place. My furniture looks kind of shabby, and no longer in that chic way, so maybe when I get some money I can head up to IKEA as well.

Everyone is exhausted after the move and I wish I could buy them beer and pizza but Kayla is shunning carbs at the moment and Steph won't let me spend my money. Bram disappears into his apartment – right next door, the corner unit – and comes out with a bottle of champagne and a six-pack. We all pull up a box and sit around, talking, drinking and stretching our aching muscles.

Eventually, Steph and Linden are the last to leave. It's just me and Bram in my apartment now, which I guess is his apartment, and it's at least another hour until my mom and Ava get here.

"So," he says, folding his arms across his wide chest and standing, his legs askance. He surveys the living room, which is a disaster zone of boxes and furniture. "This is going to be your home."

"Until I get back on my feet," I quickly remind him as I lean back against the kitchen counter.

"Well, I was under the impression that you'd pay rent as soon as you get on your feet. Doesn't mean you have to leave. I mean, you like it here, don't you?"

"I just got here."

He eyes me suspiciously. "You're having a hard time with this, aren't you?"

"What?" I ask, hoping my face looks surprised.

He gestures to the room. "This whole arrangement. I really wish you'd learn to trust me."

"I do trust you," I say, then correct myself. "I think. But I barely know you."

He takes a few steps forward and I find myself inching up against the counter. There's a heated look in his eyes that makes me worried. "Well, don't worry, sweetheart, you're going to get to know me pretty well, whether you like it or not. We're neighbors now, above anything else. You need a cup of sugar for your baking, come knock on my door. You need a roll of toilet paper, come knock on my door. You get caught up with some knob in the heat of the moment and you need a condom, come knock on my door. I have plenty." He squints at me. "You do *have sex*, don't you?"

I swallow hard and curse the heat that's coming to my cheeks. Why the hell did I have to have that wine when I know it makes my face extra hot? "Of course I have sex," I snap. "But neighbors don't need to know about each other's sex lives."

"You've got that look again," he says, his voice lower now, as he peers down at me and takes another step forward until there's just a foot between us. "The way your cheeks are pink. Do you remember what I'd said about that?"

I did. That I'd look the same when I had an orgasm. "No and please don't remind me."

He licks his lips and nods. "All right." He turns around and heads to the door. "I'm going out for the evening." He glances at me over his shoulder. "I hope you enjoy your first night here. Say hello to the little one from me."

Then he's gone and I'm alone in my apartment for the first time.

If all of our interactions are going to be a mix of overt generosity and him being, well, him, I'm not sure what the next one is going to bring.

All I know is that it's definitely going to keep me on my toes.

Chapter Six

NICOLA

"Mommy?" Ava asks me, puttering into the kitchen and dragging her Snuffy animal behind her as I'm unloading the dishwasher.

"Yes, angel?" I say, peering at one of the glasses against the morning light, checking for water spots.

"How come you don't have to stick yourself with an ouchie?"

Ah, shit.

It's been two weeks since I've moved into the new apartment and about three weeks of giving Ava her insulin shot. She doesn't mind the finger prick from the glucose monitor as much because she thinks it's like in *Sleeping Beauty* when Beauty gets pricked on the spindle – I think Ava thinks her Prince Phillip might show up. But the shot is something else. She doesn't always cry but I can tell it hurts her and it doesn't seem to matter where I put it. I guess it doesn't help that she calls it her "ouchie."

I put the glass on the table and crouch down to her level. I brush her hair back behind her ears. "I don't stick myself with the ouchie because I'm all grown up. You need the medicine to make sure you'll be grown up and big, just like your mother. But not every child gets this medicine. Only the special ones. You're one of the special ones, angel."

Ava pouts over that but then nods. "Okay." Then she runs into the living room with Snuffy at her side. My heart expands inside me. Being a mother is such a curse sometimes, discovering that ability to love so much more than you thought possible and then being tied to that love forever, no matter how old they get, no matter how much you can't protect them anymore.

I sigh and finish putting away the rest of the dishes. It's Saturday morning and I know I've forgotten to get yesterday's newspaper from the mailbox. I've been applying to every job I can find, at least all somewhat related to my field, but I've only gotten one interview. That was for a clothing store as a sales clerk and it was one week ago. I'm no longer holding my breath. Even though I know most of the ads are online these days, I'm taking no chances and checking the classifieds as well.

"Ava, mommy's going to get the paper from downstairs, okay?" I tell her as I head for the door. "Stay where you are, I'll be right back."

She nods, engrossed with the cartoon on TV. I look down at what I'm wearing – pajama bottoms, slippers and a tank top but at least I've put a bra on. I know who my neighbor is and the last thing I want is for my nipples to have a staring contest with Bram.

I'd seen Bram come and go over the last two weeks and he's checked in on me a few times. He has that perpetual smirk on all the time, like he's just about to throw a zinger or some comment my way, but so far he hasn't. I don't know if he's trying to be on his best behaviour or he's just gotten bored with bugging me.

What I do know is that the guy likes to get laid. A lot. A ridiculous amount. I'm surprised his dick hasn't broken off at this point. My bedroom is next to his and I can hear him when I'm in the living room, which makes things a little uncomfortable when Ava is up and about. So far she hasn't seemed to notice but that might be because I immediately put music on or turn the TV up when I hear him. He's pretty loud and the girl he's with is even louder. That's assuming there is just one girl he's screwing and I'm not too sure about that. It's definitely not Astrid. Last time he was with this cocoa-skinned model with a booty that had even me staring at it, hypnotized.

I also can tell the girls aren't faking it, which means Bram is pretty damn good at what he does. Their cries in the heat of passion all sound surprised, like they can't believe such pleasure could happen to them. I guess the mottos about him are true – one night in his bed and your legs are forever spread.

Meanwhile there's me, who isn't seeing anyone and the last time I got off was in the shower a few days ago with my BOB, my Battery Operated Boyfriend. He's the closest thing to a sexual relationship I've got at the moment and I'm starting to like his dependability.

I get the paper from the mailbox in the lobby and then head back upstairs. While I'm approaching my apartment, I see the door to Bram's open. My heart stills for a moment – I don't know why – but then I see a girl with a dramatic bob exit. She's wearing a black leather miniskirt that I can tell is faux leather, a crop top that looks like the glitter fairy vomited all over it and is carrying her Valentino knock-offs in her hands. She's got day-old mascara under her eyes.

Good ol' walk of shame.

She sees me and smiles sheepishly. "Hi."

"Hello," I say to her as I open my door. "I like your shoes." I mean, that's not entirely true, but I do like the real versions.

"Oh." She eyes them, flustered. "Thanks."

I watch as she walks quickly down the hall and disappears into the stairwell, as if she's fleeing the scene of a crime.

Suddenly Bram's door reopens and he pokes his head out, his dark hair tussled, the definition of bedhead. He's looking down the empty hall and then he notices me and gives me a cocksure smile. "Is she gone?"

"Yes," I tell him. "Like a bat out of hell."

"Excellent album," he says. Then adds, "Meatloaf. The singer."

"I know who Meatloaf is," I tell him, moving to go inside my own apartment.

"Hey," he says quickly, and steps out from behind his door. He's just wearing a t-shirt and his boxer briefs. They are grey. They are David Beckham's. They are that close that I can read the label. And they seem a size too small for all the junk he's packing in there.

"Oh my God," I say, covering my eyes and turning away. "Can you please put on some pants?"

"Prude," he says with a sniff. "There's nothing obscene about underwear."

Maybe not for the average man, but for you, yeah there is, I think. But don't dare say that, lest I add to his already over-inflated ego. I can't help but think what both Steph and Kayla had said about Linden being well-hung and I can deduce that it certainly runs in the family.

"I just wanted to ask you something," he goes on and he sounds just serious enough that I turn around and look at him, keeping my eyes trained up there and nowhere else. I'm not even sure if I'm blinking. "Two things actually."

"What?" I sound impatient. I just want to go back inside.

"I hope we weren't too loud," he says. "You know, I never asked the previous tenants if they could hear my, erm, antics in the bedroom. And every room. You know how it goes. But I can ask you."

"What makes you think you can ask me that?"

He shrugs. "I'm going to assume now that you *can* hear me."

"I use earplugs," I tell him. Which is true. I use them every night and shove them so far down I'm pretty sure they might come out my nose one day. As soon as I get more money, I think I'm going to take stock in an earplug company.

"Too bad, you're missing quite the show."

I give him a dirty look. "Did anyone ever tell you how inappropriate you are?"

"Yes, many times." He jerks his chin at me. "But knowing your wall is just as thin, don't feel like you have to be quiet when – if – you ever bring a man over. I don't mind. I like to listen."

I shake my head in disbelief. "Why is it so hard for you to stay decent?"

"Must be in my genes," he muses, leaning against the doorframe, jutting out his pelvis just so. I refuse to look even though I agree with his statement.

"Do I dare ask what the other thing is?" I say. I don't even know why I'm humoring him and not shutting the door in his face. I'd hate to think I find something fun and amusing about our little interactions. He's kind of like the kid in grade school who used to pull your hair.

"Ah, yes," he says with a wicked grin. "Given the lack of sexual activity in your apartment and your refusal to take even one peek at my knickers, I'm curious if you've ever had sex before. I mean, I know you have a daughter but you hear about these virgin births all the time."

"Go fuck yourself," I tell him, opening my door and quickly jetting inside, shutting the door hard behind me.

As my cheeks flame, I can hear him say on the other side, "There's the girl I wanted to see." Then the sound of his own door shutting.

What an asshat. I mean, I know he's fucking with me like that kid in grade school, only pulling more than just my hair. But man, does he know how to get under my skin. Just because I'm not fucking everything that walks – or him – doesn't mean I'm some uptight, virginal prude.

Unfortunately, I also know he's kind of right. Because in the last few years, I've been heading in that direction. Even though I'm not fat, I used to be way thinner and toned. Now, I've got cellulite on my thighs, an ass that won't stop growing and stretch marks and a C-section scar on my poochy stomach. I'm sure I could make it work for me if I wanted to, it's just that it's so hard to look back on the person I was – happier, better – and be okay with what I am now. It's like admitting defeat.

The last thing I want is to strip naked with a guy and it's unfortunate that the last guy I wanted to do that for was Bram.

Crap. Maybe I really should go hook up with some random just to get Bram's legacy out of my damn head.

"Mommy."

I look over and see Ava on the couch, staring at me curiously. I realize I'm leaning back against the door as if Bram's going to burst inside at any moment. I straighten up and shoot her a bashful look. "I'm okay," I tell her.

"Was that *Bram*?" She pronounces his name with extra care now, wanting to get that "R" in there.

"Yes," I say cautiously. I don't like how she still continues to stay gaga over him. I don't want to have to be nice for her sake and with him being the only male she really sees, the last thing I want is for her to see him as a father figure.

"Bram-a-lama-ding-dong!" she sings loudly, popping Snuffy up and down. "Bram-a-lama-ding-dong!"

Ding *dong* is right.

"All right that's enough," I tell her. "How about we use our quiet voices, okay?"

"Bram-a-lama-ding-dong!" she yells, running to her room and giggling.

I exhale, unfold the newspaper at the kitchen table and start searching for a job.

…

It's about two in the afternoon and I've circled every job I've seen fit in the paper, even those I have no experience in like waitressing. I've sent out every résumé and cover letter and crossed my fingers a million times. Now Ava is racing around the couch, stir-crazy from boredom and I feel like I need a dozen espressos to even get through the rest of the day. At least she's stopped singing her Bram song.

A knock at the door. I feel like I've spoken too soon.

I get up to answer it, giving myself a once over in the vintage mirror on the wall. I don't look half-bad. I guess it helps that after our earlier altercation, I had a long shower and made a full-hearted attempt to make myself look prettier. My hair is wavy with just the right amount of product. I've shaded in my brows more (apparently one of my better features according to most women), put on a few strokes of mascara and a plum lip stain. My skin started going crazy during pregnancy but thankfully it's calmed down and I don't have to wear foundation much. I also skipped the blush since I have my cheeks to thank for that.

I open the door and am not surprised at all to find Bram on the other side. Once he sees me his eyes widen appreciatively at my face and then at the rest of my body. I'm just in leggings and a long sleeveless tunic, but it's a step up from pajamas.

"Well, hello there," he says. He holds out a bottle of wine. "Peace offering."

I purse my lips. "Peace offering?"

"Yes," he says, shaking the bottle at me. "Have you had the Don Melcher before? It's brilliant."

"It looks expensive."

"It is," he says and smiles. "But I feel I need it make it up to you."

"For what?" I want him to say it.

"For being a right prick," he says. "And for standing there with my dick on display. I shouldn't tease you with it."

My eyes narrow momentarily.

He catches himself. "Sorry, sorry. I will behave from now on, I promise."

"Yeah, right."

He crosses his heart. "I swear. The minute I say the wrong thing, you can kick me out."

"Don't bet I won't." I sigh and step out of the way, letting him come inside. That fresh and woodsy scent, reminiscent of something I can't place, but something that once made me happy, wafts past and I can't stop myself from closing my eyes briefly and breathing it in.

Thankfully he doesn't notice as he comes in and places the wine on the kitchen table.

Unfortunately, that kitchen table seems to have had it and one leg breaks from under it. Bram manages to grab the wine before it crashes to the ground with it.

"Fuck," I swear and Ava comes running out of her room.

"What was loud?" she asks and then she sees Bram. Her eyes light up like a candle. "Bram!" she yells and runs over to him.

He stares down at her, smiling, while I quickly close the door and assess the damaged table.

"Bram, Bram, Bram!" Ava shrieks.

"How are you, little one?" he asks her, clearly enjoying her attention.

"I wrote a song for you, Bram," she says excitedly.

He looks over at me. "Oh really? So, she's written me a song, but you haven't?"

I roll my eyes and put my attention back to the table. Though the leg snapped off from the bottom, I think I can glue it back together.

"Bram-a-lama-ding-dong!" Ava starts singing at the top of her lungs. I ignore her and pull the leg out from under it then head to the "Drawer O' Crap" in the kitchen to find the crazy glue.

"That's a very nice song, Ava," Bram says. "Completely original."

"Bram-a-lama-ding-dong!"

"Don't encourage her," I mutter and then Bram is beside me.

"Crazy glue?" he asks, looking over my shoulder. "You need a new table, sweetheart."

I push past him and head over to it, Ava still singing her song and jumping up and down. "If you haven't noticed, I can't afford a table at the moment."

"I'll get you one," he says.

I bristle. "You've done enough." And I really need to keep my debt to him as low as possible. But I realize I'm sounding bitchy again, so I say, "Once I get a job, I'll head to Goodwill and see what I can find."

"How is that going, by the way?" he asks. "The job search?"

"Shitty," I say.

"Shitty!" Ava yells. "Shitty! Shitty! Bram-a-lama-ding-dong!"

"Now that seems more apt," Bram comments.

"Ava, don't say that word," I scold her and then scold myself for swearing around her again.

"Bram?" she asks.

"No, the…you know what, yes. Bram. Don't say that word. It's bad."

"Very, very bad," Bram comments, his voice suddenly husky. I don't know why but goosebumps suddenly appear on my arms and my belly feels hot.

I glance over to see him head into the kitchen and fish out a pair of wine glasses. Okay, so I guess this is happening now. Before I have a chance to tell him it's too early to be drinking, the wine is being opened.

"Mommy," Ava says while I try to open the crazy glue container.

"What?"

"Bram!" she yells and then runs to her room, singing that song again.

"Bram's always been a curse word in my family," he says, coming over with a glass of wine and handing it to me. He then puts his hand on my shoulder, squeezes it for one hot second, and leads me over to the couch. "You sit here. Let me fix your table."

"But," I protest.

"Sit!" he says, pointing at me. "Relax for once, will ya?"

Relax? He'd laugh at the notion if he tried to live my life for even a second.

But still, I sit. I take a sip of my wine (it's damn good). And I watch him as he glues the end of the leg, hoists up the table and sticks it back in place. Actually, I'm watching his muscles as he's doing so. He's in blue jeans with a tear at the knee and a grey V-neck t-shirt that looks really thin and really soft. His casual style is just as enticing as his suits, just in a different way.

"Are you checking out the goods?" he asks, not looking at me. "Because you had more than a chance this morning."

"I'm checking out the table," I tell him, turning around in my seat and focusing on the wine. "It looks good, thank you."

He plops down on the armchair beside me. "You're welcome. That's what good neighbors are for."

"Have you always been this helpful with them?"

"Only the right ones," he says then his expression dampens. "Back in Manhattan, I think all my neighbors hated me. Actually, I know they all hated me. Too many parties and none of them were ever invited."

"Do you miss it?"

He looks surprised at that. "I don't know. I don't think so. I suppose I had more of a routine over there, a scene. I knew who my friends were, even though deep down I knew they weren't really my friends. In New York, it's easy to find people who will follow you around like a bloody puppy dog as long as you're the one that fills their bowl."

"Sounds like a pain in the ass," I tell him.

"Is that right?" he asks. "I would have thought somewhere in your past, you were somewhat the same. Not the puppy, but the big dog."

I don't appreciate how personal he's getting. In some ways he's right, though. In high school and even in college, I had money, I had style and I had followers. Seems like a different lifetime now. In some ways it is. My life is split into Before Ava and After Ava. That's not to say I'm angry about it, but it's just a fact of life when you have a child. Your life changes, for better or for worse, but it changes. Nothing looks the same anymore.

"I've hit a nerve," he muses when I've said nothing. He can see it on my face, I'm sure. "Sorry."

I shrug but busy my mouth with more wine.

"Well," he says, resigned, and lightly slaps his leg, "back to the job search. Not going well?"

"Nope," I say. "I had one interview for a clothing store but they never called me back. I guess there was just something about my face they didn't like."

"But it's a beautiful face," he says softly and I look to him, surprised. He smiles gently. "It's true."

I swallow and look away, not used to compliments. "Anyway," I go on, clearing my throat. "I'm starting to lose my nerve a bit."

"Are you just applying for certain positions, certain fields? You're in fashion, right?" I nod. He goes on, "No one likes to lower their standards, believe me, but maybe you should start going for something that's just a bit beneath you."

"Beneath me?"

"Pride can be a dangerous thing," he says. "I know this. I know this so well."

There's a graveness to his voice that makes me wonder what's happened to him and his pride in the past.

"Well, like what? I've already started to look into waitressing."

"Good," he says. "Though that's a tough job, too. There's a reason there is such a high turnover rate in the industry. I have no doubt you can handle it – you're a mum after all, you can handle anything, but it's..."

"But the problem is that the lower I go, the more I won't be hired for being overqualified."

"Aye," he agrees, scratching his chin. "I wish I had some contacts here, but I don't." He leans back in his chair, looking up at the ceiling for a moment. Then he turns his head to look at me. "What about you?"

I shake my head no.

"No, you do," he says. "What about James? You know, the pierced fella that runs the Burgundy Lion. Do you think he'd hire you?"

"To be what, a bartender?"

He shrugs. "I know my brother used to work there. So did Stephanie, that's how they met. What's wrong with bartending? You're fucking hot too, so you'll make a lot of tips. If you show off your nice tits a bit, you could make even more."

I ignore the "nice tits" comment (even though a terrible part of me is kind of flattered) but I still immediately want to dismiss the idea.

"I don't think so."

"Give me one reason why not."

I chew on my lip. "I don't know how."

"They train you, you'd learn in a second." He snaps his fingers.

"They might not hire me."

"But they might. And they probably will. I can be very persuasive."

"I don't need you to fight my battles," I tell him quickly.

"No, you don't. But you do need to know the difference between fighting someone's battles and trying to help them. James will help you. All you have to do is ask."

And that's the problem. I don't want to ask.

I can feel Bram's eyes on me and I know he's reading me. I know he's figured out some way to get inside my head. "Everyone has to put their pride away sometimes," he says quietly.

I exhale and close my eyes. He's right. I don't want to ask, because I don't want to admit to someone I know that I need help. But I do need help. And a job at the Lion, as much as it's something I never planned on, would make a world of difference in my life. It might just put me back on my feet.

"Okay," I say and when I open my eyes, Bram has my cell phone and is holding it out for me.

"Call him," he says.

And so I do. With Bram there, I ask James if I can have a job bartending at the Burgundy Lion. I only get so far starting to explain my situation and he tells me not to worry, he's going to make it happen somehow.

Now I have a job. And as I sit back in my sagging couch, sipping expensive wine, I feel a world of weight lift off my shoulders.

I have a job.

And maybe, just maybe, I have a pretty good neighbor too

Chapter Seven

NICOLA

Three weeks.

I've been working at The Burgundy Lion for three weeks now and I'm finally, *finally* feeling my groove about things.

That said, in three weeks I've overcharged five people.

Undercharged twenty.

Overpoured 70% of the time.

Underpoured 25%.

Who knows what happened to that other 5%.

I've spilled three drinks.

Two on people.

One on myself.

I've fallen down once.

Not sure how.

I've been hit on countless times.

I've made $800 in tips.

I come home to the apartment absolutely exhausted and pay Lisa – who is more than happy to be back and watching over Ava when she can – or let my mom stay the night because I don't want her driving back home at that hour. The nights are late now and my feet have blisters but I'm finally making money to start balancing things out. I'm finally feeling a little bit in control. My only complaint is I work three shifts a week but James says he's working on getting me more. I'm just grateful he gave me a chance at all.

And I have Bram to thank for that. Bram the man. Bram the man next door, who still has loud sex with random chicks and still manages to piss me off from time to time with teasing or overtly sexual comments. But when he doesn't do it – on those days I don't run into him in the halls or he doesn't go and knock on my door – I really hate to admit this, but I kind of miss him. I mean it. The banter and interaction. And yeah, maybe I miss the eye candy too.

But I'm not too happy about that because I have no intention of letting that man get close. As a neighbor he's great, as anything more than that...he's bad, bad news and bad for me.

Tonight I have my mother over to watch over Ava. Sandra, the girl that normally works Friday nights at the bar, called in to work saying she had a thing and wouldn't be able to make it into work until eleven. Even though the shift was just from 8pm to 11pm, James asked if I'd like to come in and he'd pay me for four hours. Naturally I jumped at the chance – I was taking anything he was slinging my way.

"You've really made this home," my mom comments, sitting down on the couch. Just as she does so, I hear a rip. Yet another hole appears in the threadbare cushions. We both look at the tear and at each other and share a small laugh. It's taken a long time for either of us to laugh at our circumstances.

My mother really had the perfect life when I was young. She had my dad, who, yes, did seem flighty at times, who didn't always apply himself, who wasn't a go-getter after the finer things in life. But he had a good heart and a good soul.

I would have thought a forgiving soul too, but I'm not sure how much of that is true. My mother always wanted more and one day she fell in love with the world's most boring lawyer to the rich and famous. They had an affair, one that lasted years. You'd think I would have known what was going on, but I was a teenager at the time, hated everyone and was completely oblivious to anything around me that didn't involve *me*.

Eventually my mother confessed. She and my dad divorced and he took that opportunity to up and leave to find his path in life. It led him straight to India to do charity work. I used to feel slighted that he left so easily – and sometimes I still do. That little sting of rejection, why daddy left, why he didn't think I was worth sticking around for.

But at the same time I get it. He assumed I didn't need him; that I would better off with my mother and Richard, in a big fancy house in one of San Francisco's richest neighborhoods. He probably assumed I didn't need him because I never told him, never acted like it.

It couldn't have been further from the truth. Some days I think one phone call to my dad to tell him I needed him would have brought him back. But I never tried. I didn't have the guts.

I wonder if the same thing could have happened with Phil. Maybe I had done something wrong, maybe I just spent too much time focused – obsessed – with Ava, that I hadn't noticed I pushed him away. Maybe Phil needed to hear I needed him too.

I swallow back the bitter memories and they move down into my chest where I hope they stay, that blank, dark space behind my heart. I think I see my mom doing the same. When she married Richard, perhaps because of how they got together, he made her sign an indemnity clause. When she eventually cheated on him – let's face it, what they had wasn't love – she lost it all. Now she has nothing. No education, no love. She lives in a tiny house in the middle of nowhere, cleaning other people's homes to make a living. We both used to have so much, and now we have so little. I know people must think this is her karma, that it's deserved after all she did.

But what did I do to deserve the struggle?

"You better not be late," my mother warns. It makes me realize I must have been standing there blanked out like a glum zombie.

"I'm going," I tell her, walking into the bedroom to grab my purse. Ava's already asleep so I quickly get out the door so I can make my bus on time.

I have the worst and best timing when it comes to bumping into people in the halls.

Bram and his new girlfriend are just stepping out of his place.

"Hi," I say to him, immediately feeling awkward as I stand in the doorway.

"Hi," Bram says, smiling brightly, not seeming awkward at all. I'm not sure I've *ever* seen him look awkward.

Silence and a polite smile from the tall brunette on his arm. She's dressed to the nines, very classy in a long black dress and gold jewelry and Bram's wearing a sharp black suit and tie. His hair is pushed off his face and he's looking exceedingly dapper, like he did at his brother's wedding. He could be the next James Bond. Even his accent is the same as Connery's, maybe with a bit more emphasis on the rolling "Rs."

"Is this Bram?" my mother suddenly asks and I nearly jump. I look behind me and see her poking her head through the door. And I was so close to closing it.

"She's heard of me?" Bram asks gleefully.

"Who hasn't?" I say dryly as he leans over to get a better look at my mother.

"You must be Nicola's mother," he says, grinning those dimples at her and offering my mother his hand. "I can see where she gets her beauty from. A rose from a rose."

Oh, brother. While my mom seems to melt in front of him, telling him her name is Doreen and that he's far too kind, I exchange a glance with the silent brunette. She looks like she wants to roll her eyes too. Makes me wonder how their date is going to go.

"Well, I'm going to get going," I say, knowing if I miss my bus I'm screwed.

"Off to work?" Bram asks. "I can give you a ride."

"Isn't he darling?" my mother says.

"That's okay," I tell him quickly. "The bus is easy."

"You'd rather take the bus than come with me?"

I eye the girl again, rather apologetically this time. "You seem to be on a date."

"We're just going to the opera." Oh, *just* the opera. "Justine doesn't mind, do you Justine?"

Justine gives a half-hearted shrug with one shoulder, wearing a world of indifference on her elegant features.

"See, she doesn't mind," Bram says. "Come on."

I really should have protested further but to be honest, I was glad to not take the bus for a change. My stupid car was now at the back of the building – Bram had it towed there from the Tenderloin – waiting for money so I could get it the part it needs. Battling crazies on the bus had become a part of my nightly routine, but it would be nice to just relax for once.

Yet, I do anything but relax in the back of Bram's Mercedes. Bram keeps talking to me about this and that, completely ignoring his date who seems to be bored by the whole thing anyway. After a while I stop feeling bad that I have so much of his attention and start to enjoy it. He can be damned charming and funny when he wants to be.

After he dropped me off, I was immediately swept into the chaos that is working at The Burgundy Lion. James is a pretty good boss, although he's a moody little bitch sometimes. I remember what an obstacle he was with Steph and Linden when they got together and I'm glad Linden finally pushed James's opinion to the side because he strikes me as the type to get upset about everything. Thankfully he hasn't thrown a hissy fit with me yet but that's because I do my job and even when I make an epic mistake (um, like forgetting to charge a group for their massive bill), he's had the grace to look the other way. I think he knows I'm much harder on myself than he will ever be. I also think he's a bit scared of me. I don't know why. Perhaps he thinks single moms are crazy. In some ways, we kind of are.

By the time my short shift is over, I get to the apartment, by way of the bus this time, no Bram to whisk me away in his car. I'm absolutely exhausted and it's getting close to midnight. I feel terrible that my mom has to drive back to her place so late but as soon as I step inside the door, she's all bright-eyed and bushy-tailed and ready to go.

"Everything was okay?" I ask her.

She nods. "She didn't wake up, keeps on snoozing away."

"Are you sure you don't want to stay the night?"

"On that couch, are you kidding me? Last time I woke up with a back I thought I'd get when I'm 80," she says with a grin. "Seriously, Nicola, darling, first chance you get, get a new one. You know this couch is too big for most living rooms anyway. What about two loveseats? I bet IKEA has them at the right price."

Two loveseats would make the living room area look much bigger but there are so many other things to spend money on – important things – that a new couch or two seems frivolous. Besides, how the hell would I get my things from IKEA anyway, haul all the boxes on the bus?

"By the way," my mom adds as she heads to the door. From the saucy look in her eyes, I have a feeling I know what the subject will be. "I spoke to Bram again."

"Again?"

She lowers her voice. "He came home about an hour ago. He was alone if that makes any difference to you."

"It doesn't," I quickly interject.

"Nonetheless," she goes on, "he knocked on the door, just wanting to see if I was okay and if I needed anything. Actually I needed a cup of tea and your kettle isn't working so he came over and lent me his." I look over my shoulder in the kitchen and see a fancy stainless steel one on the counter. "He said you could keep it. I told him you would really appreciate it."

"Mom," I say, nearly whining, "I don't want anything else of his. He's done enough and I'm tired of feeling like a charity case."

Her smile fades. A heavy pause settles between us. "I know darling. It never gets easier, does it?"

I sigh, my heart feeling fragile, like tempered glass. "No. It doesn't."

Then, to my surprise, she quickly pulls me into a hug and holds me tight. She hasn't done this for ages. She's a lot like me, or maybe I'm a lot like her – we forget to be affectionate most of the time.

"You're a good mother," she whispers into my ear. "I'm proud of you, just like this, just the way things are now. But they will get better. For both of us. I promise."

I close my eyes, letting that glass shatter. Just a little. Then my mother lets go and the air in the apartment is cold. She gives me a loving look and she's out the door.

Slipping off my shoes, I head over to the poor, ragged couch and flop down on it.

The rip gets larger.

The apartment is almost silent except for the faint beat of music coming from Bram's place. I make a mental note to talk to him about soundproofing. Since he owns the building, he could make it happen.

There's something assuring about the fact that he's up even though the music sounds like it's getting louder and louder. It's nothing too drum heavy, it sounds more like Massive Attack or Portishead, with slow, lazy beats.

I wonder what he's doing. My mom had said he came home alone. Did that mean he didn't get laid with Justine? That it was just an opera fling? Knowing Bram though, I wouldn't be surprised if they screwed each other in a private box seat or something.

Stop thinking about him, I admonish myself, *he's nothing more than Mr. Rogers to you*. So I get up to check on Ava instead. I sit on the side of her bed and watch her breathe in and out for a few moments, her own breathing steadying mine.

Meanwhile the thumping bass continues. I go into the kitchen and eye the kettle. I meant it when I said I didn't want his charity. I pick it up, wrapping the cord around it, and go out into the hallway. I wait at his door for a second. I can hear the music more clearly here, the beginning of Portishead's "Strangers," which makes me flashback to high school and my British trip hop phase. I used to have a lot of sex to this kind of music. I kind of want to tell Bram that, just to get rid of my prude persona.

I knock on his door and wait. No response. I knock a bit louder. The music must be blocking me out. The right thing to do is to go back in my apartment and give him back the kettle tomorrow. After all, it's not an emergency. I can gain back my pride another day.

But I don't do that. Instead I try the door handle.

It's not locked. It turns with easy and against my better judgement, I push open the door slowly. The music is loud now, a light is on in the kitchen but everything else is dark.

"Hello?" I call out, stepping inside. I push the door closed to keep the music out from the hall. I tiptoe forward now and place the kettle on the kitchen counter.

It's then that the music quiets for a break beat and I hear something from his bedroom, like a groan. Could my mom have been wrong and he didn't come home alone? Suddenly I'm very aware that I'm standing in the near dark in my landlord's apartment, completely trespassing while he might be banging Justine in his room.

But I don't hear any female noises and I no longer hear his.

I slowly make my way over to his bedroom, mindful of my footfalls, as the music builds up again. His door is open half-way and the light is on. I carefully peek inside.

My mouth drops open.

Bram is lying down on his bed and from my angle I can only see him from the chest down. He's lying on top of a silky white duvet cover, completely naked. More than that, he has his dick in his hand and is slowly sliding it up and down his shaft.

Oh my God.

Oh my God.

Oh my fucking God.

I'm stunned, frozen in place as I watch him pleasure himself. This may make me a huge pervert, but to me there's nothing sexier than watching a guy get himself off. Maybe that doesn't make me a huge pervert but the fact that I'm sticking around to watch him do it, secretly I must add, most definitely *does*.

And yet I can't help it. This is my first look at him completely naked and he's one tanned, muscular machine, his body taught and golden against the white beneath him. His legs are long and toned, there's a defined six-pack on his abs that glisten with sweat, and his chest is broad and hard with a bit of chest hair that only adds to his pure, vibrant manliness.

Then there's his dick. I obviously had a hint of it before but now it was large and in charge. His own hand looked like he could barely tame it. I wasn't sure anyone could.

But right now, I'd be willing to give a shot.

I have a brief fantasy about walking through the door. What would Bram say? I bet he wouldn't even stop. He would keep going, watching me the entire time. Just before he'd come he'd ask me to get on my knees and crawl to the edge of the bed. With one large, tense hand he'd wrap my hair around his fingers and he'd tell me to slide my gorgeous mouth over his length. He'd tell me, breathless and commanding, to suck his cock.

In the fantasy I do it. I lick him from balls to purple tip and watch his eyes roll back in ecstasy. I'd do it and I'd love it.

But this isn't a fantasy. This is reality. I'm spying on Bram as he jerks off and I'm fucking wet as hell, the throbbing building between my legs along with the music. Jeez, I really need to get laid because this is ridiculous. Those cobwebs need to be cleared ASAP.

I watch for a few more moments, each one seeming to stretch into an abyss of yearning. I'm practically salivating. I feel no shame in taking it in, not in this moment. Maybe later it will dawn on me that I have a secret, skeezy soul. But now, now I watch and I want. I want to put my mouth where his hands are, feel him, squeeze him just so. Then I'd climb on top and ride the shit out of him, ride him until this need inside of me is gone.

I've got to get out of here.

I slowly back away until I can no longer see him but I do hear his groans becoming louder. I know them so well because I've heard them often but it's an entirely different animal to hear them up close, to be able to envision just what his hard body does when he's that wrapped up in lust.

I manage to leave his apartment, quietly shutting the door behind me, before I can hear him escalate. If he had come in front of me that would have been way, way too much. I might have lost all control over myself.

Once inside my own place, I close the door to my room and try to go to bed. I don't even bother washing my face or anything. I just want to drift away and start over. But I can't. My heart rate is up and I feel flushed from head to toe.

Just go back over, I tell myself. It's that dirty part of me, the one I've tried to keep buried. The wild one. The one I know Bram wants to see and wants to bring out of me. But that's not me anymore.

Still, I slip a hand between my legs and feel how soaked I am. It just takes a few strokes of my clit to get me off and I throw the pillow over my face to keep my own moans from escaping out into the air.

Somewhere behind his music, behind the wall, I think I hear Bram crying out, too, finally coming. I imagine him coming hard, his toes curling up, his head thrown back, his ass muscles clenching. It's enough to have me coming again, this one sneaking up on me in surprise.

I may have not acted out my fantasy but whatever the hell just happened was one of the hottest things to happen to me in a long time.

I know I fall asleep with a stupid grin on my face.

Chapter Eight

BRAM

When I wake up, I'm feeling strangely refreshed, something I haven't felt in a while. Maybe it was good that I hadn't brought Justine back to the apartment after Aida was over. It hadn't been my plan to shag her anyway. I mean the whole date was made on behalf of our parents. I'm not sure why my father thought anything would come from it and I'm not really sure why I went along with it but old habits die hard.

Oh yeah, it was because Justine was gorgeous. She was also one of those types that put up a battle in the "I don't like you" department, just like Nicola. It got me going every single time. But while Justine smelled like roses and indifference, I can tell I'm slowly getting through Nicola's defenses.

At least I hope I am. I've never been so unsure with a woman and while I'm finding it mildly frustrating, it's at least keeping me on my toes. I feel like every day is a new challenge and I haven't felt that way since I left New York. Shit, I haven't felt this way in a very long time.

Adding to the perplexities that living next door to Nicola brings, when I finally get out of bed and make my way into the kitchen, I'm shocked to see the kettle on the counter. I had given it to her mother last night to make some tea. Now she was quite the MILF, but then I guess her daughter is too. I'm not surprised that Nicola brought it back – I figured she would – but I am puzzled as to how she got into my place without me knowing it.

And why?

I make my way over to the door and see that's its unlocked. I have a habit of doing that sometimes, probably because when I first bought the building I was the only tenant in this place for months.

So last night – or this morning – she would have had to come inside and put it on the counter. Was it possible that I didn't hear her, that she didn't wake me up?

Or was it that…

Well, after I dropped off Justine at her place and got nary even a peck on the cheek, I took my sexual frustrations home and had a bit of a wank-fest, as you do. I had the music pretty loud, everything that reminded me of my Scottish youth: Portishead, Garbage, Massive Attack, Faithless, Tricky, you know, just to really get in there.

But the minute I was stroking it, Justine became a distant memory. Her face would go out of focus every time I tried to imagine her and in her place was Nicola. It didn't matter how many other people I tried – Brooklyn Decker, Kate Beckinsdale, that saucy, bitchy redhead that shot Jon Snow on Game of Thrones – Nicola's face replaced them all.

And why not. It's a beautiful face. She has the most gorgeous cheeks and a full upper lip that you just wanted to take between your teeth or have her slide along the ridge of your cock. The freckles just add to the appeal. There's something so wholesome about her yet she always has this wicked gleam in her sloe-eyes that hints at something wild underneath. I know she puts up a bashful and prudish front, but it's just a front. I know it is. I know how mums get, how wrapped up they can be with their child about being selfless and devoted that they forget they're still a sexual creature with multiple needs.

I want to let the sexual creature free. Out of its cage. I want Nicola to have the fun she hasn't had in a long time.

But my usual tactics don't work with her. I'm not sure what will. And to be honest, I'm not sure if even hitting on her is the right thing, let alone fucking her. The absolute last thing I need is to be entangled up with a single mum, no matter how enticing she is, no matter how precious her child is.

I just can't go down that path.

I know how that ends.

More and more though, it's becoming something I have little control over. And that, that is what scares me. Fear has no place in my life, not anymore.

I contemplate going over to her place and asking her when she dropped off the kettle. I know that within seconds I'll be able to tell whether she caught me in the act or not. I wouldn't even be embarrassed about it. I actually wish she did watch me sampling my own goods. Maybe the sight of me naked would be enough to get her to look at me a little differently. I mean, I know I'm good-looking, I know I have what it takes to lure any woman into bed and I know what it takes to get them off again and again and again. But I think her disgust for me might run a bit deeper than her hormones.

I decide to bypass the whole kettle situation and bring it up later. Even though I woke up refreshed, my head feels cloudy now so I drive up to Golden Gate Park and go for one of my Saturday runs before stopping at the boxing gym. Pounding those bags isn't as satisfying as pounding a woman, preferably Nicola, preferably from behind, preferably while pulling her hair. But it will do.

When I get back to my building though, all cleaned up and spiffy, I knock on her door only to find that awkward bird of a woman, Lisa, there instead.

"She's already left for work," she says, eyeing me like I'm about to bust down the door and steal her virtue. Makes me wonder what Nicola has told her.

"Long shift?" I ask, checking my watch for the time. It's only about three in the afternoon.

She nods, her expression un-changing.

"Well, I guess I'll catch her later."

The door shuts in my face. So polite.

But I don't plan on letting later happen on this turf. I want to see Nicola in action. At about seven I get a cab and head to The Burgundy Lion. I haven't been there since she started working and it's high time I paid it a visit. Back in New York, I was always frequenting the hoighty-toighty nightclubs and martini bars but secretly my favorite kind of place was a dive bar. There's something so freeing about those places, the freedom to be yourself, to let loose, to express desires, to lurk in the dark. Everyone is equal in the shadows with a cheap drink in hand. Now, the Lion wasn't a dive bar at all, but it could feel that way on the weekends when everyone seemed to congregate there under the sole purpose of being pissed off their rockers.

When I step inside, I'm assaulted by the smell of beer and overpriced cologne. Though it's relatively early, the place is almost packed with most of the gleaming teak booths crammed with people. There's a sense of urgency here, as if you don't get here on time, the chances of getting laid go down with the rest of your beer.

And there, in all the chaos, I see Nicola behind the bar. Her back is to me but her hair is pulled back, exposing the perfect bare skin of her neck and her upper back as it dips into a loose-cut tank top. She moves with efficiency, whatever she's doing, while a bunch of guys lean across the bar, bills wavering in their hands. They watch her every move, just as I am.

Something inside me burns hot as coals and I swallow down a surprising burst of jealousy. I can't remember the last time I got jealous but it's as if it suddenly dawns on me that I may not be the only one who wants to get in her pants. And of course I know I'm not, but it seemed that until she took the job here, she was relatively safe from roaming eyes.

I'm completely delusional, but I still stride over to the bar and stick myself right beside the guys, my hands stretched along the edge of the bar top.

The guy next to me, some punk with gelled blond hair that would give Zach Morris a run for his money, gives me the fuck off look but I don't pay him any attention. My eyes are trained on her. They might think I'm here to get a drink but that's not the case at all.

When she turns around, she plunks four bottles of beer down on the counter and smiles at the guys while she tells them the total. I want to be jealous over that smile alone, even if it's just for show. Then as they pay, her eyes flit to me, a good bartender, always looking for that next customer and when she sees me, she does a double take. She's jarred.

This could be good.

"Bram," she says and then her smile goes wider than the world and I don't feel jealous anymore. I feel fucking elated. Because that was no "give me a good tip, you wankers" smile, that was an "I'm really glad to see you smile."

Please Lord, let it have been that kind of smile.

"Hey," I say, suddenly feeling rather speechless. I clear my throat. "Thought I'd come see you in action."

The boys take their beers and turn away. I notice they didn't leave any tip, probably because I had to butt my way on in and hog all her attention.

I reach out and grab Zach Morris's shoulder. "Listen," I say to him and it looks like he wants to spit at me. "Just because you have zero chance of going home with her tonight, doesn't mean you don't have to tip her."

"Bram," Nicola warns quietly, eyes wide as a deer.

"So," I go on to the wanker, ignoring her, "pay up if you thought her service was good. I was watching. It was good."

The wanker eyes my hand on his shoulder but I've got height and breadth and he's got…bloody awful hair. He looks at one of his friends who quickly whips out a five from the change she gave back and smacks it down on the table. I take my hand away and they walk off to a booth in the corner, shooting me daggers as they go. They can shoot all they want. If I survived Nicola's death glares, I can survive anything.

"Bram," she says again, admonishing me as I turn back to her. "It was fine."

"It wasn't," I told her. "They would have tipped you but your smile for me was so much more beautiful than your smile for them. Jealousy makes dickheads do dickish things."

She rolls her eyes and flips a dishrag over her shoulder. "I've been here long enough to learn some things, you know."

"I also know you work part-time and tips are as important as blood. I did say it would be a hard job."

Now there's a hint of a smile, just a subtle lifting of her lips. "It was easy until you got here."

I lean forward more on the counter until my eyes are level with her cleavage. She took that advice of mine too. Show off those beautiful tits for tips. But like the gentleman I am, I keep my eyes trained to hers. Even in this light I can make out the many shades of brown in them, the way they all snake in vibrant lines toward her pupil, the very pupil that's widening before my eyes, as if she likes what she sees.

You better fucking like what you see, I think to myself, wishing now that we weren't here at all, but back in her apartment or mine, sharing a bottle of wine. Oh the things I could do to try and break down that wall. I'd pull out brick by brick with my teeth until she's screaming my name.

As if she can see the filthy images in my head, her cheeks grow pink and she looks away for a moment. "So now that you're here, what will it be?" she asks, her voice now cheery but false. She's back in bartender mode with polite professionalism.

"Make me something," I tell her, straightening up. "Anything. Make a Bram McGregor."

"I don't think we have enough ego for that," she says.

I grin at her. "I suppose I have enough already, don't I? I'm serious though. Make me anything sour."

She raises her perfectly shaped brow. "Sour? I would have thought you a sweet kind of guy."

"There's nothing about me that's sweet, and you know it."

But from the way she's staring at me, I can tell she doesn't agree with that. "Maybe a shot of sweet," she concludes after searching my face like a puzzle. "But it's definitely spicy all the way."

"All right then, babe," I tell her. "Take your best shot."

Even though there's a small line forming behind me (the other bartender is James and he seems swamped), Nicola takes her time trying to figure out what Bram McGregor tastes like. I wish she could find out for herself. I've seen that cute, pink little tongue at times and I think it could give me a real lashing. I tell her she should add some salt in there for good measure and I swear her cheeks go crimson.

When she's finally done she slides the drink toward me.

"This is what I call the Bram McGregor. Mainly spicy with a kick of sweet and salty."

I take the highball from her and my fingers brush against hers as I do so. I pounce.

"I found the kettle in my room this morning. When abouts did you return it and how did you get into my apartment?"

The question takes her completely off-guard but from the way she looks absolutely bashful and ashamed, I know she must have done it when I was whacking off.

"Just when I got home," she says quickly, suddenly eyeing the next person in line. "I thought you were asleep so I just put it in the kitchen and left."

Bullshit. But I let it go because even if I called her on catching me in the act, she would deny it – anything to get out of that conversation.

As she tends to the next person, I slip a fifty in the tip jar and take a sip of my drink. The Bram McGregor certainly has a fucking kick to it. It's actually pretty damn good.

I leave her be for now and look for an empty bar stool and find one by none other than Linden who is at the end of the bar talking to James as he shakes a martini.

"Fuckface," Linden says when he sees me saunter over, our usual term of endearment. "What the hell are you doing here?"

I shrug. "Bored." I look at James and pass him the drink. "You have to try this."

James's brow piercing raises as he eyes it. "What is it?"

"Your new bartender made it," I told him. "Try it."

James does so and then considers it with a tilt of his head. "Not bad."

"It's called the Bram McGregor," I tell him.

"Of course it is," Linden says with a groan.

I go on, "You should give that gal a raise. Anyone that can make something this tasty on the fly is someone to hold on to."

"Well I am trying to get her more shifts," James explains, "but it's not easy when I had full staff to begin with. I gave her the job to help her out but I'm not sure what else I can do."

"Fire someone," I suggest.

"Bram," Linden warns. "Don't get all embroiled in someone else's business. You have your own to attend to, brother."

"Well, Jenny isn't exactly working out," James admits. "I mean, she's efficient and dependable but the more she works here, the more she thinks men are responsible for the doom of civilization. I can't have a conversation with her unless some weird sector of feminism is brought up."

"She does work here though," Linden points out. "You can't really blame her."

"Like I said, fire her," I say.

"I'll give it time," James says. "I hate to sound like a douche, but I just don't know how reliable single moms can be."

For some reason the comment makes my veins feel black and poisonous, like squid ink.

"She's reliable," I tell him, my voice stern. "I'm her damn landlord, I know she is."

He gives me a look, the look that doesn't take me seriously whatsoever. I should be used to that. "She doesn't pay you rent. So you can't really compare. Look, I like Nicola and I think she's great, but what if something happens to her kid. We all know she's sick. She could have a problem and then Nicola would have to up and leave."

"Well, if you're going to look at it that way, Jen Jen or whatever her name is, could have a flat tire on the way to work, or get food poisoning, or hell, just play hooky for a day. Anyone could. Having a damn kid doesn't make you any less dependable. Don't you think she needs this fucking job?"

"Easy brother," Linden says, putting his hand on my shoulder. "Just finish your ego drink and relax. James is just speculating. He'll help Nicola as much as he can, right James?"

James nods, looking a bit weirded out, like he thought I was going to punch him or something. "Definitely. I'll help." Then he backs away and disappears around the other side of the bar.

"Scares easy, doesn't he?" I ask Linden.

"Does he ever," he says with a sigh, then finishes the rest of his Anchor Steam. He gives me a discerning look. "What are you really doing here?"

I shrug and take a sip of my drink, pretending my mouth isn't on fire. I have a sudden notion of cooling it off with an ice cube and then my mind wanders over to Nicola, wondering if she'd squirm if poured the spicy drink over her breasts then rubbed my ice cold tongue on them after.

"Oh, I see," Linden says and I immediately snap my attention to him.

"What?"

He jerks his chin down the bar at Nicola. "You're here for her."

"I guess I want to see if she'll eventually pay me rent."

A slow smile spreads across my brother's face and he shakes his head in disbelief. "No you don't. You'd let her live there forever rent free, I reckon."

"Is that so?" I challenge but I'm afraid he might be right.

"Whatever happened to my brother who moved out West, wanting to invest his money and make a name for himself, step out from under our parent's shadow?"

"I'm still him, you half-wit," I tell him, hating that he's got the power to get under my skin sometimes. It doesn't help that both of us can bring the other down with the mere mention of our mum and dad. "There's nothing wrong with trying to be a good Samaritan. You were the one always harping on me about being a selfish lout, doing nothing with myself. Now I am doing something and one of those things happens to be a good deed."

"Oh, there's nothing wrong with the deed. I want Nicola helped out as much as the next person, especially for Steph's sake. Those two are pretty close, even more so since we got hitched. I guess having babies or getting married brings you into the next step of the maturity club. But you can't pretend you don't have ulterior motives." He jabs his finger in my face. "You can't pass this all like you're interested in charity. You're losing money here, brother."

The funny thing is I *am* interested in charity but there's no use in telling my brother that. He doesn't listen to me anyway. No matter how much you change, some people will always view you as you were at a certain time of your life. I don't think Linden will ever stop thinking of me as the philandering git he knew growing up. I don't think I'll ever stop thinking of him as the annoying little shit who used to steal my stuff, the same one I used to give atomic wedgies to in the playground. And no matter how much our mother tries to cut down on her drinking and the icy shell of her exterior, no matter how hard our father pretends to be proud of us, we can't help but view them as themselves when *we* were most vulnerable.

"Be that as it may," I try and explain. I sigh. It's hopeless. "She's got a nice rack." I give up and drink my burning elixir.

But Linden is watching me closely. "Is that all?"

I nod and start to cough. He slides his water over and I gulp half of it down. "Thanks," I say, wiping my lips with the bar napkin. "And yes, that's all. Would you expect anything more from me?"

"I guess not," he says. He twists around in his stool and nods at the front door. "Hey, check it."

I glance over my shoulder. A stunning blonde with arse-length hair and a glossy smile comes in the door. She's dressed to impress in a gold strapless top that shows off just enough cleavage and tight-as-fuck jeans.

"She looks like your type," Linden says.

"Are you trying to distract me?" I ask him wryly.

His eyes turn serious. "I told you before, Nicola is a no-go for you. Steph will absolutely murder me if you two hook-up. I will never hear the end of it and she'll go on and on about ruining our dynamics. It's always about the dynamics. She keeps quoting *Friends*, when Ross and Rachel broke up and changed everything for everyone else. Drives me bloody bonkers."

"I am not bloody Ross," I tell him defensively. "Joey, maybe."

"Fine, but you get what I mean. She's concerned about everyone being nice and getting along and you know if you shag Nicola, that's just going to end poorly. Not only for her, but for yourself. How charitable are you going to be when she sets your whole apartment building on fire, huh?"

I can't help but smile. "You think I'd affect her that badly, huh?"

"Oh, you're useless," Linden says and snaps his fingers for James. "Barkeep, I need another one."

I sit there with Linden, shooting the shit for a wee bit, until Nicola comes on down the bar to us.

"Brave enough for another one?" she asks. Do my ears detect a flirty tone?

I can feel Linden get up from beside me, which brings me an ounce of relief. Last thing I want is for him to watch over everything I say to her.

"If you're serving, I'm drinking," I tell her with a wink. "It was...Bramtastic."

Her eyes seek the ceiling.

"You are unbelievable," she says. "Maybe I'll add less sweet this time, though I swear I didn't add any *cheese*."

"I'll be whatever you want me to be."

She sighs and starts to make the drink. I make a mental note of the ingredients – Patrón tequila, lime juice, triple sec, hot pepper infused liqueur, a splash of orange juice and a wee hit of the brine from a jar of pickled banana peppers. Ah, so that was the secret ingredient.

While she's piling up the garnishes on the end of a cocktail sword, she shoots me a look I haven't seen before, not on her face anyway. It's sort of pleading and puppy dog-ish. I like it. It makes me feel like she wants something from me for once instead of me always trying to give her something.

"So," she says, her voice unsure. She hands me the drink. "So," she starts again, "this drink is on the house."

"And why is that?"

"Because I need a favor."

My eyes widen. "You? You're asking for a favor? From me?"

She seems to shut down before me. I quickly reach out and put my hand on hers, giving her soft skin a squeeze. She feels absolutely radiant to touch and I don't want to let go.

But she's staring at my hand like it doesn't belong there. I remove it but lean forward to meet her eyes. "Sorry," I say to her, "I didn't mean to tease. What's the favor? You know I'd do anything for you."

Arse. That was not what was supposed to come out of my mouth. But I just smile at her, keeping it cool.

"Well," she says, looking at the counter, "I was wondering tomorrow, if you're not busy, if you wouldn't mind taking me and Ava to IKEA." She eyes me and quickly continues. It looks like just asking is bringing her pain. "I wouldn't be long. I just need a new couch and I don't think I can take the bus with it. I mean, I can try but—"

"I'd be happy to," I tell her emphatically. "It's not a problem at all. What time would you like to go?" I don't bother pointing out that the Mercedes isn't exactly big enough for a couch, even if it is disassembled into small, aggravating boxes but I figure I can always swap my car for Linden's Jeep if need be.

Her features relax and she manages a smile. "You really wouldn't mind? I don't know, whenever works for you. I'm not working so…"

Everyone knows that Sundays at IKEA are a living nightmare so I suggest we get there as soon as they open and beat the crowds. She agrees and there's a rare tickle in my stomach. I think I want to drown it with my drink.

I'm still smiling at her when Linden taps me on the shoulder.

"Bram," he says as I turn around. That blonde with the gold top is standing behind me with him, looking at me expectantly. "This is Paige."

What the hell is my brother doing? I've never known him to try and set me up before. He knows I don't fucking need it.

"Hello, Paige," I say to her with a polite bow of my head, because I'm anything if not fucking polite.

"I was just talking you up to her," Linden goes on but I'm looking back at the bar. My drink is on the counter and Nicola is way down near the other end, serving other customers. Bollocks. Linden sure fucked up that one for me. But still. IKEA is on.

I pick up the drink and take a sip – damn, that's even hotter than before – and with an internal sigh, turn around to face them. Well, since the blonde is in front of me and she looks just as agreeable as she did earlier, I guess I don't really have anything to lose.

"You oughta try this, Paige," I tell her, offering her the drink. "I dare you."

"Okay," she says, still smiling but sounding a bit nervous.

"Here, I'll drink it first," I tell her, having another sip and trying to hide the burn from showing on my face. "Sweetheart, I don't need to put roofies in your drink in order to have sex with you."

"Okaaaay," Linden says slowly. "I'm going to go now."

He heads to the washroom and I nod at his empty seat.

"Sit down and drink up," I tell her. "But if you cough once, you forfeit the dare."

"All right," Paige says, wanting to be a good sport. She sits down and I slide the drink her way. She sniffs it before picking it up. Right before she has a sip her eyes catch mine. "Wait, if I cough, what happens?"

"We don't know yet," I tell her smoothly, leaning in close so that my knee brushes against hers. It feels all too easy to do this, to pick up a chick. It's just as much fun as a good shag or two. But at the same time, there's something prickling the back of my skull, telling me this probably isn't a good idea. I think that's the same part of my brain that doesn't like me to have any fun. I call it Logic.

I watch as Paige has a sip of her drink. To her credit though, she doesn't flinch. She gulps it down with a smile. I imagine she'd swallow my cum in the same way.

Now Logic's friend Guilt decides to pop up. I'm not sure why, there's nothing wrong nor different about my thoughts. Nicola couldn't give a rat's arse what I do or who I sleep with. I'm just her neighbor, her landlord, and maybe, just maybe her friend.

For now, anyway.

And perhaps that's what's stopping me from going home with Paige. The very minute possibility that one day down the road, I could be with Nicola. It's unlikely but I'm suddenly unwilling to put it in jeopardy, not until I know for sure that the two of us have no chance together, not even for a hot fuck.

So, though I spend the rest of the evening talking and flirting with Paige, it's all in good fun. I don't see Nicola again, nor do I see Linden, so at the end of the night I ask if she wants to split a cab. She enthusiastically agrees, talking about how I must owe her something from drinking the drink so well.

But the only thing I owe Paige is the cab ride home. When we get in the back, it's quite apparent from the way she's rubbing my leg just what she thought we were doing and where we were going. I mean, I had told her something about fucking her earlier, hadn't I?

Tonight, maybe for one of the first times ever, I end up being a cunt-tease. I get the cab to take her where she needs to go but when she gets out, she's stunned that I'm not following.

"I have to get an early start tomorrow," I explain, which is completely true now that IKEA is in the cards.

She looks pissed off and I can't blame her. But still, she thanks me for the ride and tells me I should call her when I don't have something – or anything – to do in the morning. Though she put her number in my phone earlier, I have no intention of calling her any time soon.

When I get home, the events of the day have taken some kind of toll on me. I feel a million different threads of want and need inside me, but more than that, this nervous, buzzing energy that has no outlet. I start thinking that maybe it was a mistake to drop Paige off, that she could be sucking my cock right now and distracting my mind. But who am I kidding? I wouldn't be thinking of her at all and I know that it would make things worse.

I hear Nicola's door open and the small chatter of her and Lisa next door, muffled through the walls, and I wonder if I should go on over. I almost do. I get up and go to the door, one hand on the handle. I want to make sure IKEA is still on. I want to make sure she's okay. I want to thank her for the drink. I want to touch her hair, brush it behind her ears and get lost in her lips. I want to know what she tastes like – her mouth, her skin, her sweet little cunt. I want to experience every last drop on my tongue.

I'm lacking courage tonight. I stay in. Naturally the night turns into epic wank-fest part two and this time, this time I am loud. I don't hold back and I don't drown it out in music. I hope she can hear me.

I hope she likes what she hears.

Chapter Nine

NICOLA

When I came home last night, I was in a bad mood. I guess it's not much of a surprise that I wake in a bad one too. This was one of those cases that sleep did nothing to erase the worries of the day before. It's still all there, simmering, and I don't even understand why.

Luckily Ava gets up bright and early so I'm used to getting out of bed around seven am. I have no idea whether our IKEA excursion is still on for the day and I've regretted asking him since the moment it came out of my mouth.

I especially regretted it when Linden introduced some hot blonde to him and she immediately had his rapt attention. I don't know why it bothers me so much. I guess because for a second, I thought maybe there was something more between us.

And yes, I know, something more is something bad. Always will be. But when his fingers brushed against mine, sending warm currents up my limb and down the middle of my back, when his eyes seemed so focused on me that I could almost see lightning in those grey clouds, I couldn't help but imagine, just for a second, what it would be like if he were mine. Mine in bed, mine outside of it, it didn't matter. But the thoughts – the lust – was there.

Unfortunately he ruined that pretty fast. I know what Linden was doing too, wanting Bram to stay the hell away from me. I couldn't fault him and maybe I should have appreciated it. But for once, for damn once, I wanted to make all the big, bad mistakes.

The ugly, foggy light of a San Francisco morning puts things in a different perspective though. I try and shove those angry feelings away and wonder if Bram meant it when he said he would take us to IKEA. I heard him last night, moaning away. I actually went outside into the hall for a second, almost hypnotized by his cries, as if I were going to act out my fantasy for real this time. But I never knocked on his door, never opened it.

There's a knock on my door now, though. I have to blink a few times, discerning if it was in my head or in real life. Then Ava says to me, through mouths of scrambled egg, "It's the door, mommy." Her eyes get bright. "Maybe it's Santa."

"Oh, I think you've gotten those letters mixed up there," I say under my breath and get up to answer it. I give myself the once over in the mirror and decide, in my sleeping shorts and camisole, my hair greasy and my face dull, that I can't possibly look any worse. I sigh before opening it.

There's Satan all right on the other side, dressed in dark jeans, converse and white dress shirt that's the kind of thin material you wouldn't want to wear in the rain. Well, *I* wouldn't want to wear it in the rain, he can gladly do so.

He looks me up and down but there's no judgement in his eyes, only this slow burn, like a subtle version of the look I got last night. "You do remember we have a date right?"

I give him a look, back on my defenses. "It's not a date. It's a favor."

"I've been on many dates that were favors and many favors that were dates." The corner of his mouth quirks up. "Mind if I come in?"

I gesture to the apartment. "Come on in. I haven't gotten around to the coffee yet."

"You must be superhuman," he says, striding past me as I close the door. He stops by the table, his palm out for Ava. "High five, little one."

She smacks it and giggles as he goes into the kitchen and starts making coffee like he lives here. "So, Ava," he says, his back to us. "How does that song of yours go?"

"Bram, no," I warn. But it's too late. She's yelling it again at the top of her lungs.

"You know," I tell him, raising my voice to be heard over her racket, "it's lucky that you're at least one of my neighbors. I have a feeling the old man to the left of here is going to complain about her singing one day."

"He can complain all he wants, sweetheart, I'm the one in charge here."

While he puts water into the reservoir, I can't help but ask, "So, how did it all go last night?" I try to sound as breezy as possible but I feel it's a mistake saying anything. I don't want him to think I care. I don't care. "I'm just curious," I add in, as if that will make a difference. Because I *am* just curious. Nothing wrong with that.

"At the Lion?" he asks, flicking the pot on and then leaning back against the sink to face me. He crosses his arms and I do what I can to not focus on the taught bulk of them.

"Yeah."

He tilts his head, inspecting me. "You were there. You tell me."

I lick my lips and then shrug nonchalantly. "You seemed to hit it off with that girl that Linden introduced you to. I saw you guys leave in a cab together."

"Did you now?" he asks. I love the way he says "now" with his accent, like "no" but sweeter.

"Mmm hmm," I say, wishing I hadn't said anything.

"And how did that make you feel?"

What, is he seriously asking me that? I give him a look. "I felt nothing except maybe a bit of pity for the girl who will be kicked to the curb in a few days."

His forehead crinkles. "Is that so?"

"Stop answering me with questions."

He lets out a little laugh. "Fair enough. For your information, it went nowhere. She went straight home from the bar."

So the noises I heard last night…I fill in the blanks. They were all him again.

"And," he says, straightening up and sauntering toward me, his massive form seeming to take all the space in the apartment suddenly, "for your information, the date with Justine ended the same way."

"Two nights in a row and no sex," I comment.

"That's right," he says calmly. "It happens. Usually when my mind is preoccupied. Why fuck somebody if you can't stop thinking about someone else?"

Oh my shit. Is he talking about me?

Of course he's talking about you, I quickly tell myself. But still, even knowing that's probably true, there's no part of me that's prepared to handle any of this. Bram gave up screwing both those hot babes because he was thinking about me? Miss Single Mom with scars and stretch marks and who, at the moment, is wearing the ugliest night garment ever?

He's joking though. Beneath that smolder in his gaze, beneath that somewhat wicked twist to his mouth, it's all a joke like it always is. Bram the jokester, Bram forever pulling my leg.

He *has* to be joking.

"Mommy," Ava suddenly says, appearing between the two of us. It takes me a moment to tear my eyes off of him and look at her.

"Y-yes, angel?" I ask her, surprised at how my voice is shaking. I'm also surprised at all the other feelings coursing through me, the physical ones that make the situation extra inappropriate.

"You said we're going on an adventure today," she says. "Where are we going?"

Right. IKEA. I can feel Bram's eyes still on me and I don't dare look at him. I don't think I'm ready for the truth, no matter which way it spins.

"To a store to get us a new couch," I tell her.

She looks at the couch, puzzled. "But I like our couch," she says with her lower lip trembling. "It's my castle."

My heart melts and I automatically crouch to her level, pulling her under my arm. "I know you do, Ava, but where we're going we are going to get a better couch. Maybe two couches! And you know what?"

"What?' she asks quietly.

"There's a magical room there called the ball room," I tell her. "Remember when we watched that movie and you saw the kid hiding underneath all the balls." Unfortunately I think I'm remembering the movie *Traffic,* which she most certainly did not watch with me, but she doesn't need to know that. "It's so much fun. When I was a kid, it was almost as good as Christmas."

Now she's looking at me like I'm damn crazy.

"It's true," Bram says and she looks up at him. "You're about to have a very fun adventure. Are you ready, little one?"

Because she's so in love with Bram, her eyes light up and she smiles, nodding vigorously. I'd be jealous of him if I wasn't feeling a whole whack of other things, especially in my uterus. It's like it's kicking at me – *hey, Nicola, hey, he's a good one* – and I think I may have to put my uterus, vagina, and heart into some sort of holding cell where only my brain has the lock and key.

He eyes me with a lazy kind of excitement. "Are you ready?"

I take in a deep breath and manage a smile. "Let me just put on some clothes and run a brush through my hair."

"You're perfect just the way you are, babe," he says. "Though those nipples of yours seem to be vying for my attention."

I look down at my chest and see them poking through my thin top like they're trying to tunnel their way out. Shit.

I slap my hands over them and hurry on over to my bedroom, wishing I could start the morning over and yet oddly giddy about where it's been so far.

. . .

When we pull into the IKEA parking lot in Emeryville, I'm surprised that it isn't full. Then again, even though it's Sunday, it's still early. I glance at the clock on the slick dashboard of the Mercedes and it's 9:50, ten minutes till opening. I wonder if this is what middle age is going to feel like, trying to beat the crowds or snag a deal by going early.

Then I look over at Bram, whose hand is still on the gearshift, and for a split second I imagine more grey in his hair. I imagine more stubble on his gorgeous chin and lines by his eyes. I imagine him older and I imagine myself older, and a teenage Ava in the backseat.

My heart seems to expand at the thought, feeling whole, complete. Then it stutters, as if it's something it can't even begin to comprehend and I feel embarrassed that my mind even went there for a moment. Holy moly, what the hell has gotten into me?

"Let's go to the doors," I say quickly, opening the door and getting out of the car. I can tell Bram is puzzled by my abrupt departure but I need to clear my head and focus on the task at hand. Couch, couch, couch. Swedish furnishings. Mesh pits filled with balls. One-dollar hot dogs.

By the time we get to the doors though, after wrangling Ava out of the booster seat and making sure I have sliced apples, a small bit of juice, the insulin pen and glucose monitor just in case, the store is open for business. Still it's relatively quiet and we're lucky that the ball pit isn't all full. Ava is measured to make sure she's tall enough to go in and then we leave her there with the daycare, which gives us about an hour on our own, just enough to look around the store and then pick her up for lunch.

I watch her for a few minutes as she slowly approaches the edge of the pit, watching the kids who are already in it. She's never been that shy with other kids but I haven't really exposed her to them either. I guess I just don't have any friends who have kids – something that happens when you have a kid early and out of wedlock.

One child, a boy a few good inches taller that her, swims through the balls and then stops in front of her. He grins, toothless and then throws a ball at her. It bounces right at her head and before I know it, I'm ready to run to the pit, scoop Ava up and call that little shit what he really is.

But Bram has grabbed hold of my arm and he's pulling me back and to him.

"Easy, mum," he murmurs in my ear. I let him hold me and we watch as Ava picks up the ball and throws it right back at the boy. It hits him square in the chest and she scowls at him before walking off to the other side of the pit where a girl with red pigtails bounces up to her.

"He's not much different from you," I mutter as my heart rate turns back to normal.

Bram still has his hand around my bicep and he lowers it down my arm, his fingers skimming over my skin until I'm certain he's going to grab onto my hand and hold it. But then he pulls away all together. "And Ava knows just how to deal with boys like me, just like her mum has. Shall we?"

I know we won't get anything done if I keep standing in by the play center. I watch as other moms come and drop off their kids and then hurry away into the store as if they can't wait to be done with them. I'm so used to being around Ava all the time that it's hard not to have her with me if I can help it. But this is good for her and it's good for me. It has to be.

I give Bram a small smile and we go up the massive staircase and into the rest of the store.

"So," Bram muses as the floor plans make us start in the living room set ups, just where we need to be. "What kind of couch are you looking for?"

I shrug. "I don't know. A cheap one." I eye a humungous sectional right in front of us. "A small one. And one that doesn't tear easy."

Bram plops down on the sectional and puts his feet up on the coffee table, making himself right at home. "Well, I hate to break this to you but IKEA isn't exactly known for their quality. Cheap, yes."

But I'm no longer listening to him. Instead, my eyes are drawn toward his socks on display. Again, they are the ugly brown and yellow ones with the loch ness monster all over them.

"Okay," I say, nodding at them, "this is the second time I've seen you wear them. What is up with the socks?"

He looks at his ankles, as if he's surprised to see his feet there. "Oh these? Lucky socks." But when he smiles at me, there is something hard in those eyes of his. It's a look I don't see too often and even though I immediately want to dissect it and figure out what it means, I know I shouldn't. I'm the queen of deflection and that look tells me he'd give me a run for my money.

Instead I say, "Are they lucky? They are the ugliest things I've ever seen. Doesn't really go with your whole outfit."

The dark look passes and he eyes me with mocking sincerity. "Are you taking an interest in what I wear?"

"It did used to be my job," I say. "I mean, I dressed mannequins but I made sure they were the best dressed mannequins in the whole of SF."

"I believe it," he says. "For a woman without a lot of money, you sure manage to make yourself look like a million dollars." He gets up off the couch and I'm kind of stunned at the compliment. Believe it or not, it means more to me than he could know. I used to have a fashion blog years ago when it was cool and profitable, and I took so much pride in how I dressed. Now, it just didn't seem important anymore.

No, scratch that. It wasn't that it wasn't important. It's just I found it no better than the crazy glue holding my kitchen table together. I could dress up but deep down I was still a fucking mess.

Except today I actually did dress up a bit. I put on a pair of Alexander McQueen ankle boots from many years and many seasons ago, skinny jeans from Old Navy (which I got on sale for $4) and a Petite Bateau Breton striped topped. It's a little threadbare at this point but it still makes my rack look fantastic. Let's face it, it's why I'm wearing it and from the way Bram's eyes keep flitting there, I can tell he appreciates the effort.

"Thank you," I tell him, fumbling for a way to play off his compliment. "You're not so bad yourself. You know, aside from the poo and pee socks."

He bursts out laughing. "Poo and pee? You've been hanging around Ava too long, my love."

"Probably," I admit and we carry on down the aisle. So far, none of the couches I've spotted are exactly what I'm looking for and I'm getting tired of sitting down and getting up again to try them out.

Finally we come across an area where a lot of the armchairs are and there's something that catches my eye. It's a small loveseat with bright yellow fabric and metal legs. I gravitate toward it and look at the price tag. It's under a hundred bucks. I could get two of them, they'd fit with my décor and they look pretty easy to assemble as well.

"Seriously, this?" Bram asks, eyeing the couch with distain. "How are you going to have me over? I'll break the damn thing if I sit on it."

"Try it," I coax him and watch as he lowers his large frame onto the couch.

He winces. "The most uncomfortable couch I have ever had my arse in."

I sit down beside him. It's snug. Really snug. My leg is smushed up against his and that wonderfully hot, male smell of his is teasing me. But other than that, he's right. It's pretty bare bones in the padding department.

But the price is right. "I have lots of pillows," I tell him, attempting to get out of the couch. "I could make it work."

And I'm really working my abs trying to get out of the damn thing. Bram is absolutely no help. He reaches for my collar and pulls me back down beside him.

"You know if we were a couple," he says, sliding his arm along the backrest so it's hovering behind my shoulder, "this would be the perfect couch for us. We'd never get up. We'd have to sit here in each other's company for eons."

"Thank God we don't have to deal with that," I say and now his arm is right on my shoulders, his hand curling around and holding me to him.

"It isn't so bad," he says, his voice sounding a bit gritty. "Is it?"

"I can't believe you're putting the moves on me in IKEA," I joke, making an attempt to rise again. I don't make it far. I guess my attempt was rather half-hearted.

He takes his arm off and jerks his head back, an incredulous look on his face. "You think this is me putting the moves on you? Oh, sweetheart, you haven't seen anything yet. My moves make you hot, sweaty and breathless, moaning my name. They don't have you cracking jokes."

I don't dare admit that there is something breathless about our proximity to each other. "They would have me coming up with a motto though, right?"

He grins broadly and I notice that crooked tooth on the bottom, which adds a rugged charm to his already too perfect face. "Wham, bam, thank you Bram is a good one."

I shake my head. "You're too much."

"I am too much," he says and he somehow manages to get to his feet. "But I have faith you can handle me." He holds out his hands for me and when I place mine in his, admiring how small and delicate they look compared to him, he pulls me up.

"Thanks," I tell him, adjusting myself after the mini couch nearly held us captive. "By the way, you're always so tan. Is that fake or do you just get to go to nice hot places all the time?"

He seems a bit too pleased at my question. "Why, Nicola, I'm flattered that you've noticed my skin tone. First it was my socks, now the color of my skin. I'm starting to think that perhaps you're interested in more than my landlording skills." I cross my arms, one leg askance and give him the "are you kidding me?" look. He continues. "I have a few favorite spots where the sun shines even when it doesn't in this grey city." He pauses and his gaze is steady. "And I'd be more than happy to take you and Ava sometime."

Whoa. I look at him, used to his generosity and all but a trip together seems to say something else entirely. "What about Linden and Steph?" I ask cautiously.

He lazily lifts a shoulder. "They can come too. It kind of interferes with my whole seducing thing though."

I can't help but laugh. "Seducing thing?"

He flicks his finger at me. "Just you wait for it." But then he strolls over to the kiosk nearby and gets a card and one of those small pencils and writes down the product information of the couch and where to find it in the warehouse. He waves the card at me. "I got all the details of your horrid little couch."

"Thank you," I tell him and we continue on our way, even though Bram keeps looking over his shoulder at a nice futon. I nudge him playfully. "I've made up my mind, I can't afford the futon and the yellow couch is cute. And cheap."

"It's going to be a real shit to assemble."

"I'm an old pro," I reassure him. "And I've got a neighbor who seems to know how to wield a tool." I glance at his smug face and quickly add, "Not that Allen keys are all that complicated."

When we head toward the bathrooms, Bram grabs my hand and quickly pulls me aside. "I have a dare for you."

"A dare?" I repeat. I know that Steph and Linden had their first real kiss because of a dare but I'm not sure what Bram has in mind. Dares are dangerous, usually embarrassing and, well, kind of immature. I think I was eleven years old when I last had a dare and it involved trying to tip over a cow in the middle of the night.

"Yes," he says, looking far more excited than he should. "You go into the bathroom over there and sit on the toilet, pretending to read a magazine. When someone comes into the bathroom, you yell at them to get out and that you need your bloody privacy."

"What?" I exclaim, looking to where he's pointing. "It's a fake bathroom. I'm not doing that."

"You don't even have to pull down your pants," he says, almost giggling. "The person will be in such shock they won't even notice."

"Ew, no," I tell him, ripping out of his grasp and walking away.

"You really are no fun," he says, coming up after me.

I stop, whirling around and point my finger in his face. A wave of anger swarms up from my chest. "You know, you said that to me once and it's stuck in my head ever since. I am fun, I'm just not stupid. I know how to have fun, but I'm also not a whore. I—"

He raises his palms at me, eyes wide. "Whoa, easy. That is most definitely not what I was saying. You're not a whore and you're certainly not stupid, okay? It was just a joke. I poke fun at you, you poke fun at me. See…there's fun *there*."

My breathing is heavy but I take in a deep inhale and gain the rhythm back. I don't know why I overreacted like that.

"Hey," he says gently, putting his fingers at the bottom of my chin and tilting my head up so I have to meet his eyes. The last time he looked at me like this was on the wedding night. Fragments of feelings come wafting back and it feels like I'm there and in the fluorescent glow of IKEA all at the same time. "I can be insensitive sometimes, I know this. It's nothing personal. You are fun." I try to look away but he holds my face in place. "You *are* fun, Nicola. You're fun to be around, whether you think so or not. And I think you might be the cutest thing I've ever seen, picking out the tiniest, cheapest little shitpiece couches for your apartment. If that's not called fun, I don't know what is."

Now he's being too nice, the compliments making me uneasy. He seems to believe them too much. "I think I like it better when you're a jerk."

"All right," he says. "I can work with that too. You know what your real problem is, sweetheart?"

"What?" I ask, wanting to know and scared of the answer.

"You're totally underfucked," he says, his voice dropping a register. He leans in closer. "And I'm the one who can tip the scales in the other direction."

I blink, swallow hard. I don't have a comeback for that because I know it's true. I just don't want him to know it's true.

I give him a wry look, trying to shrug his innuendo off. "There you go thinking so highly of yourself. Can't you keep your ego in check?"

He shakes his head slightly, his eyes focused so intently on mine. "I have ego for a reason. And one of these days, you'll find out just why that is."

Heat flushes me from my core to my scalp. I look away and he drops his fingers from my face. I feel entirely breathless, almost shaky, like I'd been trapped in some kind of hypnotic force field in the middle of Swedish furnishings.

"In your dreams," I tell him but it comes out as nothing more than a squeak.

He just smiles at that.

"Sorry," I mumble, trying to change the subject. "About overacting. I've obviously got some issues there."

"Don't we all?" he asks. He grabs my hand and leads me along the hall. "Let's go rescue your daughter from the cootie pit."

He doesn't let go until we get there.

Chapter Ten

NICOLA

The rest of the IKEA outing is pretty uneventful and by that I mean all the sexual innuendo stops, thankfully, once we get Ava. Not that what Bram was spouting off could possibly be called innuendo. There was nothing indirect about it.

By the time we get back to my apartment, I feel all twisted up in knots. I think I need a moment to be alone with my thoughts, to gather my strength and my wits. As much fun as I had today, it challenged me. Bram challenged me. And it feels like the more I hang around my handsome neighbor, the more my resolve will dissolve.

But what a way to go.

"Well," I say to him after he's brought the heavy boxes of couch inside and once again I make a point not to ogle him while he lifts and lowers, like some impossibly rugged cave man. "Thank you so much for taking us there."

"Anything for my two favorite girls," he says, looking at Ava. She giggles and then as if she's struck by a case of the bashfuls, she runs off into her room. "And I mean it," he adds, eyes on me now. "Are you sure you don't need help with your crappy couches?"

"I'm sure," I tell him.

He nods. "All right then. Holler if you need anything." He gives me a flash of a smile before he leaves the apartment. He closes the door behind him but I don't breathe until I hear him shut the door to his place.

I collapse down on the couch and I'm suddenly sad to be getting rid of it and swapping in the new cheap ones. This couch is comfortable, it's soft, it's like a warm hug. Sure it's falling apart at the literal seams but it's been with me this whole time, there while my life became unhinged and I fell off track. I bought it from Anthropologie online and I remember Phil was so mad when it showed up at our apartment one day. He said our place was pushing him out, it was becoming too girly. That should have been a sign then. Maybe it wasn't the furnishings that were pushing him out, maybe it was me.

I don't want to let go of the couch. I want it to stay. I want to say, right here, where it's safe.

"Mommy," Ava says in her singsong voice, climbing onto the couch beside me.

"What is it, angel?"

"Is Bram my father?"

I nearly choke. "What? Your father, no. Honey. No. Phil is your father."

She shakes her head. "But I don't remember Phil. I have never seen *Phil*." She says his name like it tastes bad. "I see Bram. Bram *should* be my father."

Something in my heart cracks at that. "That's not exactly how it works."

"Why not? Doesn't he like us?"

Oh, Jesus. I smooth her hair back off her face. "I think he does like us. Maybe you can ask Santa for him this year," I add as a joke, just trying to get her to stop talking about it.

She smiles. "Okay, I will do that. How many months until Christmas?"

Shit. Obviously the joke is lost on her. I know I'm putting off the inevitable but now I feel like it's going to turn into one horrible Hallmark movie come Christmas time. I wince at the sugariness.

I hear low bass come from next door and Bram has put on some of his 90's British trip hop again. I can almost see him as a teen in Scotland, doing ecstasy and going to underground clubs. I bet he had short spiky hair and wore a beaded necklace and Adidas sports jerseys. I think I'll ask him what he was like back then.

No, I tell myself. *Get him out of your damn head. Now.*

And so I listen to myself because I rarely steer myself wrong. I pick up my phone and I text Steph.

I know it's Sunday, but I need a girls' night BAD. And not to the Lion.

She's instantly responding. **Done. I'll tell Kayla. We'll get you good and drunk. Who is looking after Ava?**

Good question.

I'll find someone.

I then call my mother and when she can't do it because she's cleaning a house early tomorrow, I call Lisa. She's got a dinner and can't do it either.

Well, shit. I guess having two people on call for babysitting really isn't enough, especially not on short notice. Maybe I'll have to forget about letting my hair down after all, which is too bad because the more I imagine myself dancing without a care and drinking my face off, the more I'm beginning to crave it. I need it, *need* it.

I can't find anyone, I text Steph.

What about Bram? Is her quick answer.

What *about* Bram? I immediately want to dismiss it. First of all, the night is supposed to be an escape from Bram and if he takes care of Ava, I'm going to be worrying about her and, by default, thinking about him all night. I also don't know if I'd trust him with taking care of a child, especially mine, especially a diabetic one.

I also don't want to ask him for another favor. So there's that.

I don't think so, I text Steph. **I'll find someone else**. Even though we both know there is no one else. I mean, I guess there's Linden, but he'd be even worse than Bram in the irresponsible department.

I lean back on the couch and start going through my phone contacts while Ava plays with her dolls on the floor. I consider Penny, James's girlfriend, and am just about to Facebook message her when I hear Bram say, "Nicola?" from out in the hall.

Great. I put down the phone and go to the door, opening it. He's on the other side with eager eyes.

"Yes?" I ask mildly.

"I just heard from Steph," he says. "I'd be happy to watch Ava tonight."

Steph? That bitch!

"She called you?" I ask incredulously. I immediately run over to my phone, all ready to send her messages with expletives and shouty caps.

"She did," he says, leaning against the doorframe. "She said you'd never ask yourself but that you wanted a girls' night out and couldn't find a sitter. So, here I am."

I don't know what to say. But Ava says it for me.

"Bram!" she yells as if he wasn't just here ten minutes ago. She runs around the couch and right over to him, throwing her arms around his leg. It's so cute I want to vomit. And remembering what she had said earlier about Bram, I think I might just do that.

"Did Santa bring you?" she asks.

Oh, God, I think. *Please stop there.*

"Okay!" I say quickly. And loudly. Both Ava and Bram jump a little. "Okay, that would be great Bram, if you don't mind," I lower my voice. "I know it's asking a lot. There's just a few things I want to go over with you, about her, uh, situation."

"Diabetes!" Ava yells, running back and forth between us, knowing what I'm trying to skirt around. "The special disease!"

"That's the positive attitude," Bram comments to her. He smiles at me. "Show me the ropes, mum."

I eye him in askance. "If you keep calling me mum, it's going to get weird."

"Right." He nods. "Don't want that mistake to happen while I'm shagging you sideways."

I gasp and place my hands over Ava's ears until she laughs and squirms away. "Language," I admonish him.

"The dirtier the better," he says, loving it. "All she knows is we're talking about carpets. Speaking of carpets..." His eyes drift down to my jeans.

"Bram," I say sternly. "If you want to help, shut up and come here."

I take him into the kitchen where I keep the insulin and supplies in a special kit. "I need you to really pay attention. This is serious. Got it?"

He says he does but he's still got a bit of that smirk going on.

"Have you even taken care of a child before?"

His smirk disappears. "Of course I have."

"Oh really?"

He frowns at me, his eyes narrowing slightly. "I'm not as incompetent as you think." There's an edge to his voice that catches me off guard. It's the same kind of vibe I got when I asked about his stupid socks.

"I hope you're right," I say breezily, trying to ignore the sudden change in him. But while I have his rapt, albeit tense, attention I go over the basics with him. "This is the blood glucose monitor."

"The spindle!" Ava cries out, running over and watching us eagerly. "That's the spindle where Sleeping Beauty pricks her finger."

"Is that so?" Bram asks and it seems like he's calming down a bit. Sheesh. I think I like the jokester a lot better. When Bram McGregor gets serious, he gets *serious*.

"It's just a tiny pin prick on her finger." I hold the device and slide in the test strip, turning it on. I then take Ava's hand and prick her fingertip quickly and gently with it. She shakes her hand after like it hurts. It probably does but she's so used to it now and she's smiling at Bram like a big girl.

"Then," I go on, showing him, "we look at the results. It says its 170, which is about right for her right now. The only time you'll have to do it will be before she goes to bed. Then it should be around 100 – 180." I take out the test strip and put it in the garbage. "Then you get rid of the strip."

"And what happens if it's not in that range?"

"You adjust her diet," I tell him. "But that's nothing for you to worry about. It's just an ongoing thing really, making adjustments. I do the test about six times a day, some times more. She gets insulin injections three times a day, in the morning, the afternoon and then before she goes to bed. I just gave her one in the bathroom at IKEA but tonight before I go, I'll give her the last one and show you, just in case." Suddenly I realize I'm out of breath and I'm grasping at my heart.

Bram puts his hand on the side of my cheek, peering at me intently. The feel of his hot skin is steadying, even though I'm starting to have a minor panic attack. "It's okay," he says in a soothing tone. "I'll be fine."

"Sorry," I manage to say, trying to breathe. "It's always hard, every time I leave. I feel like I'm leaving her fate in someone else's hands."

"And you are," he says, stepping an inch closer, his palm still cupping my jaw, his fingers gently brushing back my hair from my cheekbone. "But I've got this. You'll go out, have fun, and then you'll come back. She'll be fine, she'll be asleep and I'll be going through all your photo albums."

I somehow smile at that.

…

When seven o'clock rolls around, I'm all dolled up in a black cocktail dress suited for an episode of *Mad Men*, with red lipstick and 60's hair piled up.

"Mommy, you look like a princess," Ava says as she sits on the edge of my bed, swinging her legs back and forth while I put the finishing touches on my liquid eyeliner. "No, a queen."

"Why thank you," I tell her, smiling at her in the reflection. "Now, you behave for Bram, okay?"

"I will," she says and I believe her. One of the many beautiful things about Ava is that she's never been a bratty child. She's always been polite and considerate and even when she has the occasional temper tantrum, she's quick to stop and quick to learn from it. I certainly wasn't like that as a child and sometimes I wonder how she's turned out so good when our circumstances could be so much better. But then again, as long as she has food in her belly, a roof over her head and a mother that loves her, a child can't really want for much. Except maybe some of those new generation My Little Ponies but that's what Christmas is for.

Along with other things now, apparently.

It's not long before Bram comes by. He brings himself a bowl of pre-popped popcorn, which I think is kind of adorable, and he nearly drops it the moment he sees me.

If it's petty to have wanted that kind of reaction from him, well, I can I own up to it.

"You look fucking edible," he says in this throaty, husky voice that makes me want to clench my legs together. The word *edible* from his lips conjures up oh so many amazing scenarios.

"That's what I was going for," I tell him, not even bothering to correct his swearing.

"So, you're going out to hook up?"

I frown at him. "I never said anything about hooking up." *And why do you care? I mean, do you care?*

I kind of want him to care.

"Sweetheart, when you go out looking like a bloody movie star, the kind that young boys put on their walls and wank off to inside of a sock, you're going to be hooking up. You may not know it yet but," he waves at me with his fingers, "you're giving the fuck me vibe."

"Giving the vibe and wanting it are two different things," I tell him.

"Oh, do I know that. But I'm just saying...be prepared to be hit on a lot."

"Pshhh," I dismiss him. "If I can handle you hitting on me, I can handle them."

He smiles softly. "I suppose you're right about that."

After I show him how to give Ava her insulin shot – God forbid he needs to use it – I leave the two of them and go downstairs where Steph and Kayla are waiting in an Uber. The last vision I have of them is Bram standing by the door and Ava bouncing up and down on the couch in the background. If the couch breaks tonight, it looks like I'll be spending my Monday morning in the IKEA assembly line.

"Nicola," Steph says as I squeeze into the backseat of a Prius. "You look fucking hot."

"Yup," Kayla says, leaning forward to look at me. "Props." She gives me the thumbs up.

They don't look too shabby either, dressing in tight jeans and slinky shirts and ankle-breaker heels. Steph's, I notice, are authentic Rodarte, which makes me hella jealous for a moment.

"I am so glad you decided to do this," Kayla says later as we approach the first bar, Bartlett Hall just outside of Union Square. "I've needed girl time. I say we make up fake names and fake jobs for ourselves. I'll be Lorraine Moneypenny, a circus trainer for the pigeons that perform during Cirque du Soleil. The ones in the rafters during the shows. Then we'll ask guys for dick pics. You know, just approach random guys and ask for them, see who wants to play." She pauses mid-scheme, adding a saucy smile. "Did I ever tell you, that you two are the best wingwomen a girl could hope for?"

"Oh, hold up," Steph says, putting her hand on Kayla. "Tonight is about Nicola, not you. And I know my bestie. If she says she needs a girls night out, she really needs a girls' night out. Hot mama needs to get laid. We want dicks, not dick pics."

They both eye me, expecting me to deny it. But I don't.

I nod. "Yeah. I need to get fucking laid ASAP."

The Uber driver is smiling to himself as he pulls up beside the bar.

"Does this have something to do with living next to Bram?" Kayla teases.

"This has everything to do with living next to Bram," I practically moan and the both of them look shocked. "If I don't screw something soon, I'm going to end up screwing him. And we all know how bad of an idea that is. Even our Uber driver knows. Right?"

Uber driver eyes us in the rear-view mirror. "Sometimes bad ideas are good ideas."

"When the guy in question happens to be my neighbor and my landlord?"

The guy whistles. "Hoo, boy. Good luck with that one, missy."

I look back at the girls. "And this is why I need to get laid."

"Think you can be a wingwoman tonight?" Steph asks Kayla.

Kayla puts on her serious face, like she's going into battle. "We *will* get you some dick, honey."

Our first bar isn't really the dick-getting kind of place but it is a nice start. We each have a beer flight and share some appies and by the time I'm done with my Kolsch, I'm feeling buzzed. I'm feeling great, actually. I only thought about Bram once, too.

Actually I texted him while I was in the washroom, just checking up on Ava. He answered back that she was asleep and he was watching porn in preparation for my return and that he hoped I was having fun.

I assume the whole porn thing was a joke but part of me started fantasizing over the idea of it not being a joke at all. I mean, I know I don't have porn on my TV, I just have basic cable, but what if I returned to the apartment, all tipsy and hot and bothered and he was there, ready to go. What would I do?

I think I know the answer but it's all the more reason to hook up with someone else.

"All right girls," I announce. "Time to move on."

Next, we go to a bar called Dirty Habit, which seems to be more subdued than we'd like but still stay for serval more beers and martinis before we end up at some no name place outside of Chinatown where a rowdier crowd thrives.

Things are getting a bit spotty now. We're sitting in a booth we managed to snag after eyeing the couple in it like a hawk for an hour. There's a lot of dancing happening on the dance floor and it's becoming too hard to hear what we're each saying, so we sit in silence while the music thrums around us. I stop drinking at this point because it's getting too expensive but before I know it there's a guy standing in front of the table and whispering something in Kayla's ear.

He's pretty hot. Athletic with big round shoulders and short dark-blond hair. A nice smile. Bright eyes. Young. Wearing a Giants shirt. Pretty standard stuff but whatever Kayla is saying to him has him eyeing me appreciatively. I would have thought she wouldn't have been a very good wingwoman herself but she genuinely seems interested in Project #Dicks (hashtag needed) as she ended up calling it. I noted she called it plural, but I suppose there could always be one for her at the end. After all, Steph has her #dick at home.

Okay, I think I'm drunk. The guy is leaning forward and asking me something but I can't hear him so I just nod. Then he holds out his hand for me and takes me to the dance floor. I look behind my shoulder at the girls and I can tell Kayla is yelling "Dicks!"

"What's your name?" the guy asks, as he wraps his arms around my waist and brings me up to his chest.

"All yours," I tell him with a smirk. I can't believe that came out of my mouth.

And next thing I know, the guy is kissing me. He tastes like beer and his tongue is too sloppy but I'm into it. The alcohol, the music, the feeling of anonymity on the dance floor. I can be anyone, he can be anyone.

Yet, no matter how hard I try, he can't be Bram.

The next thing I know, we're in a cab. Steph is here. Flashes of Kayla. She's making out with some guy, sitting on his lap. I'm on this Giants guy's lap.

Then we're in another bar. Woodbury or something. There are two bars inside. We stay at the one that's just for beer and shots.

I do a lot of shots. After a while they don't burn anymore. I make out some more with Giants guy and then he takes me into the handicapped restroom, a place I know is tailor-made for having disgusting bar bathroom sex.

The guy lifts up my dress and asks if I'm on the pill. I am – I've been ever since Ava – but I lie. I don't know why. I tell him I'm not.

"You should be," he says as he pulls down my underwear. "You don't want to end up pregnant."

I look around the bathroom and stop at my reflection. She looks like someone else. Drunk and pretending to be unafraid. The girl in the mirror breaks my heart.

So, I look down at the guy who is grinning up at me and I say, "Doesn't make a difference, I already have a kid. Ava. Want to see her picture?"

That stops him dead in his tracks. He lets go of my underwear and I widen my leg to prevent it from falling to the dingy floor. I pull it up as he stares at me with panicked eyes. He's young, too young for the truth.

"Look, uh," he says, nervously running a hand through his hair. "I don't mess around with moms. I'm only 24 and I—"

"It's fine," I tell him, pulling down my dress. I'm too drunk to try and pretty up my face though, so I just punch him awkwardly on the shoulder. "Thanks for the make-out session though, it was fun."

"Yeah," he says, looking sheepish now. "I had no idea. You're just so fucking hot. And young."

I nod him my thanks and then unlock the door, heading back out into the bar.

"What happened, did you score?" Kayla asks as I walk over to her and Steph. I notice her boytoy isn't around either.

"No," I tell her. "And it's fine. I just…fuck it, let's drink everything."

We immediately order another round of beer and shots of Jameson and we drink until things go back to being blurry again.

When reality starts to fade in a bit, I find myself being walked to the door of my apartment building, my arms draped over both Kayla and Steph. We go up the stairs and now I'm standing in front of my door, wobbling back and forth, trying my hardest to look as sober as possible.

Steph goes to knock on the door but it's already open. I guess we are being loud, giggling, in the hallway.

Bram looks at the three of us and my God is he a sight for sore eyes.

"We brought her home," Steph says, motioning with her hand for Bram to get out of the way, "your shift is over."

"No," I tell them as they shuffle me inside. "He can stay."

I know the three of them are exchanging a look over my head.

"I'll make sure she goes to bed," Bram explains. "No funny business, I swear."

"Pinky swear?" Steph says and I turn to see her holding out her pinky to him. "You know I don't break those."

Ugh, Steph and her damn pinky swears. She wouldn't even be married to Linden if it weren't for one.

But Bram does a pinky swear with her.

"No funny business," Steph warns him.

"Good thing I'm not funny!" I yell as I flop down on the couch. The room is beginning to spin.

"Nic, that was, like, five minutes ago," Steph says. She reaches over the couch and pats my head. "Do you want us to undress you because Bram's not allowed."

"No one undresses me but me!" I yell, throwing my fist up into the air.

"Have fun with her," Steph says to Bram. "And remember, she's untouchable. Don't make me make your brother punch you in the junk or something."

Bram makes a scoffing noise. "Last time he tried to do that, I got him back good. You just ask him what happened on January 16th, 2005 and why he'll never eat pudding again."

"I mean it," Steph threatens and I hear her and Kayla leave and the door closing.

I close my eyes too. Drift away for a moment. The spinning has stopped and there's a beautifully cool breeze wafting over my skin.

"I'm not supposed to touch you," Bram's gruff voice says and when I open my eyes, he's crouched in front of me, a lock of dark hair over his forehead. His face is shadowy in the dark, the only light now being from my bedroom behind him.

"That's okay," I mumble into the couch. "You can touch me. I say it's fine."

"How about I bring you something to sleep in? Do you have a favorite nightshirt? I always see you in that top that your nipples try and poke right through."

"No, not the nipple shirt."

He goes to get up. With a lazy hand, I grip his shirt. "Don't leave. I'm fine here."

"I can't imagine you being comfortable."

"I'm drunk. Everything is comfortable. Except I wish I had a cheeseburger. I would eat it and use it as a pillow. Or maybe use it as a pillow and then eat it."

"I see."

I raise my brow at him. "You just want to go through my underwear."

"Oh, I've already gone through your underwear."

"Lies."

"I wore them on my head and danced around your apartment."

"Did you really?" I ask, totally serious.

"Come on," he says grabbing my forearms. "If you want to sleep in your clothes, that's fine. But I'm bringing you to your own bed and taking off your shoes."

"Can you brush my teeth too? I need clean teeth." I let him pull me to my feet and I pitch to the left, heading right for the coffee table. But I'm in his arms, his capable arms, and he's holding me to him.

"You have capable arms."

"You have an exquisite arse," he responds and half leads me, half drags me out of the living area and into the bedroom.

"I like the way you say *arse*," I say with a giggle, exaggerating his accent. "I like the way you say everything."

"I'm glad, because I foresee a lot of arse talk in the future."

"Yeah, yeah." I try and swat him away. "All talk and no arse pinching."

"You're as tipsy as a loon," he whispers into my ear. "Otherwise, I'd be all over you and in you. You wouldn't be able to walk for days and I'd just be getting started." He lays me down on my back and then starts to take off my shoes.

"Sounds painful," I comment, feeling my whole body turn into a jellyfish. For a moment I think I don't even have fingers and toes or arms or legs, I'm just this squishy, nebulous blob.

"Nebulous blob?" Bram asks.

"You can read my mind!" I'm offended at the violation of privacy.

"No, you just said nebulous blob," he says. "Aloud."

I take in a deep breath, trying to protect my thoughts from his mind-reading abilities. Then I blurt out, "I made out with something. I mean, someone."

"Okay," he says slowly, placing my shoes on the floor and sitting on the edge of the bed. "And you're telling me this because?"

"Because you can tell the things I did."

His breath hitches slightly and I roll my head to the side to peer down the bed at him. "I let a guy almost have sex with me in the bathroom. He was twenty-four and a Giants fan."

His Adam's apple bobs as he swallows. "Sounds like half the boys in the city."

"But I didn't have sex with him."

"No? Are you an Oakland A's fan?"

"I'm a Giants fan," I snipe, getting defensive. "And he wasn't *you*."

He tilts his head, studying the nebulous blob on the bed. "So why *did* you almost have sex with him to begin with, if you knew he wasn't me?"

"Because," I say, frustrated. I place my hand over my eyes. My hand smells like beer. It makes me want to vomit. "I didn't want the last person I kissed to be you. I wanted to wipe you from my lips."

A heavy silence fills the room. I feel like I'm sinking further and further into the bed and I want to panic, thinking it's swallowing me whole. Man, I haven't been this drunk in ages. I'm going to regret absolutely everything in the morning.

"I was the last man you kissed?" he asks, his voice light and unbelieving.

I nod. "Yes. At the wedding."

"And why would you want to erase that kiss?" He puts his hand on my bare leg, just beneath the hem of my dress.

I want his hand to go up higher. I want the energy to do something about it.

I also want to pass out.

It's a conundrum.

"Because," I tell him. No use in holding back now. "I saw you with that girl later. You took her behind the bushes, to where we just were. You were a fucking asshole. *Arse*hole."

I can hear him lick his lips. It sounds so loud in this room. My heart is thumping loud too, like a hammer against a padded wall. "She was second choice," he eventually says. "You turned me on like nothing else that night, sweetheart, I didn't know what to do."

"Go home and jack off like every normal person," I tell him snidely.

"You know very well that it's not always a good substitute. And certainly not for a woman like you." He leans forward and puts his warm hand on my face, his fingers trailing down the side of my cheek. It brings out a shudder in me that I can't suppress. "I only had eyes for you that night," he tells me.

He's a liar. He had eyes for everyone that night. I roll over on my side, away from him, and the room makes this *whom whom* throbbing sound. I think it's my brain. I broke it.

"I'm serious, Nicola," he goes on, voice gritty and soft all at once.

Whatever. "Only an *idiot* would fall for a line like that," I mutter into the sheets, sleep coming for me now, wanting me even when I'm feeling slighted.

A pause. I feel his weight lift off the bed and know he's standing up, bearing over me. "Even smart girls can be fools sometimes." He sounds almost sad.

I can hear him leave the room and for a moment I think he's gone and something in my chest seems to be snuffed out. Then he comes back in and places a glass of water on my nightstand and shuts off the bedroom light.

"Ava is asleep. She did fine all night. Her blood was normal. I'm sure she'll wake you bright and early and you'll feel like absolute shit. But if you need anything, you know where I am."

Then he leaves the room and leaves the apartment and I'm swept away into a spiral of beer, shame and regret.

I wish I had the drunken courage to have made him stay.

Chapter Eleven

NICOLA

"Mommy, are you dead?"

"Almost," I croak, attempting to open my eyes and roll over at the same time. I fail at both. The room swims and my head feels like it's full of quicksand. My stomach churns. I don't want to get up – I fear death by spinning room if I do – but if I don't, I'm going to puke all over my child.

I can't believe she's seeing me like this. I can't believe I was such an idiot last night.

Memories seep in.

Bram.

Bram.

Bram dragging my drunk ass to sleep.

Bram telling me he only had eyes for me.

Me, who told him I made out with someone else in order to get over him.

Shit.

Now, I'm really going to vomit.

I cover my mouth with my hand, throw back my covers and run into the bathroom, making it to the toilet just in time. Somewhere in the back of my head, behind all the vile grossness being evacuated from my body, I hope that Bram can't hear me. The bathrooms seem soundproof so far – thank God – but this is definitely something I wouldn't want him to hear.

When I'm done and it feels like I have nothing left in my stomach, I flush the toilet a few times and stagger to my feet. The mirror shows me a hot mess. No, not hot – just a mess.

My hair is somehow still in its updo, but it's completely askew and fuzzy like one giant dreadlock. My fancy eyeliner is halfway up my temple and the red lipstick is a smudge around my mouth and chin. I look like a creepy clown lady.

I look like a terrible mother.

"Are you sickie?" Ava asks. "Do you need the ouchie now too?"

"I'll be alright, sweetie," I tell her, quickly brushing my teeth and attempting to melt off my makeup with cream cleanser. I spend a few minutes trying to make everything right in the world but nothing works. I strip my clothes off, take a hot shower and then get into loose boyfriend jeans and a long grey tunic, all comfy. Anything tight today can just fuck right off.

It's 7:15 am, so luckily I'm not too behind on Ava's monitoring. I prick her finger and breathe a sigh of relief when I see the numbers in the normal. Then I get set on getting some egg and avocado in her, with a small slice of wholegrain toast, part of her carb counting to keep her levels in check.

As for me, I can't eat and I can't fathom drinking coffee, so I sit on the couch and finish a whole carton of orange juice, feeling sorry for myself. And all the while, I wonder if I'll hear a knock on the door. I wonder if Bram will come over. I wonder if he still likes me – if anything – after being such a drunken fool last night.

Even smart girls can be fools, I hear his words echo in my head. I know it's not what he meant, but I'm definitely feeling the fool right now.

When lunch time rolls around, I'm only feeling better enough to have a packet of chicken noodle soup, the fluorescent yellow one that comes in the packet and contains no chicken at all. That, plus Bragg's soy sauce, plus hot sauce, plus a hit of Worcestershire and a side of toast, and you should be feeling right as rain in no time.

Only I'm not. I lament everything I drank, everything I did, and when Bram still doesn't show, I start annoying Steph and Kayla via group message.

Steph assures me that Bram used to be worse than what I was last night and that was part of his nightly routine. There was no way he could be looking down on me.

Kayla thinks it's a shame I passed out before I could get some and when I tell her it wasn't even on the table because I was so drunk, she says that Bram was more of "the man" than she thought.

But neither have any answers and when I finally have a bit of strength, I go over to his apartment. I knock on the door and wait.

No answer. I put my ear to the door and listen but can't hear anything inside except the faint hum of his fridge.

It's completely silly to take that as a sign of rejection but somehow I do. I plod back to my apartment and decide to busy myself to take my mind off of things. Because Ava is bored and a light rain has started outside, which is something of a relief in a city that always seems to hold it in, I try and make assembling an IKEA couch sound like an exciting adventure.

She falls for it. She always does. We open the boxes and then get to work. It's only when I see the two drawn figures in the instructions saying this is a two-person job that I wish again that Bram was home. But still, I do what I can, even the instructions have me completely confused and things would be so much easier with an electric drill.

Eventually I tire out and give up. So does Ava. We retire to my room and the both of us pass out on my bed. She always loves it when I have naptime with her and I can't remember the last time I treated myself to such a luxury. Sometimes it's the easiest, most simple things in life that bring you the most joy. The good, pure kind of joy that just makes you feel human and proud of it.

I must have only been asleep for about fifteen minutes when I hear a knock on the door break through the fog. I get up without waking Ava and close the door behind me as I go across the apartment.

Even though I'm tired, my heart is lodged at the top of my chest, ready to pop like champagne. Am I actually giddy from just opening a damn door?

But yes. I am. Bram is in the hallway, his lips pursed in concern.

"How are you doing?" he asks, looking me over. "You look like shit."

"Always the charmer," I say dryly, even though my heart is beating fast and I can't help the smile on my lips.

He shrugs casually. "You told me you liked it when I'm a jerk."

"I say a lot of things," I tell him. "That's the first thing you should know about me."

"Oh, I already know a lot of things," he says. "After all, I was here last night going through your photo albums, just like I said I would. Is it strange that I think we would have been boyfriend and girlfriend in high school? I saw you with your hair short and purple, with a Lovage t-shirt. Girl after my own heart." He looks over my shoulder at the apartment. "So, are you going to let me in or what?"

I step aside and gesture for him. "Come on in. You can see over there the attempt at putting together one of the couches. I'm pretty much an epic fail today. A hangover and no cordless drill make Nicola a dull girl."

He raises a finger in the air. "Just one moment." And then he's turning around and heading out the door into his apartment. I watch his high, firm ass as he goes. He's dressed in a suit again, which makes me think he's been doing important things all day.

When he comes back in he's holding a toolkit.

"Well, aren't you a handyman," I tell him, as he opens it and starts taking out tools and placing them on the ground.

"I'm more than just a pretty face, I can tell you that much," he says with a wink and soon he produces a cordless drill. He revs it a few times and I'm glad I closed the door to the bedroom so Ava can keep on sleeping. Even so, it's not that loud.

But it's definitely *hot*. Bram takes off his grey suit jacket and throws it on the couch, then rolls up the sleeves of his black dress shirt, showing off those gorgeous forearms again and gets to work. If watching Bram jerk off was the hottest thing I'd ever witnessed, then watching him be all take charge and manly man with the tools is the second hottest thing. I guess it says I'm a pretty basic bitch to find that attractive but hell I'll own up to it.

"So," Bram says while I try and hold together one part of the frame while he connects another. "What do you remember about last night?"

I groan, not wanting to relive this. "Everything. At least the last half of the night."

"You said you made out with some Giants fan. Almost had sex with him."

I swallow uneasily and glance at him. His face is almost as neutral as his tone, though I can see this dark intensity in his eyes that betrays him.

"Almost," I remind him.

"Are you sure you didn't earlier and you just don't remember?"

"Oh, come on," I hiss and then lower my voice. "No, I didn't. I didn't *blackout*, blackout. Things just got fuzzy." I inhale deeply. "Hey, look, I'm sorry I came home such a wreck and I'm sorry you had to take care of me."

"I wanted to," he says simply and puts the drill on pause and stares right at me, his arms resting on the frame. "I wanted to make sure you were okay."

"Well." I look away, embarrassed. "Thank you for that. But I'm sorry you had to see me in such a state. I went looking for you today and when you weren't home, I figured maybe you were keeping your distance because you thought I was such a wreck."

He slowly shakes his head, an awed smile spreading across his face. "Are you kidding? That's what you thought. Sweetheart, first of all, I have some stories to share with you. Only I won't, because then you'll probably want to keep your distance from *me*. And I can't have any more of that, you already hold me at arm's length. Second of all, Nicola…as much as you hate how you were last night, as much as you're paying for it now, you were real. You were wild. Maybe you got a little carried away and in the wrong direction, I mean that could have been my tongue wrapped around yours. But you were true and honest and I'm glad you told me everything you did. Now I know why you have such a giant stick shoved up your arse. Babe, there are better things to stick up there."

So many things to ponder, I don't even know where to begin. I guess the main thing is he doesn't think any less of me, even if I do. The other things are the mention of his tongue wrapped around mine and the idea of him sticking anything up my ass. Both of those flood my head and body with a crazy kind of yearning.

I push it aside.

"Then we're cool?" I say slowly.

"We're cool," he says and he stares down at his hands for a moment. "And for future reference, you don't need to pound back the shots or whatever you gals drank, in order to feel wild and free. Believe me, I know this. I lost many years of my life never remembering the nights, all in an attempt to escape, to forget, to be something else. It never amounted to anything except guilt and regret, the very things I was trying to escape. It just doesn't work that way. Whatever you hope to drown, the booze only feeds it, makes it stronger. It has gills you see. Not to say I don't have my fun, but there's a line and I left it in New York City. I hope you learn to leave your line at last night."

I nod, impressed by this wise version of Bram. I never thought he'd regretted his party life on the east coast, I thought he had to give all of that up on account of his parents or something like that. I didn't think it was a conscious choice, nor one that he was glad to make.

"Is that why you moved out here?" I ask him. "To put it all behind you."

"One of the reasons. I just wanted to start over, really. And when Linden was hurt, I thought I might as well be close to the only person on earth I'm actually close to." He laughs to himself. "The funny thing is, Linden and I aren't even that close. But compared to my parents, he's the one who has been there through it all."

"I thought you were close with your parents and Linden was the one who wasn't?"

"Nah," he says with a shake of his head. "As you know, my father was a diplomat and my mother was all high society. What they really wanted was for me to follow in his footsteps. Not even make a name for myself in something else, but follow in his footsteps exactly. Any other achievement was ignored, maybe even looked down upon. At least, that's the impression he gave off…actually, still gives off. You'd think that maybe owning this building and investing my money would have brought him some kind of pride for his son, but no."

I've never heard him talk so frankly about his family. I want him to go on and on. Selfishly it makes me feel so much better to know that even the rich and powerful have problems. I also want to learn as much about him as possible, storing away each fact and revelation to draw upon later. It reminds me when I was in grade school and there was a kid I liked called Joey. Every little thing I learned about him – that he drank Pepsi instead of Coke, that his mother's name was Beth – I held onto like gold.

"I guess I'm kind of screwing up your investment though," I tell him.

"You're not," he says. He bites his lip for a moment and I want to do the same. It's amazing that I'm able to think or feel anything sexual at the moment, given what happened last night and my current, foggy state of mind, but the whole handyman thing really has me wanting it. Hell, at this point, I think I'd want him no matter what.

But as long as he stays on that side of the couch, as long as our relationship never diverts from being good neighbors, then I have nothing to worry about.

So, why am I afraid?

He eventually releases his lip, brows bent in thought. "Can I tell you something and you promise not to laugh?" He catches himself. "All right, well you can laugh but just don't laugh long."

"What?" I ask eagerly.

"Well, everyone thinks – assumes – that I bought the building in order to make more money in the end, to have as an investment. But that's not exactly true. It's what I want them to think but I have bigger plans." I stare at him expectantly, waiting for him to go on. "You know Richard Branson?"

"The bajillionaire?"

"Yes. That is the correct term, I believe."

"What about him? Oh my God, are you going into space?"

He laughs. "No. Bloody hell. Space is terrifying."

"Agreed." I add, "No one can hear you scream."

"Right," he says. "Anyway, Richard Branson, when he was only twenty, set-up a mail order record business. By twenty-two, he had Virgin Records. We all know what happens after that. He invests, he makes smart decisions, he never stops trying new things or learning something new. Nothing is impossible for this guy, not even space apparently."

"So you want to become the next Richard Branson," I say. "That's a great goal but it's not exactly a strange one."

"It's not just that." He licks his lips and looks off into some imaginary future. "Branson has said, there is no point in starting your own business unless you do it out of a sense of frustration. I bought this building out of frustration but not because I saw an opportunity for myself but because I saw an opportunity for others, one that wasn't there before." He looks at me and his eyes are bright sparks of grey and blue. "There is a distinct lack of affordable housing here in the city, especially for those in need. I've never seen it so bad before. Normal people can't even afford to live here, so what about the poor, the ones struggling with families, those that have lost their jobs, their savings, their everything? Where do they go? The Tenderloin? To live on the streets with the crackheads, to share shelters with thieves and addicts? I don't think so."

He's starting to sound worked up and he takes in a deep breath. "I wanted to make a difference. It's a really long process because you need support from the city. You need investments from people who want to help a charity-type cause. You need a lot of things. But I'm here, I have the building and nothing but time."

"What happens to the people already living here?"

Bram smiles shyly. "Most of them are already people in need. No one here is paying full-rent. I'm just not sure how long I can afford to keep this up without the city's involvement. So that's what I'm working on now. Had a meeting at city hall today."

"Oh." I think that's one of the most surprisingly noble things I've ever heard. "And you're hoping that the tax break you got for letting me live here will allow you to be able to do it for everyone in the building?"

"Tax break?" Then he grins. "Oh, no I lied about that."

My eyes bug out. "What? Why?"

He shrugs. "Because there was no way you'd believe me if I told you I wanted to help you out of the goodness of my own heart. And if I told you the other truth, you would have run the other way."

"What other truth?"

"That I wanted to win you over."

I blink. "That's why I'm living here? You wanted to win me over?"

"I've done outlandish things for a girl before, but nothing like this," he says, almost to himself. "But yes. I wanted to help you and I wanted you to think of me just a little bit differently. I wanted you to get to know the real me."

"But the real you is still an arrogant manwhore," I point out, feeling far too many emotions about this whole thing. Strangely enough, none of them are bad.

"Perhaps, an arrogant manwhore with some endearing qualities." He waves the drill at me. "Like, being handy."

"You certainly are handy," I comment, still feeling out of sorts. Dizzy swirled around. It must still be the hangover. It can't be learning that Bram did this all for me because of, well, *me.* "I still don't know what this has to do with Branson though."

"He's a huge humanitarian. He's been able to do so much with his fortune. I want that. I want both – the money and the means to help."

"Why is this such a secret? I would think your parents would be proud of you for this. I mean, your father is a diplomat, he must have many ties to charitable organizations."

His mouth quirks into a quick smile. "Even Linden doesn't know. No one does, except the city and you."

"Why not?"

"Because people like to hold onto their ideas of what you are and who you are. They put you in a box and no matter how hard you try to show them what you're really like, they can't wrap their heads around it. They won't. They only want you to be a certain way, the way they see you. To change that messes with their heads. I'll always be Bram the fuck-up to them, the party-animal, the playboy. It doesn't matter if I tell them my plans or not, they'll never take me seriously. I could do this for fifty years, I could become the next Branson, and they would still see me in the box they put me in."

I can't help but relate to his every word. I know that the moment I tell people I'm a single mom, I'm slung into a box that I have no hope in escaping. I don't think many people have met me and then seen that I'm more than just my title, my circumstances.

Not like Bram has seen me. The thought hits me like a bullet.

He's studying me and when I meet his eye, my face perhaps held in surprise, he clears his throat. "The only problem with the whole thing is that Branson has had a fifteen year head-start. I pissed away my twenties and early thirties on booze, drugs and women. While I obviously enjoyed it at the time – as you know, women are still my weakness – I could have done so much if I had just gotten my head on straight at an earlier stage."

"You know they say it's never too late," I tell him.

"In some ways it feels like it," he says. "You know I had a great idea a few years ago for a social media site comprised of just pictures. Pictures of me. You know, after a swim, running on the beach, taking off my shirt. I called it Insta-Bram."

I watch his face carefully, knowing he has to be joking. "Insta-Bram?"

But his expression is stone cold serious. "Has a nice ring to it, doesn't it?" Then he breaks into a wide, shit-eating grin that lights him up. "Hey, I gotta let my ego come out to play sometimes."

I shake my head. "You're the worst."

"I'm the best." He taps the side of the couch frame. "Come on, this couch won't build itself."

So we get back to work on the shitty little couch and when we're nearly done, it really does look like the cheapest crap I could have bought. I'm starting to think about throwing them out and just keeping my torn-up but reliable one.

"I'll need your help with this," Bram says, muffled. He's inside the large swath of fabric that is supposed to slip on over the frame, covering him like a yellow ghost from head to waist. "I need to zip onto those white pads that are somewhere out there."

I spot the pad behind me and dip down until I'm under the couch material with Bram. It's like being inside a very tiny tent and there's barely enough room for both of us to stand under here. Our faces are bathed in a yellow glow.

"Here," I say, holding up the edge of the pad that has a zipper pull. I'm wildly conscious of how close I am to him and I try to keep my breath contained, my voice down. It's getting hot under the canopy and all I can smell is his beautiful skin.

Shit, shit, shit, I think to myself. Get out of this situation.

But I don't. He pulls down the zipper track inside of the fabric and I hold up the mattress pad and we struggle for the zipper pull and the track to connect. His brow is furrowed in concentration, I'm trying to hold everything just right and I feel like neither of us are breathing.

Then the zipper catches and slides along and the pad is attached. I think we both breathe out a sigh of relief and then he ducks under the pad, lifting it behind him so we're still under the tent of fabric, but both pressed up against each other.

He's smiling. I'm smiling.

And a flash of danger comes across his eyes.

Maybe it's lust.

But it's all danger to me.

Beautiful, delicious danger.

For once, for once, I'm ready for it.

But before that thought even has a thought to process, the look in his eyes smolders, drunk with desire and he grabs my face with one hand, the other hand going behind my hair and he's kissing me.

Kissing me.

Kissing me.

I thought I was ready for this but I wasn't.

His *kiss.*

It's more than I remembered. It does more than knock me off my feet. His tongue is insatiable, explicit as it thrusts into my mouth hungrily, his lips crazed and needy. It's wet and violent and makes the want inside me throb, over and over. His hand at my head is gripping my hair as if he's holding on for dear life and each tug shoots fire down my nerves. Every part of my being feels alive, soaking it all in, desperate for more of his touch, more of him, more of everything.

He pulls back half an inch, just for a second, just enough time to let out a moan while his other hand holds my face in place, captive. His heady-lidded gaze fixates on my eyes, then my lips, as if I'm some sort of apparition.

Then I grab his shirt collar and yank his lips back to mine. The need in me builds and builds and I'm dying to wrap my legs around him, to feel every inch, to feel his want for me. I think I whimper. I gasp. I kiss him with the same kind of abandon as he's kissing me, his mouth all encompassing as if wanting to swallow me whole. I wouldn't mind his mouth somewhere else.

As if he reads my thoughts, he grabs me around the waist and quickly lowers me backward to the ground, the padding inside propping my shoulders up. We're lucky that the couch frame or coffee table wasn't in the way but I'm not even sure if that would have mattered. To hell with all the furniture.

With rough, eager hands he shoves up the tunic so my breasts are exposed and then pulls down my bra until my nipples are hardening in the air.

"I knew you'd be so fucking perfect," he says, breathing hard. The feeling makes my nipples even more sensitive and a low moan escapes from my mouth. "Oh, sweetheart, if you keep making noises like that, I'm afraid I'll come all over you before I can come inside you."

Our top halves are still inside the fabric and he places his wide, hot tongue on my stomach, trailing a path up and over my breast and to my nipple. He swirls his tongue around before flicking it. I moan again, unable to keep it inside, my hands gripping onto this soft, thick hair like a lifeline.

"It's like licking a fucking buttercup," he says between groans and I look down. My breasts, heaving and wet from his tongue, also glowing yellow from being inside the fabric.

Now he's undoing my jeans and sliding his fingers down the front of my underwear. I want to spread my legs to give him easier access but he's pulling down my jeans and locking my thighs together. His finger pushes in through the slit and I close my eyes to the feeling, succumbing to him.

When he finds me soaking wet, I'm almost embarrassed at how desperate my body is.

"You're gushing," he says, in a low voice that connects with me on this primitive, visceral level. "Oh fuck, babe, you have no idea how badly I need to be inside your tight, pink little hole right now." And with his words, two of his fingers slip inside me and I gasp, automatically clenching around him.

"God, you're greedy, aren't you?" he whispers. "Totally underfucked and I'm about to change all of that for good."

Oh, God. Please do.

He bites at my breast, plunging his fingers in further and my back is arching, wanting so much more, harder, longer, deeper. I want to be stripped naked, bare to the marrow, and I want him to take me so fucking completely I'll never need anything else again.

"Mommy?"

Ah, fucking shit!

"Damn," I cry out softly and Bram immediately retrieves his hand, zipping back up my jeans. We exchange a wild, bashful look between us and then, once my shirt is on properly, he lifts the couch fabric up and over us.

Ava is standing at the door to my bedroom, rubbing her eyes and looking sleepy. Thankfully from her position, she couldn't have seen all that much.

"Hi, sweetie," I say to her, trying to catch my breath.

She peers at me and Bram. "What are you doing? Your hair is all windy."

"Just putting the couch together," I say, smiling way too broadly. "Bram stopped by."

"Hi, Bram." She yawns and then plods along through the living room and sits down on the couch. The normal couch. The couch that doesn't practically force two neighbors to have sex in it.

I look over at him as he pats down his hair with a smile. What the hell just happened? I'm still turned on as hell, my breasts feel heavy with desire, my clit throbs from where his thumb was pressing. Good Lord, I need him to continue.

But maybe this is a good thing that we stopped. Getting carried away would have been a bad idea.

Right? I realize I'm just asking myself and I don't have the answers. I just want to get fucking laid by this Scottish sex god beside me.

"Well," I say to Bram, clearing my throat. "Thanks for your help."

He nods and slowly gets to his feet, pulling me up to mine as he goes. "Sure. But I wasn't done helping you, you know. I was just getting started."

I know what he's saying and as much I want to ask for more, I'm not sure how and if I should.

"Well, thanks for the help you did give. You know, with the couch."

He shoots me a wicked smile and then runs his fingers – his same fingers that were inside me just moments ago – underneath his nose and breathes in. "I'll be back for more of this," he says thickly.

Then he turns and leaves and I'm standing beside an almost finished piece of shit couch, wondering if my legs are ever going to stop shaking.

Chapter Twelve

NICOLA

I don't see Bram for the rest of the night and when I wake up the morning, my body's still groggy from the previous hangover and my insides ache for the brief moment that some part of Bram was inside me. It all feels like a dream, a really good wet dream, except I never got a chance to come and now I'm feeling embarrassed and sexually frustrated to boot.

Jesus, the things he said to me were so fucking hot, I don't think any guy had been so explicit and we had barely gotten started. I wanted to see where that filthy mouth would have taken us – figuratively and literally. I wanted him to come back for "more of this."

But as the morning stretched on, I'm stuck with one almost finished couch, another in a box I can't even fathom putting together and I'm this close to taking the largest blunt object I have – probably my dildo – and smashing the shit out of both of them. Fucking IKEA! But it's not really the store's fault (not really), it's mine for getting so wrapped up in him already. It's like one little touch, one little taste, and I'm ready to give him more. Although,

I would say neither his touch nor his taste was *little*. His tongue is strong and long and his fingers even more so.

Even though it's Tuesday, Lisa can't make it in to cover my shift today since it starts at 3pm but luckily my mother can. I'm starting to feel awful for dragging her out here more often. Shift work just isn't as predictable as the jobs of my past but she's a trooper and loves spending time with her granddaughter as much as possible.

"Hey, darling," she says to me as she comes inside. She stops and immediately eyes the IKEA crap in the corner before waving at Ava who is lying on the original couch, buried in cushions and mindlessly watching TV.

Ava gives a half-hearted wave back, as if she can't muster the energy. Normally I'd freak out that there's something wrong with her but I just measured her blood levels and she's in perfect range. She's just a bit blah – must be picking it up from her mom.

Yet my mother says to me, "You're looking good." As if it's a surprise, as if I normally walk around looking like a bag of crap. Hmmm. Maybe I do.

"Oh, thanks," I say. I'm just wearing my normal bar uniform of black cleavage-producing tank top and jeans but she's peering at me like I'm hiding something.

"Really,"' she says, pinching one of my cheeks, something she hasn't done since I was a little girl. "Whatever you're doing, keep it up. Don't forget you're still young, you know, no matter how old this troublemaker makes you feel." She jerks a thumb at Ava who pays no attention.

"Yeah, yeah," I tell her. I grab my leather jacket I've had since the Dark Ages since SF decided to be a real asshole this week and drop the temperatures to about minus a million. I'm getting ready to head out the door, when my mother says, "Should I expect a visit from Bram?"

Even though the door handle is in my grasp, I let go and step back to face her.

"Mom, listen," I tell her. "Bram's a very nice guy."

"A gentleman," she says with a weirdly knowing smile.

"Sure," I say. "I mean, he's a real good guy. And also, not…anyway, my point is, I don't care if he brought you over a kettle or seems to show an interest in me and whatever, he's just my neighbor. He's never going to be anything more than that."

"Oh, Nicola…" she goes on, throwing her hands down at her sides.

I grab one of her hands. "I know you and this is pretty much the first guy you've met since I've been with Phil, other than that guy Ben, but he didn't stick around much either, but really…Bram and I? We are just friends. I don't know what the future holds but for now, he's doing me a favor and I'm trying to make it as easy as possible on him." I pause. "You know what I mean? And don't do any of your mom meddling things that you usually do. That's not going to work, okay? It may jeopardize the landlord-tenant relationship we have going."

"What makes you think I would do any of that?"

"I can see it in your eyes," I tell her. "I see it in my eyes too, sometimes."

She throws her hands up in the air and walks over to the couch, plopping down beside Ava. "All right. I understand. Mom can't have a little fun. But I'll tell you, one day your daughter will be old enough to be dating boys and you're going to care as much about the process as she does. Only she won't let you."

"Sounds fabulous."

"It's true. It's what happens to all us moms. Time keeps chugging by and you all keep changing but the love never does. You'll always be my little angel and she'll always be yours. And all mothers just want their angels to find men worthy of them. Even more than that, someone that will look at them like they're magic." She looks at me, plopping her legs on the couch. "If you find a man who looks at you like you're magic, you hold on to them. I had that with your father and I never should have let him go."

I swallow hard. "But you have to think the man is magic, too. It goes both ways."

She nods. "Yes you do. It has to be both ways and when you find it, it's alchemy in its purest form. Don't cast it aside for anything else."

I don't know what else to say. I tell my mom to call if there are any troubles and I leave.

I don't see Bram in the halls. I don't know what I'd say if I did. I'd probably ask for a ride and would end up getting more than I bargained for.

...

Unfortunately I don't end up working the shift that night for very long. The night is slow and at around eight, James tells me I can go home. It's great I still get the tips and a few more hours of my paycheck, even if I'm not there – he can be a really good boss sometimes. But the hassle of public transportation doesn't help and also, I guess I just really wanted to be out of the apartment for a long time. It's easy to forget about Bram when I'm so far removed.

I walk down the hall to my apartment, shrugging off my leather jacket and am about to stick the key in the door when I hear laughter.

My mom's laughter.

Ava's laughter.

Bram's laughter.

Oh, hell no. I silently whip out the powder compact and give my face the once over. Hair is disheveled a bit but I look okay otherwise. I take a deep breath and open the door.

Inside my apartment are Bram, my mom and Ava. They are all sitting on the same couch.

Only it's not my old couch and it's obviously not the yellow shit piece. The yellow shit piece and the other box are stacked up by the door, right beside where I'm standing. All three of them are on this sleek, dark grey sofa that I've never seen before.

Actually, as I shut the door behind me and peer at it closer, it looks like the same futon Bram had his eye on in the store.

Oh my God, did he buy me a new fucking couch?

My eyes fly to his and from the way he's grinning at me, the tip of his tongue held devilishly between his teeth, I know that's exactly what happened.

"You're home early," my mom says and she looks bashful, as if I caught her doing something she shouldn't be doing. She adds quickly, "Bram came by with this couch for you, isn't that so nice of him?"

"It's very nice of him," I say, walking over the couch and kneading the top of it between my hands. It's soft but sturdy. I like it a lot, but God how his charity is starting to make me uncomfortable at times. I think that's why he does it. Screw the Richard Branson aspirations. I think Project Nicola Price aka Eliza Doolittle is more because he enjoys how much it bothers me. He's becoming a regular old sugar daddy when I sure as hell never asked for one.

I look over at Ava who is smiling at Bram like he's her damn hero. "How do you like the couch, angel?"

"I like it very much," she says emphatically.

All right, so I guess that settles it. "Where's the old couch?" I ask him, oddly sad I never got to say goodbye.

"A charity organization came to take it away, going to a half-way house," he says. "So don't worry, it's going to a good cause. And tomorrow we'll just return the other couches to IKEA."

Oh, so we have plans for tomorrow now? I do my best to keep a stupid smile from showing on my lips.

"Well, now that you're home, I better be going," my mother says, easing herself off the couch. She gives Bram a flirty look. "Nice talking with you, Bram."

"Always a pleasure," he replies, his brogue extra thick. Extra hot. Damn, he needs to stop showing off his accent.

My mom gives me a quick hug, says bye to Ava and just as she's out the door, she winks at me.

I totally pretend not to see it.

But once the door closes, it feels like I'm being locked in a tomb with Bram and suddenly I want my mother back because I am afraid like nothing else at what could happen tonight.

Because he's here. He's sitting on my couch – my new couch – and he's staring at me so intently that my bones feel like melting away. That look can only mean one thing.

"Mommy," Ava says, snapping me back to attention. "Can I stay up with you guys and watch Dora?"

"No, sweetie," I quickly tell her, grateful for the opportunity. "You have to go to bed now. How about you go brush your teeth. Did your grandma use the spindle and give you the ouchie?"

She nods and then runs off to the bathroom.

"You know what's going to be nice?" I say to Bram. "Her starting kindergarten in the fall. She'll be so tuckered out, there's no way she can stay up late."

"That will be nice," he says. "And easier on you, especially if you start working days. You think you'll still be with the Lion?"

I shrug, glad that we're talking about other things and ignoring the throbbing elephant in the room. "I'm just taking each day as it comes, to be honest. But yeah, I guess I should keep looking shouldn't I?"

He purses his lips and drums his fingers along the back of the couch. "Since bartending wasn't your career choice, you can always start incorporating your dream job back in. You know. Your passion."

I nod. "I'll try." Actually one of things I've been wanting to do lately is start sewing again like I used to do as a teenager, but I'll have to save enough money to get a sewing machine. It's funny how much I feel like a teen again with Bram around. I want to sew, I want to listen to 90's trip hop, I want to just let my hair down and be a bit wild and free.

For the first time in a long time, I wouldn't mind losing my heart. Just as long as I can get it back. When you're a teenager and you fall in love, you think you'll never move on once it's been lost. But you always gain it back, you always fall for someone else. No boy holds it for too long. Your young heart is a wild, elastic thing. Now, I fear that age and time and experience stretches it too hard, too far, and it will never snap back.

But why am I even thinking about love. My mind should be in the gutter, if anything.

"Do you hate the couch?" Bram asks as I go into the kitchen to put on some decaf.

"Not at all!" I tell him. I shoot him a sheepish glance over my shoulder. "Sorry, I'm just surprised. Like, really."

I look back at the coffee grounds I'm trying to measure and I can hear him get off the couch. I can feel him come toward me. The man carries his own force field and maybe it's just my hormones or my deprived imagination, but I swear I can feel every hair on my body standing to attention as he approaches.

"It's a really nice couch," I say meekly, talking for the sake of talking. Oh man, when I get nervous, I can talk anyone's ear off. "I think we saw it in IKEA, right? I guess you could have returned the yellow couch earlier."

"Aye," he says and now his voice is like a growl. He stops right behind me and I can feel his breath on my neck. "I could have. But I wanted your approval. I told the halfway house that you may change your mind, so they're holding it somewhere."

I swallow. "Okay. Um, well, no. It's for a good cause as you said and I guess we can return to the store tomorrow or some other day for the rest and..."

I trail off because his lips are on the bare spot between my neck and my shoulder and his kiss, so soft, so slow, is literally stealing my breath and my thoughts. I am pure silk in his hands and I have to brace myself on the counter so that I don't slither to the ground.

But he has me too. He places those warm, large hands around my waist, making me feel so impossibly dainty and one hundred percent his. I lean back into him and he presses his pelvis against my ass. I can already feel the hard contours of his erection, straining for me.

"Mommy," I hear Ava call from the bathroom. Kid has the worst timing I swear.

I raise my shoulder, trying to shrug Bram off. "I don't want her to get the wrong idea," I tell him.

He takes his lips and hands away and I can feel his eyes on the back of my head. He clears his throat. "There is no wrong idea, Nicola. There's only a right one."

I twist around to face him but he's already halfway across the room and going for the door.

Shit. Did I scare him off that easily? The expression on his face is tense and I wonder if I somehow offended him.

"Good night," he says and just like that he's gone.

Holy moly. I stare at the closed door a few seconds until Ava runs over to me. "Mommy, can I have toothpaste that tastes like bubblegum? I saw it on the TV."

I absently ruffle her hair. "When you finish this tube you can."

I'd never seen Bram so moody before though it doesn't surprise me. Beneath that easy-going exterior, sometimes I can see the darkness in his eyes, hinting at something underneath. We all have that in us.

Later on, after I put Ava to bed, I find that I can't sleep. I toss and turn, staring up at the ceiling, pulling the duvet over me as the chill from the Bay wafts into my room. I masturbate soundlessly, getting off to Bram everything – Bram on me, inside me, around me – but that doesn't help at all. It just makes things worse because I'm so aware of how there's no substitute for the real thing.

Finally, I get up and go into the living room. I sink into the couch and I'm suddenly so grateful for it. Not only is it stylish, but it's functional without being too overwhelming - meaning, now my guests (aka my mom) have a proper place to sleep when they stay over. And the dark grey color, it kind of reminds me of Bram's eyes. Especially when they get all dark, like they did earlier, like storm clouds rolling in.

I'm about to flip on the TV and maybe watch something stupid just to take my mind off things when I look at my phone. It's just after midnight.

Would Bram be awake right now? It might be crazy, but I feel like going next door. Just to see if he's up. Just to see…

But I don't want to wake him if he's not, especially since he left so abruptly. After all he's done for me, I don't want to get on his nerves. Well, maybe just a little bit, but only because it's so fun.

Maybe I'm finally understanding why he likes to bug me so much.

I sigh, staring at my phone. That kiss, such a simple kiss on my neck and I just wanted to give myself over to him, his forever to have. It surprised me how eager and willing I was to just let him have me, with no regard for my heart or for our relationship or for anything. And I know, I know, I should be using my head above all else. It's kept me safe over the years.

But I just want to pretend that everything will be all right. That giving myself to Bram will answer all my prayers, even if just for a night.

I pick up the phone and text him. **Are you awake?**

I wait, staring at it in my hands that are trembling slightly, wishing I could take it back. I wait and there's no response. He'll probably get it in the morning when he wakes up and I'll have to come up with some sort of excuse as to why I texted him.

Then I hear his door closing out in the hall and there's a quiet knock at mine.

I freeze, my hand to my chest and stare at it for a moment, knowing that if I open it, everything could change.

"Nicola," I hear his throaty voice whisper.

I get up and go to it, opening it a crack. He's standing in the hall in just a pair of thin, black pajama pants. Very thin. I can't help but stare at his crotch for a moment.

"Hi," I tell him softly, tearing my eyes away, my pulse starting to awaken with lust. "Did I wake you up?"

"I've been awake for a long time," he says, his hand resting on the doorframe.

"What have you been doing?"

A heavy pause settles between us.

He licks his lips. "Thinking about you."

Before I can say anything to that, his eyes burn with urgent need and he bursts into the apartment like a man who sees what he wants and will do anything to get it.

And what he wants is me.

Chapter Thirteen

BRAM

I couldn't wait a second longer. What little patience I had left for Nicola had snapped and I let loose like a rubber band that's been stretched to the end.

I grab her face, that fucking perfect, sweet face and kiss her more wildly, more violent and desperate than I've ever felt before. Her mouth feels like silk as my tongue thrusts inside, wanting to claim every wet inch and her skin feels like heaven, clouds, that beckon you to grab and squeeze and make yours.

A small whimper escapes her lips and into my mouth and her hands are on my bare chest, trying to push me back but I can't wait. While I'm still kissing her, I reach back and quickly close the door behind me, silently, aware that Ava is asleep. I have no intentions of waking her up, of having any interruptions. I'm going to get deep inside Nicola tonight and fuck her so raw, so hard, until she has no choice but to see the animals we are.

I grab her roughly and with a grunt, flip her over my shoulder, like a caveman would, like a hunter would bring home a meal, and take her into the bedroom where I throw her on the bed. She bounces on it and I shut the door behind us, making sure it locks, then take the condom foil out of my pocket and toss it on the bed before sliding off my pants.

She's breathless and wide-eyed as she stares at my naked, massive erection for the first time. It's just the reaction I want. Actually, she's looking a wee bit intimidated but that's not so bad for the ego either.

"There's no time for foreplay," I warn her gruffly as I get on the bed and crawl toward her, my thick shaft bobbing between us. "But I'll get you wet all the same." I put my hand on her shoulders and push her down onto the bed while I settle over top of her, my hands on both sides of her face. I run my thumb over her lips, pushing it in until I get between her teeth.

"It wasn't just tonight that thoughts of you have kept me up," I tell her, wanting to know how badly she's gotten under my skin. "It's every night. It's all the time." I remove my thumb and press my body down on top of her, so she can feel how hard, long and ready I am. Her eyes widen but they aren't afraid. It's like her body has been ready for this and her mind is struggling to catch up.

She's eager, even though she doesn't know what will happen next.

I reach over for the condom packet, my heart pounding loudly, and spread her legs apart with my knee. The scent of her already drifts up and I breathe it in deeply, sweet and musky, more addicting than any perfume.

Quickly, before I lose it, my body hair-trigger sensitive, I sit back on my heels and rip the condom open, sheathing the thin latex over my length. I watch Nicola's face, her eyes taking me all in and I remind myself that even when I'm turning down an extra beer and sweating for hours at the gym, this moment is all worth it. I take the best damn care of my body and she can't seem to take her eyes off of me.

Once it's on, I shake a drop of sweat from my brow – Christ, I'm burning up in here, my skin feeling like the sun – and lower myself down on her, keeping all my weight on one arm as my free hand slinks between her waiting legs.

"Just making sure you're ready for me," I murmur to her, my lips and teeth finding the soft, delicate lobe of her ear and tugging on it just so. I bring my hand up to her pussy and grin against her cheek. Not only does she feel just as plump and silky as before, now she's positively drenched. Fuck, I should ditch my plans and just lap up every last decadent drop but then I know I'd be blowing my load in the first minute. There's nothing so primitively sexy, so fucking raw, than eating a woman out, licking up every ounce of what makes her *her*. When you combine that with the pleasure you're giving her, I dare any real man not want to lose control. Turning her on turns *me* on.

"You're so fucking wet," I tell her as I push two fingers inside her tight little hole. The way she squeezes around them, holding me, makes my eyes momentarily roll back in my head. Fuck, and that's just my fingers.

Her breath hitches and she arches back, her round, pale breasts heaving upwards. I run my tongue over her nipples, hard pebbles that respond to my every touch, and she groans loudly. I push my fingers in further and the groan deepens. She's like a fucking smorgasbord, a buffet, a feast, and I have no idea where to start but every single item is bound to be delicious.

I can't take much more. I make a fist around my rigid shaft and position it at her entrance. Her eyes flutter from being closed to being open wide as I slowly rub my swollen head up and down her shiny cleft. It feels too incredible.

"Oh God," she says breathlessly. "Just get inside me already."

"Impatient," I comment. "I like that."

She pauses for a moment. "Just…it's been a long time. I may have been revirginized."

The stupid smile on my face spreads even wider. "You say all the right things. I'll go slow."

And even though going slow is the last thing I want – fuck, every nerve in my body is ready to slam right into her hot depths and ram her until she's up against the headboard – I do it anyway. I slowly start to make my way inside her.

No, it's more like force my way inside her because she's that damn tight, like a wet little vice that grips every heavy millimetre of my cock.

"Shit," I growl, looking down to see myself as I push into her. My head has disappeared into that sweet pink dream. So slippery, so surreal. "This is a test of my will," I tell her.

"Easy," she says through a shaking exhale. She lies back and I wait until she relaxes a bit more before I ease in further. She's so hot and wet as I slowly work my way inside that I begin to shake. I pause, for myself this time, and take in a deep, ragged breath.

"Am I hurting you?" she asks quietly.

"Sweetheart," I say, my voice low and throaty. "You're only hurting my resolve."

She smiles at that and relaxes more but it's not enough.

"Open yourself," I tell her. "I'm only halfway there. I want you to take all of me."

She blinks. "Shit, I thought I was."

I shake my head, more droplets of sweat falling off and landing on her breasts.

She takes in a deep breath but I know how to speed up the process. I place my thumb on her clit and rub it around, her juices spreading. I work at her until I feel her widen and then I push in further. She gasps but she puts her hands at my ass and presses her fingers in, controlling my speed. But she's still pulling me forward.

I'm holding my breath, forgetting to exhale, so wrapped up in this dizzying plunge, feeling like some conqueror taking over a new land. She spreads out beneath me, so soft and lush, like paradise and she lifts her knees higher, opening herself wider, and finally I'm in all the way, my balls pressing up against her and I feel this close to blacking out. She gasps but grips me with tight, blistering fury.

I groan loudly, unable to keep quiet. For all of my reputation as a lady's man, I know I won't be able to make a good impression this first time. The need in me is too sharp, too hard, too much. I slide out slowly and watch my thick shaft shiny with everything she has then plunge back in. My whole body shudders.

But even if I'm going to come soon, and fuck it's going to be amazing, I'm not doing so without her. I steady myself and with force I grab her thighs and yank her up and to me, holding on tight with one hand, my fingers digging into her soft flesh, while my other hand goes for her clit again.

She moans, loud, and then has the strength to place a pillow over her face to muffle the cries. I have to admit, it's hot when she watches my dick slide in and out of her but it's also hot when she can't see anything at all.

"Don't hold back, babe," I whisper, breath ragged and deep. "I'm not. Not this time. I can't."

My hips roll back and forth and I plunge in and out, from tip to the last thick inch of my cock. My rhythm becomes faster and faster and I know I can't keep my cum at bay for much longer. Her pussy is so tight, so eager, I feel like I'm on fucking drugs, like I'm sticking my dick into some sexual trip I may never sober up from.

I work my fingers into a frenzy and her muffled moans get louder and louder while I slam into her harder and harder. Her back is arched, nipples pink peaks, and I know she's close.

"Fuck!" she cries out. "Oh, Jesus."

Because I'm starting to pound into her so hard, shaking the bed, shaking her breasts, I can't tell if she's spasming or not, but then I feel her clench around me, off and on, and I know she's there, lost in the spiral.

I take in a deep breath and let out a low, guttural cry as my coiled muscles let loose and the orgasm rips down my spine, shooting out through every nerve ending. I'm fucking her so hard I think I'm going to push her bed right through the wall, right into my apartment and then I'm white-hot, wild, undone.

I come hard, blasting my load so fast and powerful I fear I might just tear a hole in the condom. I'm shuddering so hard that the bed is still shaking, even though the pumping of my hips has slowed. Through my blissful, electric haze, I can still hear Nicola moaning into the pillow, gasping and making nonsensical noises. I may be doing the same, it's hard to tell when you have no control over your body, no real awareness of what's going on except you're a million miles above the fucking planet and you have no idea when you're coming down.

When my arms start to tremble, I slowly lower myself so I'm on top of her, the wet slick of my sweaty chest pressing against hers. It's so animalistic, that feeling, like we're operating on a level of instinct and desire, eons before the mind comes in. It's silly to say we're on a soul-to-soul level, but it's not far off.

"Sorry," I say as I take the pillow off of her face. "I couldn't hold back. You're fucking kryptonite."

She stares at me, her face completely flushed pink and glowing, her eyes heavy, like she's in a dream. She's never looked more beautiful. I want her like this all the fucking time.

"I can't even..." she says, her voice airy and she smiles.

"Next time, it will be different," I tell her, smoothing her damp hair away from her face. She's got wild, mad bedhead and just adds to this crazed goddess look she has going on.

She shakes her head once. "Good Lord, I hope not. That was...that was...there are no words."

"Oh, it will be just as amazing," I assure her, kissing her lightly on the lips. She tastes like salt. I breathe in deeply and the smell of our sex, both musty and new, almost makes me hard again. If it wasn't for the fact that I have to pull out and remove the condom, I don't think I'd ever have to come out.

But I do. It's only polite.

I move back a bit and pull out, gripping the condom to make sure it doesn't spill all over her. I get up and head to the en-suite washroom, making sure I'm all cleaned up before coming back to bed.

She's nestled under the covers, the top of it barely covering her breasts and in the glow of her nightstand lamp, she looks positively sated. Perfect.

"Mind if I get in?" I ask her, not knowing if she just wanted me here for a fuck or for something more. I hope to fuck it's for something more.

She gives me a lazy smile and then lifts open the blanket. I sigh inwardly with relief and get in.

I'm not much of a cuddler but now that I'm in bed with her, naked, it feels sinful not to be touching every inch of her soft body. She's such a fucking goddess with those freckles and pouty pink lips and creamy skin and I know she has no idea. It totally adds to the appeal.

I pull her toward me and kiss her shoulder, still warm and damp. My fingers get lost in the mess of her hair. I don't know what to say – I've never been much for pillow talk – I just want to hold her in my arms as I sleep and hopefully wake up in a few hours for another round.

But she feels slightly tense, hesitant. She's rubbing her lips together like she's got something on her mind and I have a feeling I know what it is.

"You know," I say slowly, running my fingers over the bridge of her cute nose, over her luscious lips. "Contrary to popular belief, that actually meant something to me."

She swallows and tilts her head to look at me. "Yeah?"

I knew it. My reputation will follow me everywhere.

"Yeah." I kiss her neck and murmur into her was. "And I don't shag more than one woman at a time. I'm fucking you now and I'm going to keep doing so for as long as you want my cock around. I know you said only an idiot would fall for this line, but I only have eyes for you and there's no sense in screwing someone else if I'm going to be thinking of you the whole time."

She nods. "Okay. Well, you don't have to worry about that with me."

"Don't be so sure," I tell her. "I've seen you at work. I've seen the way men look at you, the same way you do. But as long as I can be the only man who conquers you, I'll be happy. And I'll do my damndest to make you happy."

She smiles softly. "You almost sound sweet there."

"Just give me a few more minutes and sweet will be the last thing on your mind."

But in a few more minutes, we're both asleep.

Chapter Fourteen

NICOLA

"God, you taste delicious, sweetheart."

I hear Bram's husky, jumbled words at the same time I feel his tongue slide between my legs. I jump at the contact but his hands grip my hips, keeping me in place. I raise my head, blinking hard and see his thick head of hair as his tongue snakes along my cleft, licking slowly.

"Jesus," I mutter softly, sinking back into the bed. "What a way to wake up." It's early morning and the sky outside my window is grey blue, even though there seems to be no clouds or fog in sight. I'm surprised we're up. I felt like we fucked all night but even though I ache and my lips and pussy feel rubbed raw, I also feel surprisingly alive. My brain is bright behind my eyes, my nerves are buzzing, my skin seems like it can feel every atom in the air. It's one hundred percent clichéd to say I feel like a brand new woman, but I do.

Bram groans into me and his tongue plunges inside. I arch my back, wanting him deeper, my legs opening more and more for him. His fingers grip my hips hard and with his other hand he slips a finger along my clit, rubbing it just so.

God, I'm going to come at any moment but I also want him to last forever. Can this please be the way I wake up for the rest of my life?

Last night was too incredible for words – another cliché, but true. I'd never had a man want me so badly, I could practically feel the primal, animalistic need that matched my own. And naked, gorgeously, beautifully, exquisitely *naked*, Bram was a whole other beast. I honestly didn't know if he was going to cause me a lot of pain or not, but from the way he so slowly, deliciously, eased himself inside me, I felt nothing except a pinch and then this incredible feeling of being so full, like I'd been missing him my whole life.

The only problem is, now I feel a bit bereft at the absence of his dick. I want him inside me, all of him, not just his fingers and his tongue. I want him to make the bed shake again, for my breasts to jiggle as he slams into me. I want that wildness, that wickedness, that damn smirk as he knows exactly what he can do to make me scream even though I've been screaming into my pillows, lest we wake up Ava. And judging from how enthusiastically he's licking me, like a fucking ice cream cone, I'm about to let loose. I grab the pillow out from under my head and hold it on my face as he pushes me over the edge. All the tight coils in my body release and I'm riding wave after wave of insane pleasure, my limbs jerking from the power of it all.

Holy hell. Wham, bam, thank you, Bram.

He lifts his head when my spasms begin to fade. "That's how I like to wake my woman up."

I give him a look, my head swimming, my body floating. "What if I want to wake you by giving you a blow job?"

"We don't even have to compromise," he says as he crawls on top of me. The iron-stiff length of his cock rubs against my slickness and I hope to God I have enough condoms in my drawer. The fool had only brought one last night. I'm not sure what the hell he was thinking.

I'm about to bring it up – I may take the pill religiously but condoms are a definite must, especially with a player like Bram – when I hear a shuffle on the other side of the door and then the sound of the door trying to open.

"Mommy, the door is locked!" Ava yells. "Let me in."

I exchange a look with Bram and realize he doesn't have much in the way of clothes other than his pants. I leap out of bed, slip my house robe on and throw his pants at him. I open the door a crack, keeping Bram out of view, and slide my way through.

"Hi, angel," I tell her, my back to the door, holding it shut as I peer down at her. "You're up early."

"Why was the door locked?"

"Oh, that was an accident," I tell her.

Then the door opens and Bram appears and thank God his erection is gone.

"Bram?" she asks. "Do you live here now?"

Bram gives me a cheeky grin and then squats down to her level. "No, little one, I'm still next door. I just spent the night."

"Okay," Ava says brightly then walks off to the bathroom. I know Ava isn't old enough to get an idea of what adults do in situations like this. She's thankfully far too innocent for that train of thought. But after Phil, I've been very careful about what guys I've brought over. There haven't been many, but I was with a guy called Ben around the same time that Steph and Linden were first getting together. He was nice, which was why I was with him, but there weren't any sparks. But Ava liked him and the more time he spent over, the more attached to him she got. Then when we broke up, it pretty much broke her little heart. Since I've learned she wants Bram to be her daddy as a Christmas present, it's pretty safe to say that she's going to get her heart set on him.

As for me…I don't know. I watch as Bram saunters into the kitchen, my eyes glued to the swing of his slim hips and narrow waist and that long expanse of muscular back. I regret not making any claw marks on it last night, but there's always next time.

Oh God, please don't let that have been just a one-night stand, I think, suddenly afraid that he might revert. I know what he said last night about only wanting to fuck *me*, but for the life of me I can't imagine where this will go.

Then again, I told myself I wouldn't analyze this to death. That's not "fun." That's not wild and free. I was just going to enjoy the ride and worry about what may come later.

"So," Bram says as he puts on the coffee. I love how comfortable he is in my apartment, even though weeks ago it was annoying as hell. "When is your next shift? Do you have time to go to IKEA today?"

"IKEA!" Ava yells. "Balls!"

I laugh. "Yes, Ava, balls."

"I love balls!"

"Just like your mum," Bram notes, biting his lip to keep from laughing.

"Hey," I wag my finger at him. "Let's keep this morning rated G."

"Balls!" Ava yells. "Bram-a-lama-ding-dong!" She runs back to her room and I hear her bouncing on the bed.

"I don't know where she gets her energy," I say with a sigh, going to get the medicine and the glucose meter.

"At least you can say she's been doing great ever since she was diagnosed," he says. As I brush past him for the cupboard, he grabs me around the waist and pulls me to him. "How are you?" He lowers his voice. "You seemed to enjoy the way you woke up."

I can't help my smile. He keeps his grip firm on me and searches my eyes.

"I did," I tell him. "Better than coffee. Speaking of, you better hurry up or I'm going to gauge your eyes out."

"Ah," he says. "You're one of those angry ones who aren't even human until their third cup. Good to know. Wake up Nicola with good head and coffee immediately after."

"That sounds like heaven."

"Heaven can be arranged," he says and places a lingering kiss on my neck, kissing up until right under my jawline. "I think I've found my heaven right here."

I keep my head back and eyes closed and that ache between my legs flares up, wanting just as badly as before. But there's no way that can happen today, not with Ava in my care. Unless IKEA has a sex pit, we'll have to hold off on the bedroom stuff until it's dark.

"So," he goes on, pressing me to him and inhaling deep. "Oh, sweetheart, you smell so good. It's distracting as fuck."

"So," I say to him, trying to keep him on track. "About today."

He pulls away and eyes me. "Yes. Are you free?"

"Today is a day off," I tell him. "I'm all yours."

"Good," he says. "Because even if you weren't, I intended to make you mine anyway. Remember all those things I said about you being totally underfucked? Well, it's going to take a long time and a lot of practice until I have you on the right side. But you can deal with that, can't you, babe?"

Now that sounds like an offer I can't refuse.

...

Though it's the afternoon when we pull into Emeryville again, it's a weekday and IKEA isn't as busy as I thought it would be. To be honest, I'm actually excited to be back. It's like when we were here before that was a totally different Nicola and Bram. Now we're here and though we aren't *together* together, this time I know what his cock feels like when it's inside me – I no longer have to wonder.

Unfortunately, because we aren't the first ones there, there's a bit of a wait for the daycare fun center to fit Ava in, so we make the most use of our time by going into the dreaded customer service line and returning the couches. Apparently they don't have any issues in taking them back and I'm sure the assembled couch will find itself in the "as-is" section, where the desperate and lucky souls go hoping to find that holy grail of all furnishings, the IKEA item that's already been assembled.

Finally when it's time for Ava to get into the daycare, we're pretty much done for the day and ready to go home. But Bram points out how excited Ava is about going and I can't say no to free child minding, so we agree to take a look around the store again while she has her fun for an hour.

After we wave goodbye to her, Bram pulls me close, his fingers firm against my wrist, his thumb delicately stroking the skin there. He whispers in my ear. "You remember the dare from last time?" he asks.

I give him a steady look. "It was a few days ago, so yes. And still no. You can call me no fun again, but I am not going to sit on a showroom toilet and pretend to take a dump."

He smiles. "No, that wasn't quite it. But it is a dare. One you'll enjoy if you're brave enough to believe me."

My eyes narrow. "I don't know..."

"Come with me," he says and he leads me upstairs and back into the showroom area. We stride down the halls, past couples flopping down on couches and finicky women testing the smoothness of drawers.

Bram tugs at the tulle skirt I'm wearing. "Glad you wore this."

I look down at it and the contrast with my Zara biker boots. "Thanks, I think it's kind of ballerina punk."

"No, I mean I'm glad you wore a skirt."

"Why?" I ask and suddenly he's jerking me into one of the showroom apartments. He takes me right around the corner of a sliding wood door and we're in one of the bathrooms.

"No," I tell him, planting my feet firmly. "What did I just tell you?"

"Relax, it's not what you think," he says and with one swift motion he grabs me by the hips and hoists me up onto the sink. I squirm even though I'm hidden from most shoppers. If anyone explored this faux apartment and turned the corner, they'd totally see me.

But Bram just hikes up my skirt so it's bunched around my waist and pushes my underwear aside. The sudden burst of air and exposure makes me freeze, as does the cold faux marble on my ass. He positions himself between my legs, grinning up at me the whole time.

"Seriously, no," I tell him. "We'll get caught and kicked out."

"But what a way to go," he says and then I feel the tickle of his hair on me and the hot zing of his tongue.

I don't even know how this is going to work. How can I relax and enjoy this knowing we could be found out at any minute? This isn't pleasurable at all, this is nerve-wracking, it's dangerous.

Jesus, this feels good.

I grip his hair in my hands and lean back, my head against the mirror as his tongue and lips get their fill of me.

A moan escapes me but I don't care. The sound is taken away into the buzz of the store. Just feet away, there are people staring at this apartment, pondering their home furnishings and yet behind a simple piece of removable wall, my pussy is on display for them all to see.

Bram's not taking his time like he was this morning though. His mouth is hot and fervent and as his tongue snakes in and out of me, I moan again, guttural this time, feeling like a very bad, very wild thing. When he takes his finger and plunges it inside, stroking my G-spot while his lips suck on my clit, I'm a goner.

"Fuck," I cry out, too loud. But Bram keeps going until my limbs stop shaking. For a few glorious seconds there I think I'm above both time and space—the seventh dimension where Bram-powered orgasms send you.

"Wow," I manage to say, lifting my head up. I expect to just see Bram but that's not all I see. While he's between my legs and staring at me with concern, probably because I look like I've just seen a ghost, there's an elderly couple standing behind him with their mouths hanging open.

The woman shrieks and the man covers her eyes and pulls her aside and out of our view. Bram quickly hops to his feet, bringing me off the counter and making sure I'm covered.

"Oh, shit, oh shit, oh shit," I swear, adjusting my skirt. I grab onto Bram's shirt. "What do we do?"

"They look like the types who'll call security," he says and even though I'm freaking the fuck out, there's a hint of amusement in his eyes. I'm not sure I like that. I don't ever want to encourage this kind of fun again. "I guess we better run?"

I turn around and bang on the fake wall of the bathroom behind us. "Can't you break through this or we can tunnel our way out? I don't want to go out there," I plead.

He grabs my hand and kisses the back of it. "On the count of three, we run. Got it? One, two, three!"

Somehow my legs move and he pulls me forward and we burst out of the fake bathroom and into the fake apartment. There are a few people staring at us, wondering what's going on, but what's the most frightening is that the elderly couple are talking to an Ikea worker and pointing right at us.

"Keep going!" Bram yells and my legs keep moving even though the rest of me seems frozen in icy panic and we scamper out of the apartment and down the hall toward the stairs at the very end.

I hear a "Hey!" of someone shouting after us but we don't dare look or stop. We keep going, taking the stairs two at a time and run right to the daycare.

It hasn't been an hour but Ava is running around close to the entrance. I call for her, waving frantically while trying to not appear like a crazy lady and Ava is good enough to run right over to us without any coaxing.

"You're back already?" she asks.

"Honey, we have to go right now. Do you want to run with us? Pretend we are being chased by dinosaurs?"

She nods, always up for any sort of dino-related adventure.

"What kind of dinosaurs?"

"The bad ones." I grab her hand and the three of us jog out of the store and away from anyone who may want to ban us for life. Of course we end up getting lost in the maze that is the parking lot, but once we find the Mercedes, we hop inside and speed away.

I keep looking back at the yellow and blue building as it gets further away, imagining that angry IKEA workers are chasing after our getaway car with pitchforks and torches. It isn't until we're on the freeway that I burst out laughing. I can't help it. Tears spring to my eyes and I'm just shaking from it all, howling like a lunatic.

Bram looks at me in shock, as if he thinks I've lost my mind, but then he breaks into laughter too. Soon Ava is laughing, even though she doesn't know why. Maybe she hasn't seen her mom belly laugh in a really long time. Maybe she's been infected by the strain of lunacy that's been going on between Bram and I. Maybe she's just happy her mother looks wild and free.

We laugh all the way back to the apartment.

Chapter Fifteen

NICOLA

The one thing about sleeping with your best friend's brother-in-law is that you're not exactly sure how to approach the subject, or if you should say anything. But because it's me and it's Bram, it's almost impossible not to spill the beans. I'm bursting at the seams to tell someone.

When we got back from Ikea, Bram cooked me an amazing chicken and roasted vegetable dinner that both Ava and I loved and then the three of us spent the evening watching *A Bug's Life*. When it was time for Ava to go to bed, well then Bram and I had a fuckfest fest all night. Even though I'd gotten off at Ikea – and finally lived out my secret dream of sex in public – I'd become more turned on for him, all of him, than ever before.

But now it's the next day and Bram is in meetings and Lisa is coming to look after Ava while I work. If I don't tell someone, even Steph, what's been happening for the last forty-eight hours, I'm going to lose my mind.

I don't know, Steph's text back to me reads after I've begged her to meet. **I'm kind of zonked and I had plans with my pajamas and Netflix tonight.**

I need to talk to you, I text back. **You need to hear about who had sex at IKEA**.

There's a pause.

Then. **WTF? Who had sex at IKEA? The store??**

Come to the bar tonight and I'll tell you. And yes the store.

OMG. Was it you? OMG. WAS IT BRAM?

See you tonight.

Fine. Gah, you bitch!!!!!!!! Tell meeeeeeeeee.

Later.

FUCK.

And that's how I convinced Steph to come hang out with me while I did my shift at the Lion. Fortunately it was a slow night but not slow enough to be sent home, so Steph sat at the bar and I eased my way into telling her the big news.

"Just spill the beans already," she says, pounding back beer number two. So much for wanting to stay at home and watch Netflix.

"All right," I say and I can feel myself blushing.

"Wait," Steph says, holding up her palm. "I already know. I already know. Look at your face. You're a giant tomato! It will always give you away."

I sigh and lean in, dropping my voice. Even though there aren't any people close to us, I don't want it to fall into the wrong ears. I'm not exactly a kiss and tell kind of girl, even though that's just what I'm about to do. "I slept with Bram."

"What?" she shrieks, and James looks over from the other end of the bar.

"Steph, shut it!" I warn her, leaning across the bar to smack her arm. "I thought you figured it via my tomato face."

"Yeah but to hear you say it!" she exclaims. She wriggles in her seat. "Okay, okay, details. All the details. Tell me everything. Does he have a big dick? Is he like Linden?"

"Calm down," I tell her, knowing she was going to bring Linden into it somehow. "Okay, I guess it all started with IKEA."

"IKEA!" Steph says with a smile, putting her fist down on the bar as if IKEA was the name of a good friend of ours.

"Yeah, well, he took me there, you know I told you, to get a new couch."

"Yeah…and you had sex on the couch!"

"No. Just wait. Okay, so it was all fine. He was flirting with me, you know how he is, so damn direct about it."

"Just like Linden," she says dreamily, her chin propped up on her hand.

"*Not* like Linden," I tell her. "Anyway, so later, back at home, he comes over to help me assemble the couch. I can't remember if I asked him or not. Oh yeah, I needed a drill! Anyway, Ava is having a nap in my room and we're talking…and…you know, he's not at all what I thought." I don't want to divulge any of the private stuff he shared with me about the charity, but I say, "And I think he's not at all what you think. Or even Linden. He's a lot deeper than that."

She snorts. "Bram? Deep? Come on, the only way he's deep is when he's trying to calculate all the women he's been with."

I have to admit, I'm getting a bit defensive. "Not true at all. I mean, yeah, there's women. Or there was."

"*Was?*"

"But I'm getting ahead of myself—"

"You are getting *way* ahead of yourself."

"Anyway we were talking and…God, I don't know. I just…I know it's stupid of me but man, you know, all this time with the flirting and innuendos and I just wanted to see what it was like to be with him. You know? It started to become all I thought about, just looking at him, listening to that damn accent—"

She sighs loudly. "Yeah, that accent."

"He was making me feel things I hadn't felt in a really long time."

She gives me a steady look, her lip pouting slightly. "How come you never told me about this? I thought you hated Bram."

"I did! But, he kind of won me over. And I guess I figured it was just stupid to have a thing for someone like him."

"Oh, honey, come on. Who doesn't have a thing for Bram? He's Bramtastic."

"Oh my God," I exclaim. "You're just as bad as he is!"

She shrugs.

"Look," I point out, "you were just threatening him to not even look at me, you were threatening me and Kayla about breaking up the balance of the group. There were a lot of threats. I didn't want you mad at me or, God forbid, lecture me."

"I know I said those things," she says, "but that's only because I care and I just wanted to warn you. But honestly, you're like all-aglow and stuff. I haven't seen you like this in a very long time. I know you're being careful with him… aren't you?"

I nod. "Well, I'm not falling in love with him, if that's what you mean."

"Good," she says. "Not that I don't want you to fall in love, I would just be extra wary with a man who seems pretty good at breaking hearts." She pauses, watching my face fall. "But that aside…you slept with Bram. My brother-in-law."

"Yup."

"So, you were assembling the couch and he just, what, took you right there?"

I laugh. "That's not so far off. We were underneath the fabric of the couch. You know how IKEA is, you have to put together everything. We were zipping this foam thing to the lining and…I don't know. Some kind of look passed between us and the next thing I knew, he was kissing me, his hands were everywhere. I was pushed back onto the ground and my shirt was up and he was…it was pretty fucking hot."

"And, and…?"

I shrug. "And Ava interrupted us."

"Cockblocker!"

"Steph," I warn. "That's my daughter you're talking about. And yes, she's a cockblocker."

"But tell me you at least got to feel what he was packing."

"I told you I slept with him. Obviously dick was involved."

"Hashtag dick."

"And well, when we were fooling around under there, he did, you know, put a few fingers in me."

"This is so awesome. Give me another beer."

I pull out an Anchor Steam, pop off the top and slide it on over. I fill her in on the rest, including me texting him and wondering if he was awake.

"So you took control," she muses. "I don't think I've ever seen you do that. You know, with a man."

She was right about that. "Well, I initiated it. Once he arrived, he was in control the whole time. And it was nice. He's a bit rough, you know, a dirty talker too. At least with what I've experienced. I don't think he's quite as vulgar as Linden."

"Give it time."

"Anyway."

"And you got off right?"

"Fuck yeah. And every time after that."

"And when does IKEA come into this again?"

I can't help but smile slyly, looking away. The memory of that moment is seared into my head to the point it's impossible to shake loose. "We went back to return the couches. When Ava was in daycare, he hauled me into one of the showroom bathrooms..."

"No..." she says, eyes wide.

I nod. "Yeah. He put me up on the sink counter and went down on me."

"In the store!"

"Yup."

"And there were people around?"

"There were. I didn't see any of them until after. Then we got caught."

"You got *caught*?" she squeals. Loud. Loud enough that James finally starts walking toward us.

"Steph, you're so loud!" I hiss at her.

"What's going on ladies?" James asks, always the nosy one.

"Nothing," I say quickly.

"Nothing," Steph adds. "Except that Nicola here is a secret exhibitionist."

"Steph!"

James looks me up and down. "Are you sure about that?"

"She might start dancing on top of the bar," Steph adds.

"You can do whatever you want," he says, "as long as it brings in the customers." He stares at the both of us for a moment, trying to suss out what's going on but when we give him nothing, he leaves.

"And with that," I say to her, "please don't tell anyone about what happened."

"I'll keep my lips shut," she says. "But obviously I'm telling Linden."

"No!" I swat at her arm. "You can't tell him of all people! I don't want Bram to think I'm flapping my mouth off."

"Oh, and you don't think he's doing the same thing right now? Scoring with the impenetrable ice queen?"

"Ice queen?" That almost smarts as much as "no fun."

"You know, that's what they call any girl who won't give up their cooch on the first date. You're like their white whale."

"Great, a whale."

"Moby Dick, stupid. Anyway, Linden will know by the time I get home, I guarantee it. And it won't be on account of me." She gives me a look. "And you know, it's fun to share. It's good for you. I mean, you don't see me holding back what Linden does in bed."

"I know," I grumble. "And I don't need another recap about what you guys did with the sparkly butt plugs you bought in the Castro, either."

She shrugs. "I bet Bram is just as much into that kinky shit. And when he shoves his cock in your pussy and a plug up your ass, I guarantee you're going to call me up and shoot the shit."

"I really hope you're not being literal," I comment dryly.

Steph doesn't stick around for long after that. She gets this look on her face when she's tipsy and needing to get laid. I wish I didn't know what that look was but I've seen it too often when she's thinking about Linden.

I'm about ten minutes from finishing my shift when I get a text from Bram.

Are you still at work?

I can't help but get a giddy little thrill just from a simple text. I feel like I'm in high school again.

Yup, just about to finish though.

I'll come get you. I can't wait any longer. Been thinking about you all day.

Now I'm grinning ear to ear. I'd forgotten what fun it was to flirt via text.

All right, if you want to.

See you soon.

It's not long until I'm stepping out into the mist, bringing my jacket around me closely, while Bram pulls up in his Mercedes.

"Get in, beautiful," he tells me after putting down his window. He looks so dapper in his suit, I almost have to pinch myself that he's here to get me.

I slide on into the Mercedes. "Brrrr it's cold out," I say, rubbing on my arms.

He leans over and flicks on the heat. "You know, you'd think growing up in Scotland, the drizzliest, dampest, wet crotch of all places would have prepared me for San Francisco but I don't know how you people do it. Your seasons make no sense."

"Tell me about," I say, still feeling the chill. Wearing a skirt doesn't help but he puts his broad, warm hand on my thigh and presses down.

"You're cold as ice," he notes. "You should have had a few shots of Scotch while you were waiting for me."

I tell him I wasn't waiting long. Then the car pulls off of Van Ness Avenue and starts heading toward Golden Gate Park. "Where are we going?"

He doesn't say anything. I look over at him and he's grinning in the dark and his hand is sliding further up my thighs.

I squirm as the hairs on his arm tickle my sensitive skin. At the same time I can't help but part my legs, wanting to give him easier access.

"Where are we going?" I ask again, my breath hitching as his fingers push aside my panties and slink their way between my folds. I know I'm wet already. My body gives this man the most immediate reaction. Even the way he says "fuck" gets me going.

"I'm going to take you for a little ride," he says. There's a husky undertone to his voice that drives the message home.

This is all still so new to me. I try not to dwell on my insecurities – does my breath stink after that shift, am I wearing a matching bra and underwear, am I going to be any good? The car revs, the vibrations going right through me and I lean back in my seat and close my eyes.

I'm actually close to coming – his fingers have skill and my body has no patience, not with him – but he brings the car to the side of the road going through the park. In any other circumstances I'd think he brought me here to murder me. Or I would have been afraid of the riff raff and secret society that breeds in the park after dark. But I know Bram won't hurt me and I know I'm safe pretty much anywhere with him. He knows how to take care of himself pretty well.

"This is a bit creepy," I still say to him. "Great place to hide a body."

"Great place to shag a body," he says, turning the car and the lights off until we're enveloped in near darkness, and twisting in his seat. I hear his seatbelt come undone. "I'm not taking any chances after what happened in IKEA. Now, I'm getting in the backseat and you're going to get in right after."

I don't make any attempt to argue. He gets out of his seat and walks to the back. He opens the door and sits down, undoing his belt and zipper. In the dim light from a nearby streetlamp I can see the length of his hard cock as he takes it out.

Jesus. He's just fucking ready for this at any time.

"Are you going to get back here and suck me off or what?"

Wow. Okay. First the cock makes an appearance, then his filthy mouth.

"I'll be right there," I tell him, trying to keep my voice from shaking. Even though it's fun, it's still nerve-wracking. I feel so silly playing the role of the sexy minx and it's apparent that's exactly what he wants from me.

I open the passenger door, get out into the cold air and then open the back one. I'm about to step inside when he says, "Strip."

"What?" I say peering into the car at him. His eyes gleam with desire and control.

"I said, strip. Take it all off, now. Then get in the car and put my cock in your mouth."

I blink. I can't tell if he's role-playing or not, but he sounds dark and commanding and not at all the happy, grinning Bram that had picked me up. To be honest, it makes my nerves stand on edge.

"Bram," I tell him.

"Do as I say."

I sigh and then start to take off my jacket.

"Slowly," he says.

"It's freezing out."

"Do it slowly," he grinds out. "And I promise to take it slowly with you."

Well, at least I can't turn my nose up at the reward.

So I slowly remove my leather jacket, tossing it onto the floor of the backseat. Then my tank top until I'm just in my bra.

"Gorgeous tits." He nearly growls. "Jeans next."

I take off my boots and socks, then slide down my jeans until I'm just in my bra and panties, standing by the side of the road. No one has driven by yet but that doesn't mean they won't. The air is nipping at my skin, making it buzz and the grass underneath my feet is cool and wet. I feel like I'm slowly becoming alive again.

Then I look down. My bra and underwear do not match whatsoever. You would think I would have remembered the cardinal rule I used to follow when I was younger – when sleeping with a guy, always make sure your bra and underwear match. That and always carry mints or gum on you, don't wear too sticky lip gloss and make sure you exfoliate every inch of you, even when you don't think you'll get lucky because those are usually the days that you do.

"You're a damn goddess, you know that?" he says. His voice is so rich and deep, it could command me to go streaking down the road right now and I'd probably do that. "Remove your bra."

I reach behind me and do as he says, my breasts coming free and feeling absolutely heavy with lust and need. A breeze picks up and washes across them, making my nipples even tighter. It's like nature itself is lending a hand in turning me on.

"Now, your knickers," he says.

I slide them down my legs but my hips sashay back and forth in a sexy little dance, like I'm actually enjoying this. I'm starting to think my body has a mind of its own and it wants Bram's dick all the time.

"That's right," he whispers. "That's my girl. Now, come in the car. Slowly."

It's good timing too because I can see a pair of headlights coming down the road. I duck, covering my breasts until the car passes and when it's gone I exchange a sheepish look with Bram.

"They're gone. Get your fine arse in here."

I slide on in, the seats warm against my ass cheeks, and I close the door. The backseat of his car is small and he's taking up most of the room. Actually, his cock is. I can see the glisten of precum at the tip and for some reason it makes my mouth water.

He rubs his thumb over his swollen head until it's shiny and then he leans back, holding his cock tight around the base.

"Just lick," he says. "Just your tongue. From bottom to top. Slowly. Pretend you're molasses."

I get as comfortable as I can being naked in that backseat, utterly conscious of my scars and cellulite and any rolls even though we're mainly in shadow, and I lower my head over him. I bring my tongue up from the bottom, only touching where his hand is and then drag it up his hard length. I feel every pulse, every vein, every ridge. He's hot to touch and he tastes clean, like soap. When I reach the top, that hit of salt from the precum sinks into my mouth and I find I'm loving it. I don't even realize it's caused such a response from me until I catch myself in mid moan.

"You like that, do you, sweetheart? You like the taste of my cum?"

I nod and lick him again, this way going back down.

Now he's groaning and pushing his cock up against my tongue. "You know what they say, the worse something is for you, the better it tastes."

I give him a sly look, pausing just to say, "And I know you're bad for me."

"Very bad, and yet, oh so good."

I lick him fully and completely, all the way around.

"Now put your lips over the head and just suck on the tip. Slowly." I do as he says but his hand goes to my hair and he grips it hard, tilting my head slightly. "Don't be afraid to look at me while you do."

Shit. Eye contact has never really been my thing, especially during sex, but if it turns him on then I want to see it on his face. I stare at him with lustful eyes and he watches me right back. His gaze is intense, primal, consuming.

Finally he breaks it, closing his eyes and leaning his head back against the seat. "Fuck, you're so fucking good."

I pause, wiping my lips with the back of my hand. "Do you want me to keep going?"

He shakes his head, breathing heavily. "No," he says huskily. "I want you to flip around so you're on all fours. Your arse facing me."

Well, okay then. I hesitate but he raises his chin and looks at me, those eyes gleaming with so much desire that I find myself getting wet all over again. Just a look, just a suggestion and I'm all his.

"So fucking perfect," he says. His voice is beyond guttural I can almost feel his vibrations. I'm a ball of nerves and temptation as I feel him shift from behind me and place his hands on either cheek. "So bloody ripe."

"Ouch!" I cry out. Did he just bite my ass?

"Sorry," he says, though he doesn't sound sorry at all. "It's taking a lot to not eat you whole. But I can't hold off for much longer."

He begins to massage and grip my skin then I feel the long, warm wet snake of his tongue as it slides up and down each cheek. I shiver from the sensation, wanting desperately for him to go lower.

Instead, he spreads my cheeks apart and I flinch, not prepared for that.

"Relax," he murmurs. "You've got a good thing going on here."

To him, maybe. But I can't relax, not when I feel a wet finger slide down my crack, probing in a place that should never be probed.

"Relax, Nicola," he says again. "Trust me."

I swallow, not sure if I'm brave enough for ass play, even though he talks about it all the damn time. But then his fingers go lower and slip between my folds, stroking them.

"So fucking wet," he says, briefly teasing my clit before plunging his fingers inside me. "So fucking ready."

I hear him shift and the sound of a condom packet being torn open. Then the swollen head of his cock slides up and down my ass. He pushes briefly in the wrong spot but before I can tell him off, he moves further down and I hear an amused grunt from him. Testing me.

His hands go back to gripping my hips and he moves me over an inch and back into him. He eases the tip of his dick inside me and then pushes a hand between my shoulder blades so my ass is raised, the angle better.

Bram lets out an animalistic moan as he sinks in and I can't help but respond in the same way. From this angle he makes me feel so damn full, I can feel myself stretching beautifully around his thickness, soaking up every second that he's inside me.

He slowly begins to slide out and then pushes back in, holding me in place until I start to slip. Then my hands are up against the door of the car, my face pressed against the fogged-up window as he slams into me again and again.

One hand of his goes for my clit, rubbing wild and messy, making me crazy and the other one goes back to my ass cheeks.

He briefly rubs between the crack, then positions his thumb at my ass and slowly pushes in.

I nearly freeze from the intrusion but I automatically clench around him. This is definitely dirty, this is definitely taboo, but my body is so turned on that it only makes matters worse. The more he pushes his thumb inside me, all while his hard cock is spreading me below, the more wild I feel, the more free.

I could finally let loose, be anything, anyone. And I wanted to be animal. He was making me one.

I groan loudly. I want to growl. I want to demand he fuck me even harder.

"You like that don't you?" he growls. "It's making you wetter and you're already so fucking tight." He pushes his thumb all the way in and I gasp. It's both so wrong and so right at the same time and fucking hot as hell.

"You're creaming around my cock, babe," he murmurs, making a thick, primitive sound from somewhere deep inside. "You're ready to come."

And just like that, his finger presses down in one slick motion and I can feel how wet I am and how every inch of me feels so damn full and I am coming. I'm coming loud.

The orgasm rips through me and I know I'm trying to hold onto the car door or maybe I'm just trying to hold on in general because I feel like I'm being flung somewhere very far away where there are stars and music and my skin is blistering as the need melts off of me. I feel reduced to nothing but a shining light and then Bram is still going, still working away at me even though my muscles are rocking with spasms, muscles clenching around him.

"I'm too sensitive." I try to tell him this and catch my breath at the same time but he doesn't stop and it sounds like he's operating on pure instinct now, driven to fuck, to come.

And somehow, I don't know how, but my sensitivity melts away and even though I'm still full and swollen, I'm coming again for the second time.

This time Bram comes too. It seems violent, surreal, bigger than the both of us. His sounds, those gorgeous, crazed sounds, fill the car and as I come down from yet another high – the greatest high – he's holding my sweaty back against his damp chest. He kisses down my spine in between trying to catch his breath.

"Fuck," he swears, trying to clear his throat. "That was unbelievable."

"You're telling me," I tell him, my own chest heaving. I peel myself off the car door and nearly collapse onto the seat. "I've never come twice in a row like that."

"Then next time we'll have to shoot for three," he says, smiling against my skin. He places his hand around my waist and then slowly pulls out. I automatically feel empty without him.

We sit down next to each other in the backseat, the air filled with the hot and musky scent of our sex. I'm totally naked and drenched. He looks both slick and disheveled at the same time.

"Let me know if you want a ride next time," he tells me as he opens his door.

"Will I ever." I quickly slip on my clothes and he drives us the rest of the way home, no more pit stops.

When we finally make it there, however, we disappear into his apartment for a quickie. I know, I know. We just had mind-blowing sex and should leave it at that. We're fucking greedy, what can I say. And it's bad of me since Lisa is on the clock, but I can't help it. Even just leaving his car, his hands were all on me as we climbed the stairs and though car sex was as steamy – and ground-breaking – as anything, there was something about the comfort of a bed that called to me.

Plus, you know, the man was making me damn insatiable. When I was with Phil, I rarely felt this turned on all the time. Even when we first started dating, everything was so controlled and, let's face it, my physical attraction to Phil was never off the charts. He was cute, albeit skinny, but I think I was more attracted to his indifference and brains than anything else. And it's not like he made me feel like the sexiest woman on earth. If I ever gained a bit of weight – and this was back when I was so damn thin – he'd comment and it would set me off for days.

So where sex with Phil had been adequate – I mean, it produced Ava – it was never that bone-melting, must have, orgasms all night, kind of sex. Not like it is with Bram. I wonder if this is what sex in general is supposed to be like or I just got the luck of the draw with Bram. I'm going to assume it's mostly the latter.

Finally though, it's time to return to my apartment. Bram says he'll freshen up and then come over to sleep once Lisa leaves and I'm ready for bed.

"Sorry I'm late," I tell Lisa as I step inside. "Missed my bus."

She looks a bit cross but says, "That's okay." She gets up off the couch. "Ava was an angel, as always. Her levels were fine, too."

"That's great, thank you."

She walks past me to the door but stops and stares at me with a discerning eye. "You look different."

"Do I?" I ask. I checked my hair and makeup in the car back from our "shag spot" and after the quickie, so I don't think I particularly look like I've just had sex or done something wrong.

"You're all flushed," she notes.

"Must have been the walk from the bus stop," I tell her, wanting to add that it's cold outside but I don't want to keep talking and make her suspicious. It's not that I'm trying to keep us a secret, it's just that I don't know what *us* is yet. And screwing your landlord doesn't look very good to the outside eye.

She opens the door and then jerks her head toward Bram's apartment. "You know, your neighbor has some pretty loud sex."

I nearly choke. "Oh yeah?"

She nods gravely. "Yeah. I don't know how you sleep with that racket. Got to admit, he makes for a good show. And whatever woman he's with."

I feel my cheeks burn. "Have a good night, Lisa. Thanks again."

I have no idea now if she suspects about Bram and I, but I know at some point she's going to put two and two together. I make a mental note that just because we're in

Bram's apartment, doesn't mean I can cry out his name at the top of my lungs. I should ask him to gag me next time and then that thought itself turns me on.

But when Bram comes into my bedroom later, I'm exhausted and it seems like he is too. He doesn't push me for sex, he just wraps his thick arms around me and holds me to him. It's nice. It's so nice, just to be held, to be wanted.

"You comfortable?" he whispers in my ear.

"Very," I tell him. "I'm used to Ava crawling over me or just sleeping on me like a sack of potatoes. But this, this is very nice."

"Good," he says. "Because I don't plan on letting go."

"I had no idea you were such a cuddler, Mr. McGregor."

"Oh, there's probably a few things you don't know about me, sweetheart," he murmurs. "But you will, in time." He kisses my earlobe. "Besides, it's hard not to hold onto you. I'm afraid if I let go of you for one minute, you may just slip through my fingers. And then where would I be?"

"Jacking off?"

"Aye," he says. "But you can't do that forever."

"Really? I've tried."

"You really need to show me your dildo collection one day."

"Only if you promise to behave with them."

"Nicola," he says in mock indignation. "I can't believe you think I would do anything that would jeopardize your fair virgin beauty."

I giggle. "Shut up. Who knew you were such a dork?"

"Not many do, so please keep it between us and I won't tell anyone about your dildo collection."

"It's just a few toys," I say, playfully slapping his arm and settling back into the mattress. It feels so, so good just to be in his arms. "Besides, I think everyone I know has an idea. Steph says men think of me as an ice queen. Ice queens don't get laid."

"Mmmm, that's not true. They do get laid. It's just on their own terms. This was on your terms, Nicola, and you know that. Maybe I oughta thank you for letting me between your legs. Or maybe I oughta congratulate myself for saying all the right things, though for the life of me I don't know what they were."

"I'll just say, whatever you're doing—"

"Which is you," he interjects. "Over and over again."

"—keep doing it."

"And tonight?"

Now I feel a bit guilty. "I'm actually kind of tired."

"Same," he says, propping up his pillow. "But that doesn't mean I won't wake you up in the middle of the night the only way I know how."

I smile at that and let this absolute feeling of peace settle over me. The moment, as simple as it is, is pretty much perfect. It is perfect. I've got my daughter in her own room, responding well to the insulin and shots, taking the whole thing like the trooper she is. I've got a wonderful apartment, more than just a roof over my head. I've got the opportunity to really get my life on track, to start over and end strong, and I'm doing just that. And now I've got Bram, this wonderful beast of a man who keeps my brain guessing and my body coming.

I do catch myself on that last thought though. Because as much as I have him in the moment, as much as his arms are around me, keeping me calm and warm as the cool night air wafts in through the open window, and as much as I had him earlier tonight, I don't really know what the future will bring. I don't even know what we are. He said he wouldn't date or fuck anyone else and I believe that, just as I wouldn't even think of it myself.

But what does that mean? Are we in a relationship? Does he do relationships, like boyfriend and girlfriend, or am I just some sort of a monogamous fuckbuddy? I want to say that I don't mind just being a fling, especially if I'm the only one he has. But the truth, the damn scary truth, is that I'm falling for him. It's not love, I know it's not. It's not hitting me over the head, it's not stealing my heart.

But he is stealing my thoughts. He's training my body to want him and only him and all the time. He's making my heart beat faster when he's around, he's making me smile like an idiot when I even hear his name. He's making me look forward to each and every day because I know he'll be in it and when I imagine a day without seeing his handsome face, there's this strange sensation in my chest, like my heart is bereft.

My heart can't be involved though, it's too risky, it's too soon. I don't want love to swoop on into my life and turn it upside down, not now when everything is starting to go right. In my experience, love is a destructive force, tearing hearts to shreds and forcing people to pick up the pieces. Even the best love stories are violent tales.

I have to wonder if Bram has ever been in love. If he's actually gone that distance and bid farewell to his heart. If he's been serious enough about someone else to share a part of his life with them to move in, to have something that has a label attached. I wonder if he's ever been down this road and if it's something he's even open to.

"Have you ever been in love?" I ask, my voice sounding far away, as if in a dream. I can't believe I'm actually asking those words out loud, but there you have it. If my brain doesn't turn off, stuff will eventually come out my mouth.

I can feel him flinch beside me so that cancels out any hope that he was already asleep. Sometimes I have no idea how long I get lost in my thoughts. Is it moments? Minutes? I tilt my head to see his sharp gaze in the hazy darkness. "Don't worry," I go on. "I'm not in love with you," I assure him.

"Oh," he says, clearing his throat. "That's too bad." He swallows and then rolls on his back so he's staring up at the ceiling. "Yes. I was in love. Only once. I had it pretty bad too but…I was young. Shit happened. I panicked and I fucked up. I fucked up big time. I was just such a bloody idiot. It's a real fucking shame, you know? Because I think love is the sort of thing you should reflect on and feel good about. That's what love is, isn't it? A good thing? But I can't look back on her, on what happened, and feel anything but shame." His chest rises and falls with a deep breath. "What I wouldn't give sometimes for that chance again to just fix things…make them right. But we rarely get a second chance, do we?"

I know it shouldn't bother me, but the way he's talking about this woman is making my heart cower, like an early frost has stormed on in. "What's her name?" I ask.

He hesitates for a moment then says, "Taylor."

So, Taylor did a real number on him. I hoped that whatever we were – whatever we could be – would be enough to erase her from his mind.

"That's a nice name," I tell him, feeling stupid as I say it.

"She was a nice girl," he says. "But that's all in the past and in the past is where it will stay. What about you? Your baby daddy?"

I chew on my lip for a moment. "Was I in love with Phil? You know what? I don't know. I guess so. Maybe it was just infatuation? Stubbornness? Like I'd become so determine to love him I thought I did. Is that possible? Anyway, whatever we had, it still ruined me in the end so maybe it was love or maybe it was just loss. I don't know."

"Maybe it was love or maybe it was just loss," he repeats slowly. "I like that. That makes sense to me. Because sometimes you don't know, you just know what you had is gone and you know how that makes you feel."

"Yeah," I say through a heavy breath, remembering how damn low I felt after Phil left. How scared. Now, I don't know if my heart itself was breaking because love was lost or if it was just what Phil was to me that was gone. "I guess you know if you know."

"That's true," he says. His arms tighten around me. "Now, why are you getting all philosophical in the dark, huh? Do you need a spanking to set you right?"

I giggle and push his face away from my neck as he attempts to kiss me. "No, I'm good."

"You're the opposite of good and you're going to be punished."

He suddenly flips me over and climbs on top of me, his hand smacking the side of my hip, his mouth all over my neck and shoulders. I can't help but laugh as he kisses my worries away.

Chapter Sixteen

NICOLA

Three weeks pass by in a flash. Three glorious, beautiful weeks. There are some more shifts at work, I've bought a sewing machine and some fabric with the extra cash, the weather is starting to get warmer and Ava has become obsessed with bugs (thank you *A Bug's Life*). But for the most part, these three weeks have been one naked, hazy, sweat-slicked sex fest.

Bram is insatiable and the more he screws me every which way, the more insatiable I've become in return. Every single moment that we're alone, he's inside me – cock, tongue, fingers – and I'm starting to feel like the sexual goddess he keeps saying I am. It makes me wonder how I've even survived for so long without this in it. I understand now why sex is so goddamn important to people – it gives us life, it makes us feel more alive.

And it brings us connection. It's not just a fuck or a shag. It's not just orgasms and exploring each other's bodies. We're exploring each other's souls as well. I know that's a cheesy way to think about things, but it's true. The more I sleep with Bram, the more we talk, the more we don't even need to talk. We just feel each other on this other level, this current of intimacy that's scary as hell but addicting all the same.

Naturally, I don't know if he feels the same way that I do. That I'm falling. Bit by bit. That I feel like I understand him on levels I didn't think possible. But I at least know that sometimes I catch him looking at me and it's like he thinks I'm magic.

I keep thinking back to what my mother said about that, to never let it go once you've found it. God forbid anything from trying to derail what we are and where we might be headed, but I have no intentions of ever letting go.

The only hiccup in the last few weeks is that while I've been busier with more shifts, Bram has been busier with more meetings with the city, organizations, and investors. It's great that his idea is going full-steam ahead, but it does mean we don't see each other as much as we used to. It's usually just nights and that's probably why we cling to each other in the sex-soaked fog like we do.

Tonight though, it's Monday and I don't have to work. Bram's free this evening, so he's bringing over some Thai takeout for us. Even though takeout food is the worst thing for Ava, he goes out of his way to make sure she has steamed rice and vegetables with no msg and nothing but a little soy sauce, just so she won't feel left out.

The three of us are sitting around my kitchen table and I'm currently fanning my mouth with my hand because I think I got a load of chilies in my bite of Pad Thai. Bram is watching me with amusement, perhaps even more amused than normal.

"Sorry I don't have a tongue of steel," I tell him, slurping back a gulp of white wine to cool the burn.

He lets out a small laugh. "It's hot even for me." He looks at Ava then back at me. "Do you girls want to hear something fun?"

"Yes!" Ava says enthusiastically.

Since he included both of us in that question, I figure it can't be perverted. And so, I'm intrigued.

"What?" I ask, putting my chopsticks down.

Now he's grinning to himself, like he's about to tell a joke and is already laughing at the punchline.

"Bram," I remind him, "what's fun?"

"Okay, okay," he says, biting his lip. He's so damn handsome sometimes I forget my own name. He goes on, "How would you two like to go on a little adventure together?"

"Are we going to IKEA?" Ava asks.

"We are *never* going to IKEA again," I tell her. "That's a bad word in this house now."

She pouts a little but eyes Bram expectantly.

"Definitely not going there," he says. "But we are going somewhere that Ava has probably dreamed about going. I must warn you though, little one, you must be brave."

Her eyes widen, but she nods, serious. "I can be brave. I get the ouchies, I *am* brave."

He leans closer to her and whispers, "There are giant bugs there."

"Bugs!" she cries out. "Oh, I want to see the giant bugs."

Okay, I have no idea what he's talking about but I totally don't want to see *any* giant bugs.

"Are we going camping?" I ask him, trying not to shudder.

"No," he says. "But before you say anything, just know that I've booked you off the next four days from work."

"You did *what*?"

"Don't worry," he attempts to placate me, "I've already talked to James, it's not a problem."

"Yeah, but it's still money lost!"

"I said don't worry." He reaches out and puts his hand on mine, giving it a squeeze. "Please. You deserve this trip. You both do."

"I'm not sure anyone deserves a trip to giant bug land."

"Even if it's located in," dramatic pause, "Disneyland?"

Oh my God. Did he dare say the word *Disneyland* around Ava? That's like conjuring up Beetlejuice, except instead of Michael Keaton appearing, Ava turns into a rocket of a child, like she's fueled by one million tons of sugar.

"Disneyland!" she shrieks. It's ear-piercing. "Disneyland!"

I eye Bram who is clearly enjoying himself. "Please tell me you're serious, because if you don't take her to Disneyland now—"

"I am completely serious. And I'm glad you're all for it."

"Well, of course, I am. Who doesn't want to go to Disneyland?"

He shrugs. "I'm sure most adults don't. Didn't you see Louise CK's sketch? Personally, I think those adults are no fun, but I've got to say, sweetheart, I'm glad you're not one of them." He looks at Ava who is practically bouncing out of her seat. "And I can't imagine a better place for Ava to have some fun too."

I try to go back to eating my food but I can't. I'm just so overwhelmed. Giddy. Maybe just as excited as my daughter. Later, when Ava is playing in her room and we're in the kitchen putting the dishes away, I turn to him, grabbing him by the wrists and pulling him close.

"You didn't have to do that," I tell him, my guilt seeping in.

"I know I don't have to do anything." He kisses me on the forehead. "I want to. I can't wait to see you act like a kid."

And I can't wait to have him there with me. "How did you know that I've always wanted to go to Disneyland with someone I'm...with?" *Eep*, almost said something else there, got to keep going. "The last time I was there I think I was eighteen and with a girlfriend and everywhere you looked there were couples making out. I've *always* wanted to be one of those annoying couples."

"We can annoy the shit out of the whole park," he murmurs, kissing me lightly on the lips. "But, perhaps, I need some practice first."

I sink into his kiss, letting it fuel me, feeling the need swarm over my bones. I nearly forget that he was being a cheeseball. I break away, placing my hands on his chest, feeling his hard muscles underneath. "Thank you," I tell him softly. "Ava has always wanted to go...I've never been able to take her."

He nods. He knows. "Good thing is that, by waiting, she'll not only remember it more but she'll enjoy it more too."

"So when are we going?"

"Tomorrow morning," he says. "Bright and early. So get your arse packing." He places a wide hand on my ass and squeezes. "Or I'll get your arse spanking."

I grin at him. "Maybe I can have both?"

He grabs me by the bottoms of my ass cheeks and lifts me up in the air until my legs are wrapped around him. He then takes me to the bedroom and we lock the door, hoping we can at least steal a few minutes with each other.

. . .

When Bram says early, for us it actually means the crack of dawn. It's just about 6:30 am when he knocks at my door. Ava is in the bathroom brushing her teeth with her new bubblegum toothpaste after it took about ten minutes to rouse her awake. She only perked up when I mentioned the word "Disneyland." I can't blame her though. You know those old Disneyland commercials with the kids bouncing around in their pajamas in the middle of the night, yelling, "I'm too excited to sleep!" Well, that was pretty much last night in a nutshell. Zero sleep was had in the Price household.

I tuck my shower-damp hair behind my ears and open the door expecting to see Bram.

My mouth drops open.

It's Bram all right, dressed in jeans, boots, and a simple tee with a sleek leather duffel bag at his feet. But it's what's in his hands that has me practically swooning.

Okay, I'm totally swooning.

"Is that for Ava?" I ask, almost breathless.

He nods proudly, maybe even a bit sheepishly. In his hands is a child-sized princess dress, the pink Sleeping Beauty one that Aurora wears at the end of the movie. It even has the crown and veil attached. I think I might just die right here.

"I hope it fits her," he says. "It's hard to find those Disney Stores anymore."

"I can't believe you did that," I tell him, my heart thumping around in my chest. "That's the nicest, cutest, sweetest thing I think anyone has ever done for her."

"Well," he says, rubbing his hands along his jaw. "I did it for her and I did it for you."

I swallow hard, surprised at the burning in my eyes. No lie, I'm *this* close to crying. It's crazy how such a simple and somehow ridiculously romantic gesture undoes me. No one has ever thought of my girl with such regard.

And there goes a tear, rolling hot down my cheek.

"Oh, sweetheart," Bram murmurs, stepping into the apartment and enveloping me into a hug. "Don't cry. It was nothing. I just thought she'd like to dress up as a princess on the ride down."

"But you remembered *Sleeping Beauty* and the spindle and the needle and it's soooo pretty." I'm a blubbering, incoherent mess as I cry into his arms.

He puts his hand at the back of my head and holds me there. "Well, I'm glad you like it." I know he sounds so breezy about the whole thing but, then again, how can he understand what this means to me? So many years and no one has done something like this, no one has ever thought of me and Ava that much. It's then that I realize how tired I am, how much I've been pushed to the side, how much I've pushed myself to the side. It feels so fucking good to have someone care about us.

Just then, Ava comes out of the bathroom. She slowly walks over to us, her head tilted. She points at the dress.

"What's that?" she asks, hope sparking in her eyes.

Bram crouches down to her level. "Who is your favorite princess?"

"Aurora," she says smartly. "She pricked her finger on the spindle, just like I do."

"That's because you are a princess," he says, displaying the dress in front of her in a shimmering waterfall of magenta, pink and gold. "And this is your princess dress."

Her mouth makes an *O* and her eyes widen comically. "What?" She looks at me, almost begging for it to be true. I wipe away a tear with my hand and nod.

"It's all yours, angel."

She carefully takes the dress from Bram's hands and examines it. "It must be made out of cotton candy," she muses, absolutely dazzled by it.

"Can you go try it on yourself or do you need my help?" I ask her, knowing full well she needs my help.

"I can do it!" She runs off to her bedroom.

"Say thank you to Bram!" I yell after her.

"Thank you, Bram!" I hear her say from the other room.

A half an hour later the three of us – with Ava dressed as a princess – are in Bram's car and we're making our way down the 101, lucky that the traffic jam is on the other side. The three of us can't stop smiling and the day is full of such promise that it almost makes me dizzy.

Six hours later, after countless toilet breaks and pit stops and the never ending, "Are we there yet?" we pull off the freeway and onto Katella Avenue. This is Ava's first glimpse at Disneyland and I'm pointing out the top of the Matterhorn and Space Mountain, the Monorail and the Ferris Wheel and California Screaming Coaster in the distance. She looks absolutely terrified at those rides but I assure her there are many of them that she'll love and at that she starts boogying in her seat.

Bram didn't spare any expense and got us a suite at the Disney Grand Californian Lodge, located right in Disney's California Adventure Park. When I was young the park didn't even exist, so it was as much fun for me as it was for Ava to step inside the hotel and have everything be brand new. And let's face it, even if the park was here when I was younger, there was no way we could have afforded to stay there. The same goes for the Disneyland Hotel. Though it's dated now, it's still an arm and a leg for a room and when I was young, my parents believed in spending as little on the hotels as possible. Who cares if you were sleeping in a Super 8, as long as you were spending all day and evening at the park.

But Bram cares, and in turn, I care. The beds are clean, fresh and comfortable, the room tastefully decorated in the style of some grand lodge near Yosemite or Mammoth Lakes and we have a view through ponderosa pine and over the bear-shaped rock peak of the Grizzly River Rapids.

I'm pretty much exhausted because I've been on a six-hour road trip that has drained me like nothing else but Ava slept for a lot of the drive and now she's bouncing around the room, losing her goddamn mind.

"No rest for the weary," I say to Bram, feeling bad since he had to drive the whole way.

"I don't know if you've noticed, sweetheart, but I have stamina for days."

That he does. I go about making a day pack for Ava including the right snacks, water, her insulin kit, floppy hat, a spare pair of shoes and, of course, sunscreen. Then we head on out to enjoy the park.

Because we're tired, we plan on only spending the day in California Adventure. Ava doesn't know the difference between the two parks, plus there, she got to head into A Bug's Land and go nuts for hours.

As she does just that, Bram and I hold hands and watch as she plays in the different areas, pretending to be bug-sized, darting in and out of water fountains. When it's time to go on a ride, she grabs my hand and pulls me onto a Chinese take-out box that zooms around in a circle. Though these aren't the rides I ever dreamed of riding, she's having the time of her life. If it was up to me, of course, we'd be hitting up California Screaming and The Tower of Terror, but seeing everything through my little girl's eyes makes it that much more fun.

We end the day with Bram and I grabbing a beer and wine in the faux vineyard before we hop on the Cars Mater's tractor ride (which, in hindsight, isn't the best idea after a drink). Bram and I have been taking turns on and off riding with Ava and though she's less likely to shriek like a banshee around him, you can still tell she's having a lot of fun. Scratch that – she's having the time of her life.

The first two days at Disneyland and California Adventure are pretty much the same. We wake up early and head to the parks, breathing in the smell of churros, popcorn and turkey legs all while the tinkling music fills the air. We hit up all the kiddie rides – for some reason they have the longest lines – and then gorge on whatever food we can find. Somehow we manage to convince Ava to ride the Grizzly River Rapids with us and we all got so completely soaked that she was the only one who ended up loving it. Thankfully, the hot SoCal heat dried us off in minutes.

And of course she meets all her favorite characters including Eyeore and Sleeping Beauty. Bram and I both posed in some of the photos with her, though that wasn't my doing. He volunteered to be in the pictures and Ava looked like she was over the moon about his wanting to be a part of it.

The truth is, I'm still a bit uneasy about the whole thing and I'm glad that there are pictures of her on her own as well. As much as I'm falling for Bram – and I know I am, I mean how can any woman worth her salt not love this man? – I don't know what the future brings. I would hate to have us break up, break apart, or whatever it's called, and then be stuck with these photographs. At least now if that happens, I can burn them, pretend he never existed, and still have photos of Ava left over.

I think Bram can kind of sense my train of thought though, because he's being extra attentive and yet distant at the same time. I don't want to bring it up with him the whole, "what is this, what are we?" talk because that tends to ruin the very carefree and fun thing you have, so I don't.

But that night, as we're lying in bed together after some slow, passionate love-making, Bram says, "I know why you're hesitant with me."

I stiffen, not sure what direction this is going to take. "What do you mean?"

"Oh come on," he says. "You think I haven't noticed the way you practically flinched when I asked to be in the photos."

I take in a deep breath, wishing he didn't bring it up. "Look, it doesn't mean anything so don't take it personally."

"Well, I am going to take it personally," he says. He turns over to look at me, propping his head up with his hand. "You don't want me in the pictures because you still think I'm going to up and leave you, that this is just a bloody fling."

"No, not exactly," I say feebly. "It's just that…okay, maybe it's a bit of that. But you have to understand that it's just been me and Ava for a long time."

"Steph had said you were dating someone else for a while between Phil and…well, this."

Did she now? It had me wondering how often Steph and him talked.

I sigh. "His name was Ben. He was a nice guy and that was that. Neither of us were really into the relationship."

"But Ava liked him, didn't she?"

I give him a steady look. "What makes you say that?"

He shrugs with one shoulder. "Because you seem scared that the same thing will happen again. That Ava will grow attached to me – that even you, yourself, with your damn heart in a cage – will grow attached to me too."

I feel my skin go hot. "My heart is not in a cage," I say, defensive. "And Ava has been attached to you from that moment we first went in your car. The damage with her has already been done."

"But what about the damage with you?" he asks gruffly, peering at me even closer. "And how can what we have be called anything close to damaging?"

He really doesn't understand, does he?

"Because...." I grapple for words. "Because, when you invite someone in and they leave, they take a part of you with them. It ruins the foundation. Don't you see? It's damaging when you pull the bricks out and the whole building collapses."

He rubs a hand angrily over his face, letting out an immensely loud sigh. "Hearts aren't bloody buildings, Nicola!" He throws the covers off of him and gets out of bed, pacing back and forth. He's nude but for once, my eyes are drawn to the tension in his face. I don't even think to look at his dick.

"I'm sorry," I hiss at him, sitting up in bed. "I know they aren't but, God, I wish you knew what it was like to be me. To just know what it's like to be dealt the shitty hand."

He stops and gives me an incredulous look. I regret saying anything. He's that wide-eyed, his brow knitting with anger. "You think you're the only one who has been dealt the shitty hand in life?" He leans forward with his hands on the mattress, looking me dead in the eye. "My mother never told me she loved me growing up. My father was never proud of me, no matter what I did. I had to live with that, deal with that. I was shipped off to boarding schools half the time because no one in my family knew what to do with me. You want to talk about the shitty hand, well I got it. I was fucking unwanted. And yes, I had money and I had everything else at my fingertips. But that doesn't mean dickshit when you don't have someone to tell you they love you."

My breath is caught in my lungs. I can see his pulse ticking along in his throat, the desperation in his eyes that want so much for me to see him, the real him, to understand. And I do. Not in the exact same way, but I do.

He swallows and looks away for a moment. "Hey," he says, his voice low. He climbs on top of the mattress toward me and I'm reminded of the first time we made love. But instead of that carnal desire as he approached me, there's something else. That extra level of connection that I thought may have been only in my head.

"Nicola," he says, placing both his hands on either side of my face, gazing into my eyes with such deep focus. "I know you've been burned. But I've been burned too. Maybe our ashes can make something beautiful together."

He kisses me then with such force, such passion, I feel like the wind has literally been sucked out of me. I want nothing more than for something beautiful to rise from us together. I have my demons and apparently he has his.

We waste little time in getting intimate. He's inside me and instead of the lazy, luxurious romp we had just before, this one is crazed and desperate. It's like he's handing himself to me, afraid if I don't take it now, he'll lose me forever.

But he won't lose me.

Because I am absolutely in love with this man.

And that realization is terrifying. Because he was so, so wrong about hearts and buildings being different. They are the same. They are structures that keep us safe, that shield us from the elements. And the minute they start to falter, everything else is at risk.

A heart can be condemned, just as a building can be.

A heart can be destroyed by a sledgehammer disguised as rejection, by a bulldozer masquerading as a careless word. A heart can be blasted to pieces and ruined to the ground.

But even knowing all that, I need to move forward. I need to take that chance. I need to trust in Bram and trust in myself that giving myself to him, opening myself to love and letting myself fall for the first time in my whole life, doesn't have to end in rubble.

It can reach the clouds, pierce the sky. It can be that bridge from the life I had before, from that person I knew before, to something so much better.

I don't tell him this though. I don't dare. I keep these feelings – *I love you, I need you, I crave yo*u – and the fears – *you'll break me, you'll wreck me, you'll condemn me* – all to myself. But I let him inside that night. I let him in deep. I want him to discover these parts on his own, without the fanfare, without the expectations.

And when he comes, his eyes holding so much magic, and I think that maybe he knows.

Maybe he finally knows just what he is to me.

Chapter Seventeen

BRAM

"Hey, fuckface," Linden says as I answer the phone.

"Hello, Linden," I say politely. I'm in the middle of a meeting with the board of directors from San Francisco's Inner City Initiative and even though a coffee break has been called, there's no way in hell I'm going to greet my brother like I usually do.

"Caught you at a bad time, eh brother?" he says. "I'll call back later."

"What do you want?"

"Just wanted to check in with you," he says, sounding defensive. "Jeez, your own family can't see how you're doing. I haven't talked to you since you got back from your Disneyland excursion. Which, by the way, thanks a lot. Now Steph is harassing me wondering why she hasn't been whisked off to the happiest place on earth. I don't know how you did it with an actual child in tow."

His comment makes me flinch, as most of those types of comments usually do. "I did it for Ava," I tell him, "as well as Nicola."

"Fine, fine," he says. "I'm just saying, you're a saint. And I never thought I'd call you that. She must be really getting under your skin. Don't tell me you're going to pull a Jerry Maguire and go all ga-ga over the kid. I can't imagine Ava telling you how much the human head weighs."

No, but she would tell me the names of a lot of the dinosaurs from the Jurassic period. But I don't mention that to Linden. I don't want to give him any ammo.

"If it makes you feel any better," I tell him, lowering my voice so the people at the end of the table sipping their water and making small talk, don't hear, "I am ga-ga over Nicola. She's a shag like you wouldn't believe." I had to throw that part in there or Linden might accuse me of being a body-snatcher victim.

"I bet she is. Why else would you still be around?"

I breathe out slowly through my nose, trying to not let him get to me. I knew my brother would never understand any of this, any of what I feel and anything that I've been through before. There is so much he doesn't know about me, so much that no one knows, and lately I've been feeling like it's all boiling too close to the surface.

"You just watch out, Linden," I tell him. "Pretty soon Steph is going to start harassing you for wee babies and then where the fuck are you going to be? You're going to be taking them little shits to Disneyland and I'm going to be having the last laugh." I pause. "And yes they'll be little shits, because you were an epic shit when you were young and that will be your bloody karma."

He's silent for a change. "I'd say the same to you," he eventually says, "even though I know no girl in her right mind would ever want you to be her baby daddy."

And again, straight into the gut. I take another deep breath and remind myself that Linden has no idea.

No idea.

"Is that all you wanted to do?" I ask him, trying to sound unaffected and bored. "Trade barbs with me?"

"Where are you anyway?"

"Busy," I tell him, not about to get into the specifics. He and my family still don't know about the potential charity work, about my building and ideas. No one outside of Nicola knows and I much prefer it that way. Although tonight there is a black-tie gala for a fundraiser that attracts some pretty important local people. If Linden followed the news or local politics at all, he might get an idea.

Thank God he just sticks to flying helicopters, though that's obviously no small feat on its own.

"I see," he muses. "Well, whenever you're not busy and you're not shagging the single mum, come by and we can dip in some beers." There's a patch of silence. "Sometimes I miss you, brother. Just not this time."

"Fine," I tell him. I whisper into the phone, adding, "Fuckface."

I hang up and then realize that the people at the end of the table – Mr. Arterton and Mr. Bayswater – have heard what I've said.

I give them an apologetic smile. "Wrong number."

Thankfully the rest of the meeting goes well. Everyone is on board with my idea. It's just that no one has the money. It's kind of the same story everywhere I go. I guess things are a bit easier for me because the money has already been put down – I've bought the building and that's a huge chunk of fundraising I don't have to ask anyone else to do. But I need to have income coming in in order to pay the mortgage and that's where people are always coming up short. They believe in it – they just don't have the means to help.

I leave them feeling particularly despondent about the whole thing. When I get home though and see Mrs. Williams in the hallway, the aging and disabled woman with too much heart and not enough strength, I'm reminded of why I'm doing this. I do want to help, to feel like I'm of fucking use for once in my life. Maybe it's partly selfish – I don't think you can make money unless you are – but it's giving everything purpose.

And so is Nicola. She's not working today since we have the gala tonight, so before I even head to my apartment, I do what I usually do and go to hers first. I have a key now – well, I've always had one – but now I'm using it because I'm her lover and not her landlord.

Lover. It's not exactly the term I want to use to describe what I am to her, but I'm not sure what else will do. It's funny how lover is seen as more appropriate than boyfriend when lover has, well, deeper connotations. But Nicola has seemed a bit cagey ever since Disneyland, which was a week ago, and I don't want to push her.

The truth is, I consider us together. I consider her my girlfriend, though I wouldn't dare say it in case it freaks her out. Still, she has to come around sooner or later. I know I've not been completely honest with her and I know I have a few skeletons in my closet that could bite me in the arse. I know this. I just figure it will all come out in time, and when I'm ready. I want to establish trust first, a strong layer of it, that won't shatter when she really gets to know me.

It's close. She's close. I'm just not sure what I can do to make her let go with me. She's come so far, become so open and free and, fuck, so sexually awake. But until I really get through her defenses and her fears, I don't think she'll trust me one hundred percent.

Still, when I open the door and step inside her apartment, breathing in that familiar smell, that combination of coffee and plastic toys and her sweet skin, I have hope that the trust is there. That this is the day she lets go and gives herself to me completely. And I'm not talking body – I've had that all along. I mean her heart and her soul, the rarest things of all.

"Hi," she says brightly when she sees me. She's dressed in just a towel, though her hair is all done and piled on top of her head and her makeup is perfectly applied. Too bad all that does is make me want to throw her on the bed, open up that towel and proceed to mess up all that time and effort.

But I don't. I ignore my cock twitching in my pants and stride over to her, grabbing her by the shoulders. That delicate shower-soft skin so intoxicating beneath my hands then I kiss her on the neck. She smells like a dream. I could be buried here.

"You smell incredible," I tell her.

She giggles, squirming a bit. I know my stubble tickles her but that's always half the fun.

"Don't get carried away," she warns. "It took an hour to get my face and hair just right."

I pull back and inspect her. "Don't you always look this way?"

"Ha ha," she says. "I need to get dressed and put in my earrings. But I'll be ready in about twenty minutes. Ava's just having a nap and Lisa should be here soon."

"It takes you twenty minutes to get dressed?" I ask her, as I sit down at the kitchen table and split open a banana from the bowl.

She disappears into the bedroom, her voice carrying. "You know me. And you know I want to look good for this. I don't think I've ever been to a black-tie event before."

"That's not true," I tell her mid-bite. "There was Linden's wedding. And I know you'll get a kick out of this, but guess where the gala is?"

"Where?"

"That same yacht club on the other side of the bridge. Same as the wedding."

I look over and I see her paused in the doorway of the bedroom, a long olive green dress in her hands.

"You're kidding me," she says.

"Nope."

She looks impressed as she considers that. "Wow. It's like we've come full circle."

We'll see, I think to myself as she disappears into the room.

Thirty minutes later – not twenty – we're in the back of a black town car and heading across the Golden Gate Bridge. The sun is setting over the pacific, illuminating the stray patches of fog and low-lying cloud that clings to the downtown buildings. It's absolutely beautiful.

And so is Nicola. She's wearing a floor-length red gown with gold detail. It has a low back that just begs for me to lick up and down her spine, but a modest front. The material feels better than silk and thinner than a condom between my fingers and I deduce she's not wearing any knickers either. I can see the outline of her breasts and it's no wonder that I'm hard the entire ride. She used to lament that she couldn't go without a bra because she had child-bearing breasts, but she's become a little more free in that department and I'm grateful for it. In my opinion she has incredible tits.

Actually, she has incredible everything. As we get out of the car and enter the gala, everyone there dressed to the nines, the tuxedoed waiters going around and handing out canapes and shrimp cocktails and foie gras and truffles, there's no doubt that she's the most beautiful woman around.

And to think, to fucking think, she has *no* idea.

"You're so gorgeous it should be illegal," I tell her after we grab two flutes of champagne off a server and slowly walk around the grounds.

"You're so handsome, it makes girls stupid," she says and then jabs a thumb at herself. "Myself included."

I know she's completely joking but it's something she used to say and believe so often, back before we hooked up, that it smarts just a little.

But I brush it aside and we continue to do the rounds. The truth is, situations like this have always made me a little nervous. I'm okay once I know someone, but here I don't know a soul. I paid for both of us to be here and now that we are, I'm not sure who to approach. I've done my research and met with a lot of people thus far, but no one looks familiar.

It isn't until a bit later, when some speeches start being made about the fundraiser and the need to further develop

San Francisco into a city that's accommodating to all people with the emphasis placed on jobs, that I see Mr. Bayswater from earlier today. He wasn't the one who invited me and I had no idea he would be here, but then again, I was so busy talking their ears off earlier about my plans that I probably wasn't listening.

To my surprise though, at the end of the speech, he mentions my name. I have to do a double-take and Nicola nudges me in the side. I swallow, straightening my bow-tie, and stand up to show myself as Mr. Bayswater has asked.

Thankfully, I don't have to say anything, he just mentions my project and what I'm trying to achieve and then moves on. But when the speeches are all done for the night, I find myself being accosted by a reporter and a cameraman.

"Are you Bram McGregor?" the woman with caked-on makeup and glow-in-the-dark veneers asks. When I tell her I am, and that I'm the man that Mr. Bayswater mentioned earlier, she thrusts the microphone in my face and starts interviewing me.

I don't recall giving her permission to do so but this is a great opportunity and I use every second of it. Actually, it feels really good to be discussing it with the potential of it really getting in people's ears, all while Nicola looks on proudly in the background.

The whole interview takes about five minutes and the reporter – Chelsea Chain, such a fake-arse name – says they'll probably whittle it down into a quick soundbite for the section they are doing. Doesn't matter to me. I finally feel like I'm behind something that could have legs.

"That was fucking hot," Nicola whispers to me once the reporter moves on to someone else.

I glance down at her while she slides her dainty hands underneath the lapels of my tuxedo. "Was it now?"

"Oh yeah," she says, looking hungry and not for food but for cock, the best kind of hungry.

I know it's probably a risk in asking her this, lest it conjure up some bad memories, but I say to her, "How about we go back into the past and finish what we started?"

Hesitation washes over her brow for just a second, her glossy lips held in a pout, then a sly smile tugs them apart. "Sure."

I grab her hand and lead her through the crowd, remembering the path that took us around the building and to the garden.

Sure enough, there is no one back here and the sounds of the gala are muffled, sounding far away. Fucking brilliant, the stone bench is still here too.

"Make yourself comfortable," I tell her, sitting her down on the bench. "And by comfortable, I mean scootch over to the end here and get on all fours."

"Wait," she says, lifting a finger. "Did you screw that blonde chick here?"

"No," I tell her, knowing she'd ask that. "It was in the bushes over there. And it wasn't very fun to be honest. No one wants a thorn up their backside. At least, I don't." I pause, giving her a delicious grin. "But perhaps you're game for something a lot bigger than a thorn." I wiggle my thumb at her.

She rolls her eyes and I know she probably won't graduate beyond my thumb for a long time.

She's still not moving though, so I tell her again and she finally gets on all fours and backs up till she's at the end of the bench. I stand behind her and flip up her dress so it's gathered around her waist. Her arse looks so fucking amazing, I can't help but cup her cheeks in my hands, my fingers digging into her soft flesh. My need is wanton, elicit, and real. I squeeze and kneed them for a bit before my dick starts to ache in my pants, begging for attention. Then I unzip myself free and bring out a condom from my jacket pocket.

"Always prepared," she comments and wriggles that decadent arse in front of me.

"Stop teasing me," I warn her, smacking her lightly on the cheek. "I'd rather not come all over your dress." I see her shake her head slightly. "Okay, I would totally love to shoot my cum all over that expensive piece of fabric you're wearing and cover you in it from head to toe. But I won't."

"Because you're a gentleman."

"Oh that's right." I smack her other cheek. "The best kind."

So I have her right there on that stone bench, the way I should have had her last year at the wedding. I take her rough and hard and wild and we don't care who the hell hears us because we can't be filtered.

But the truth is, I'm glad that it didn't happen that way, that we didn't have sex at the wedding. I would have never gotten to know her and knowing me, she would have just been another shag. Sure, I would have seen something challenging in her, maybe I would have been compelled to let that wild child out. But it was her resistance to me, her devotion and dedication to her child, to everything but herself, that made me obsessed with her to begin with. It may have taken time for our paths to cross again, but I'm eternally glad they did.

"Everything in due time," I say after we've both come and we're catching our breath. I zip up my pants and dispose of the condom in the nearest trash can.

"What?" she asks, her voice dreamy as she straightens out her dress. She looks so unbelievably beautiful after sex that I often have to pinch myself. Or herself. And then pinching just leads to more sex and the circle continues.

I grin at her. "That's my motto. I told you last time we were here that I didn't have one, and well, now I do. Everything in due time." I pause. "And yours is live with no regrets."

She nods and walks toward me. "What do you mean, everything in due time?" There's hope in her eyes, something that wasn't there earlier.

"I mean," I say as she wraps her arms around me. I gaze down at her, lost in her charm, in her very soul, "that if we had shagged back then, we wouldn't be where we are now. That in some way, we were meant to be together. That we were meant to part and then come together again. Maybe we both had to change in the smallest of ways in order for this work."

"Well, I got fired. I wouldn't say that change was in my hands," she says. Her tone is joking but there's this depth to her stare, a wistfulness over her brow.

"In due time, it all works out," I tell her. "This is working out, isn't it?"

For one wee second I'm deathly afraid that she might tell me it's not working out. My heart seems to rattle in my chest.

But then she smiles, so softly, and places her hands around my neck. She licks her lips, nervous. "It's more than working out, Bram," she whispers. She swallows and traces my face with her delicate fingertips. I close my eyes to her touch, to her, to everything she makes me feel.

"Bram," she says, sounding hushed. "I'm in love with you."

She's in love with me.

In love.

With me.

My chest bloody aches. It's not what she's said. What she's said makes my soul want to sing, maybe scream a little. Tell the whole world that for some fucking reason, Nicola Price is in love with me.

It's so much, so heavy, so…bloody undeserved.

But my chest aches and my gut feels heavy, weighted, because I know I can't say the words back. Because I'm just not there yet. I'm almost there, but I won't lie to her. I wouldn't lie about something so rare and complicated as love.

In due time, I want to say again, I will feel the same.

But I can't say that either. Things are far, far too complex than she even knows and if she knew the things I'm keeping from her, the things I've kept from everyone, she'd probably take it all back.

"Bram?" she asks, studying my face. "Did I say the wrong thing?"

I clear my throat gently. "Do you believe it?"

She blinks, shocked. "Of course I believe it. I…I love you."

I shake my head once. "Then you didn't say the wrong thing. I'm just surprised, that's all. Surprised but grateful. It's an honor for you to say those words to me."

"An honor?" she repeats, letting go of my neck. "Why are you talking like you need a sword and a horse?"

I shrug, trying to be playful but I can tell she's hurt, rejected like nothing else.

"Listen," I tell her, trying to bring her to me but she wriggles out of my grasp and walks a few steps away. I follow her, putting a strong grip on her arm and holding her in place. "Don't walk away. This is nothing to get upset about."

"I just told you I love you!" she cries out, her expression pained. "And you didn't say anything in return."

"Nicola, please." I smooth her hair behind her ears and hold her face in my hands. "I adore you. I want to spend every minute with you. I want to spend my future with you. But I'm a man of a past I have yet to shake, even though I'm working on it. You're bringing me out of the past and into the future, where I belong."

I try to kiss her but she moves her face out of the way. "It's that woman, Taylor," she whispers and I try not to freeze at the mention of her name. "It's her, isn't it? The one you fucked everything up with."

"Not really," I tell her and I'm being honest here. "No. It's not like that. Honestly, I'm not in love with her, I swear to you, and that was many, *many* years ago."

The can of worms is tipping. I should just come clean now. Come clean and explain and if she loves me, if she really loves me, she'll understand. It's nothing we can't overcome, not at all. If anything, she might relate to me even more.

But I don't say anything because I am more of a coward than I'd like to admit. I'm too damn proud and too bloody afraid to mess this up any further, even though it feels like I already have.

"Nicola," I say to her again, my voice hard, "please believe me when I say I'm not in love with anyone but I swear to you it will be you and soon. I just need time to come around and when I do, it's going to be magic."

"Magic," she repeats.

"Please," I say, "you can't fault me for being honest with you. I always have been and I won't stop now. I am honored beyond belief that you actually love me, me the perpetual fuck-up, and I'm going to hold onto your love like it's gold." I kiss her softly, sweetly, and to my utmost relief, she kisses me back. "I'm never letting go of you either. You're stuck with me, sweetheart. Forever."

She nods but I can still spot that heart-breaking rejection in her eyes. I've seen it before and on a much larger scale.

We walk back into the party and I don't let go of her for a second, even when she tries to leave. I keep holding on because I feel I'm so close to losing her and I can't let that happen.

I can't.

I won't.

But I also can't help but wonder what's going to happen, all in due time.

Chapter Eighteen

NICOLA

"Nicola, can I see you for a moment in my office?" It's Thursday night and though the expected crowd isn't quite here yet, I'm still surprised that James is calling me away from the bar. I have to admit, I don't like this one bit, and as I follow him into the back rooms where his office is, my hands are clammy. Last time I was called into a place like this, I was fired.

I wouldn't be surprised if that happens. It's been a weird week so far. First, I told Bram that I loved him and he didn't respond in kind, which, although I appreciate his honesty, I'd be lying if I said that it didn't absolutely ruin me. It's all I've been able to think about, even though he's being extra attentive with me now. And he was hella attentive before.

Also, his interview he did at the gala was featured on the news and now the whole world knows about his little project, well at least California since it was apparently turned into a story about the lack affordable housing in the entire state. The minute it went live, Steph called me up, then Linden called Bram and a few days later, his parents called, having heard about it from friends of theirs.

And just as Bram predicted, no one in his family is taking him seriously, at least that's how Bram tells it. But I'd gone out for lunch with Steph and Kayla the other day and I can see their image of Bram has changed dramatically, and in the best way.

Of course, I had to tell them about my epic rejection and from the way they flinched, it's like they felt it too. No one asks for unrequited love.

No one asks to be fired in the same week, either. I sit down across from James, my eyes flitting to the walls behind his desk where he used to have a Faith No More concert poster at The Warfield from 1995, but now he just has a motivational speaking type one. You know, with the schmaltzy sunsets. He's going to start turning into Murray from *Flight of the Conchords* if he's not careful.

"Just get it over with," I say to James, putting my face in my hands. "Like a Band-Aid, right off!"

"What?" he asks. "No. Nicola. I'm not firing you."

I peek at him through my fingers. "No?"

He shakes his head and gives me a placating smile. "No. I'm promoting you."

"What?" Now I've really snapped to attention. "Why?" I've seriously done nothing but spill drinks this whole week.

"Because you've proven to be reliable," he says, "more reliable than a lot of people here. I think I can trust you and you're good at what you do."

James has never been so nice to me before. You know, other than giving me the job to begin with.

"Seriously?" I ask, just to make sure this isn't some joke.

"Totally serious." He sighs and leans back in his chair. "We're coming into the summer season soon. June is next week, and this place is just going to get busier, all while more of my people will be wanting days off. Aside from that Disneyland trip, you never ask for days off. And even then, it wasn't you asking. It was your charity man."

"So, I guess you saw the news too?"

He nods. "I have to admit, Linden's brother is the last person I would have expected to have a heart of gold but apparently he does. But, I guess I don't have to tell you that."

I manage a small smile, even though it reminds me that I'm still living rent-free.

"And with a promotion, you'll be able to pay your own way now," he adds, as if he can read my mind. "That is, if you want it. I'm not going to lie, being an assistant manager isn't a walk in the park."

"Assistant manager?"

He nods. "It's longer hours and more responsibility. You won't just be serving drinks anymore. Though I think you'll get the hang of it pretty quickly."

I'm probably a terrible person for thinking this, but I'm not sure if I'm ready to take this job. I'd gotten used to spending my time with Ava during the days and when she's down for a nap, I get to work on the sewing machine. Hell, I'm even wearing a top I sewed up the other day. It's not perfect but I'm getting my groove back and – more importantly – my passion back. Having that in my life reminds me that there's more to it all than just having a paycheck.

Now with working full-time, I'm not sure I'll have that much time to myself anymore, let alone Ava. But I know the right and responsible thing to do would be to accept it without question.

Still, I find myself saying to James, "Do you mind if I have a day to think about it?"

He seems caught off-guard. "Okay, sure. Take the whole week. Just...well, it's not my business..."

And whatever he was about to say, I can tell it's not his business.

I prod him anyway. "What?"

James shrugs, his pretty boy face blasé. "I think you could have a lucrative career here. And I know things are all cruisey at the moment for you, but eventually...that could change."

He's basically hinting that I can't have a free ride forever and I hate to admit that he's right, because he has such an annoying way of offering up his opinion when it's not needed, but he is right. I just don't tell him that.

"Well, I better go pour alcohol down some people's throats," I tell him, getting out of my seat. "And thank you. Really. I'll let you know tomorrow."

The night doesn't end up being as busy as we anticipated. Steph and Linden get there just before James says I can go home, but I'm too tired to stick around. There's a lot on my mind.

I get home just after midnight to an empty apartment. Ava is spending the next two nights with my mother in Livermore because it was just easier that way. Part of me is surprised that Bram isn't in my apartment waiting for me like he usually is, but it could be he wants me over there for a change.

With that in mind, I pour myself a glass of pinot gris, enjoying that first cold mouthful. Nothing could be sweeter. Then, once I remember to breathe a little, something I think I'm doing a bit less of lately, I go into the bedroom and change. I throw my homemade top and skinny jeans to the side and slip on a lacy red camisole with matching short shorts. Since I'm only going over there to screw, why dress up?

I go back into the kitchen and while I'm finishing up my glass of wine, I hear the strangest sound coming from Bram's apartment.

Yelling.

Then crying.

Two voices, one that must be Bram's but the other is female.

My blood runs still and my heart kicks down a few gears.

What the fuck is going on?

I head out into the hall and now I can hear it more clearly.

A woman yells, "Don't you throw that back in my face. You could have been there!"

Then Bram yells back, "I tried to fucking be there!"

"Well, it was too damn late." A pause and it sounds like she's crying. "God, Matthew doesn't need to hear this."

Who the fuck is Matthew?

I try to swallow the brick in my throat. Things seem safe out here in the hallway. If I knock on his door, everything is going to change. I just know it. This woman, that voice…it all means something, it all means too much.

Part of me just wants to go away. And I should. Go back in the apartment and drown out the voices the way I used to drown out Bram when I first moved in.

But I don't do that. I knock on his door instead.

"Fuck," Bram growls.

I hold my breath.

The door opens.

Bram's face falls at the sight of me. In his eyes, I can read everything. I can read the change.

I can read the end.

"What's going on?" I ask, barely able to speak.

In the background, I see a woman with long dark curly hair appear. She's tall, on the curvy side, maybe a bit bigger than me, and pretty, with smooth honey skin. Her dark, dark eyes are tinged with red.

Taylor.

In an instant, I know it's her.

And she knows something about me. It probably helps that I'm wearing lingerie.

"Nicola," Bram says. "This isn't a good time."

I jerk my head at the woman. "Who is she?" I try really hard not to sound like a jealous bitch but I'm totally failing.

Bram's face falls even more. "She's the woman I told you about. Taylor."

I cross my arms, trying to act stronger than I am, trying to pretend that the name doesn't shatter me. "The one that got away?"

The woman frowns and then steps forward.

"Hi," she says, looking me up and down. "Are you his girlfriend?"

I look at Bram. *Am I your girlfriend?*

Was I?

"I live next door," I say by way of explanation. "And heard yelling so I thought I'd come over."

"I'm so sorry about that," Bram says. "I'll talk to you later."

I stare at him for a moment and I feel a world pass between us. Maybe time speeds up or maybe it slows down, but I feel myself clinging to the idea of what we were together.

I love you, I think. *What are you doing? What is this? Please let there be a perfectly rational explanation for everything. Make me believe it.*

"Mom," a young boy's voice says, and before it can really register, a little boy about six or seven in shorts and a t-shirt appears between Taylor and Bram.

"It's okay, Matthew," she says, putting her hand on his head. The kid stares at me with tired eyes and he yawns big and loud.

There's something so damn familiar about this kid that I feel like I'm barely holding onto reality. Though his skin is darker, his eyes, his brows, the shape of his jaw, even at a young age, are all too similar. He's even got on the same socks as Bram. Yellow and brown. The Loch Ness Monster.

I look at Bram and realization slowly falls on me, like those first falling stones from an impending rockslide.

"This is Matthew," Taylor says to me. "Bram's son."

And now the rest of the earth gives way.

I'm falling on the inside, down, down, down, buried by the truth.

On the outside I am frozen solid.

I take in a sharp intake of air and can't seem to let it go. It freezes in my lungs, burning liquid nitrogen.

"I was going to tell you," Bram says, rubbing his hand over his face, his voice strained. "But I didn't know when. It's so damn complicated."

"Bram," Taylor warns him. "Not in front of him."

I can't even form words. My mouth opens and closes like a stupid fish until finally I burst out, "You have a son?"

"Nicola," he says, shooting Taylor and Matthew an apologetic look before stepping out in the hall and closing the door halfway. "I can explain."

How many breakups have started with "I can explain"? How many times has the explanation never really mattered?

"Why did you lie?" I croak, shaking, feeling like I'm being fileted.

"I didn't lie," he says. "I just didn't tell you…I didn't bring it up, I was going to but—"

"But what?"

He swallows hard and lowers his voice, "Because I did to Taylor and Matthew what Phil did to you and Ava. Because I wanted you to trust me before you knew about things I've done and the person I was."

I suck in my breath, trying to find an ounce of strength to turn away.

"I did trust you," I tell him. The words crumble out of my mouth. "But I don't anymore."

I step backward and he grabs for my hand and I'm ripping myself out of his reach. I run right into my apartment and slam the door, locking it. Bram knocks on it viciously, calling for me, but I don't want to see him, I can't see him.

And I can't be in here.

I yank on a pair of jeans and a t-shirt, grab my purse and I'm opening the door. Bram stands there, a face etched with panic, pain, and I push him out of the way.

"Don't, Nicola!" he yells at me.

But I'm running.

I'm already gone.

...

I have nowhere to go.

I'm on the street, walking fast, trying to get to the nearest bus stop while texting Steph with shaking hands.

I need to talk to you now. Something happened.

What? Her response is immediate. **I'm still at the Lion.**

I'll come there. Catching the bus.

I'd come get you but I had too many beerz. Is this about Bram?

I don't answer that and the minute I walk into the bar, she sees it on my face. I haven't been crying though. I'm not exactly even sure what to feel except that terrible, dreadful realization that your life, the one you were starting to love, will never be the same.

All of it, wiped away.

"Oh, honey," Steph says, getting off of her barstool and wrapping her arms around me. "You're shaking, what happened?"

Beside her, sitting down, is Linden, staring at me curiously. Sometimes he looks just like his brother.

All of a sudden a wave of rage washes over me.

I point my finger at him. "Did you know?"

Linden looks bewildered. "What? Know what?" He looks to Steph for help but she's just as confused.

"Did you know about Bram?"

His eyes narrow. "What about Bram? What did he do?"

"You know, that he has a fucking *kid*!" I practically spit out the words. They sound venomous coming from my mouth, like it could poison me. "He's a *father*."

Linden's eyes go wide. Steph's seem about to fall out of her head.

"So, did you know?" I go on, feeling angrier by the second. "Was I the only one in the dark?"

"Wait, wait," Steph interjects, putting her hand out in front of me. "Kid? Father? Are you pregnant again?"

I glare at her. "No! I mean Bram has a kid, a freaking *child*, with someone else. His name is Matthew. He looks just like him. I just fucking met him in his apartment, visiting hours with his mom or I don't know what the fuck. What the fuck?"

Linden is slowly shaking his head. "No, that's not possible. He doesn't. I would have known." He looks at Steph. "We would have known."

"Would you have?" I counter. "Does anyone have any idea what kind of past Bram had?"

"His kid and the baby mama were in his *apartment*?" Steph repeats, looking freaked out. "Why?"

I throw my hands out. "How should I know? I thought maybe Linden would."

"No," Linden says adamantly. "If Bram had a child this whole time, I would have known about it. Are you sure he knew? He could have just found out."

I want to collapse onto the ground, but I manage to lean against the stool instead. It's only then that I notice the three of us are the only people in the bar aside from James who was talking to our other bartender, Sandra, in the corner.

"He's known. Oh, he's known. He's alluded to it before. He's talked about this girl, this Taylor, as the only girl he loved, a girl he made a huge mistake with. Guess that mistake was Matthew…" My heart aches. "Or the mistake could have been leaving her." I close my eyes and take a deep breath in through my nose. "Those damn stupid socks."

"You mean the Nessie ones?" says Linden.

I nod. "I had no idea why he wore them, he just called them lucky."

"That's what he said to me when I made fun of them."

"Did he get defensive?"

"Yeah, kind of. But he sometimes does when you don't really expect him to."

I let out a ragged breath and sit down on the stool. My legs just won't stop shaking. None of me will. My own blood feels rattled. "That's Bram, isn't it? Does what you least expect him to. I saw those socks on Matthew. There's no way that was a coincidence. He knew about Matthew from the very start." His words run through my head. "He said he did to them what Phil did to Ava and me."

"What a fucker," Steph says, putting her hand on my shoulder. "I'm so sorry, what are you going to do?"

I shrug. "I don't know. I don't know. I just ran. I couldn't be there."

"I don't blame you," she says just as James comes by.

"What's going on?" he asks.

"Nothing," Steph says. "But Nicola needs a shot of whisky and fast."

"Make it two," Linden says quickly. He looks a bit shell-shocked. I guess it can't be easy knowing you've always been an uncle, you just didn't know it.

"And James," I add in. "If you're still offering me that assistant manager position, I want it."

He smiles at me as he pours the shot. "Good to hear." But I don't smile back.

"I guess we should say congratulations," Steph says softly. "But it just doesn't seem right, right now. I'm so sorry, Nicola." She searches my eyes and they become sadder by the second. "I know how much you're in love with him."

And that's what really stings. That I love him. That he doesn't love me. And that *this* happened. One person's love isn't enough to keep two people together, I knew that much already.

James hands me the shot and Linden and I down ours at the same time. It burns but not enough. I want it to burn away the gauze over this night.

"I'll have another," I tell James and then Linden and Steph chime in with their requests.

Suddenly, there's a knock at the door to the bar and we all turn around to see Bram standing on the other side, looking pitiful.

"Don't open it," I hiss to James. "Tell him you're closed."

James looks at Linden. "What's going on?"

"Nothing to worry about," he says and nods at the door. "Let him in. I want a few words."

"Shit, it's not going to be one of those nights in here, the ones that never end?" James asks. "Because when they do end, I end up calling the cops."

But Steph is already up and crossing the bar. She stops at the door, glares at Bram through the glass and then unlocks it.

"What do you want?" she asks him, opening it a crack.

"I need to speak to Nicola," he says. He looks over her shoulder at me. "Please."

Linden taps me on the arm. "Go on," he says. "Talk to him. I'll have my words after."

Talking to Bram is the last thing I want to do. The situation can't get any better. His words have the power to make it even worse. And no matter what happens, what's done is done and I know things are going to suck for quite some time.

"It's fine, Steph," I say to her. I walk over to the door and she reluctantly backs away, her eyes never leaving Bram's.

"I'm pretty sure we pinky swore on something," she grumbles and then goes on to join Linden back at the bar.

"Nicola," Bram says. His eyes are red, filled with worry, mouth twisted bitterly. He looks like shit, like he's been ravaged by something terrible. But it doesn't make me feel a thing, not even glad. "I need to explain." His eyes flit to a booth. "Should we talk inside?"

"No," I tell him and squeeze myself through the door, taking great pains not to brush up against him in any way. How weird one's body goes from being a magnet, something you couldn't stay away from, to being something you can't imagine touching ever again.

I thought that being outside I'd be able to breathe, but it's a strangely humid night and the mist feels like it's choking me. I shove my hands in my jeans, my arms stiff and close to my body as I stare at the ground.

"So you found me here," I say to him. "Explain, then."

"I would have told you – "

"No," I say sharply. "Just forget it with the things you woulda shoulda done. You didn't, okay? You didn't, and it's too late for that. So just start from the beginning. You have a son." How ironic it is that under any other circumstances, that would have sounded beautiful.

He breathes out, long and hard. "Yes. Matthew is my son. Seven years ago, I met Taylor. I fell for her fast and I fell for her bloody hard."

"How wonderful," I can't help but comment.

"Please, listen," he whispers and then clears his throat. "I fell for her because she was something good. She's a good woman, I know you don't want to hear that but it's true. She brought me a sense of normalcy and purpose during a time that I didn't have any. I was a fucking wreck back then, you have to understand. All the drugs, the parties. I was far gone down the tracks. I shoved everything I could up my nose, I drank everything I saw. I pissed away money. I made a lot of enemies and bought a few friends. You would have never even given me the time of day. I was just the worst rubbish walking the streets."

He swallows thickly. "But Taylor saw something in me that I didn't know was there myself. And for a period of time I was in love and on my best behaviour, anything to be with her, the woman who made me feel like I wasn't a worthless piece of shit, even though at that point I most certainly was. I thought love conquered everything, Nicola. I thought wrong. Because she ended up pregnant and my first instinct, my first thought was I needed to run. I needed to get out of it, to leave her with the responsibility."

My veins are starting to throb with rage. I'm relating to Taylor more than I'd like.

"I couldn't be a father. I really was a worthless shit. And I started to think she was a crazy loon for ever believing in me. I loved her, I really did, but it wasn't enough to make me stay. It wasn't enough to make me not cheat."

I gasp. "You fucking cheated on your pregnant girlfriend?"

He looks at the ground, his shoulders sloping. "I'm not proud of it. But I did. That's how I fucked up. And I fucked up a lot."

I'm starting to feel sick. "How could you be such a pig? God, do I even know you at all?"

He raises his eyes to meet mine and they're flashing with shame. "That was a different me. I've told you what I was like."

"I didn't know you were that horrible." I can feel my lips curling with disgust.

"Well, I was, okay!" he yells. "Now do you understand why people can't ever give me a chance, why they never let me become anything more than what I was? I was a horrible fucking person and I did terrible things. Maybe I didn't rape women or rob banks or deal drugs, but I was horrible in other ways. I hurt Taylor in a way I could never repair and I hurt my relationship with Matthew from the get go. Because by the time I started to smarten up, by the time I started to pull myself together, it was far too late. Taylor didn't want anything to do with me."

"Smart woman," I mutter.

"And Matthew was kept away. I tried, I tried and I tried to get them into my life but she wasn't having any of it. So I did what I could, which was to send money every single month. I paid child support and then some. I made sure Taylor and Matthew had the best life possible."

"But you never gave them a dad."

"I *tried*," he says again, his brogue thickening the more upset he gets. "But it was too little, too late. And I don't blame Taylor at all. All I could do was send the payments and send the presents and hope that I could somehow make her life just a little bit easier."

I've got this bad, sick tickle at the back of my throat. My brain wants me to think of something horrid and I'm shoving it aside for now as Bram is talking, pleading.

He goes on, running his hand through his hair. "About three months before I came out here, Taylor and Matthew moved. They'd lived in Jersey and suddenly everything was getting returned to sender. It made my move out here a little easier, I guess. But I never stopped putting money away, hoping that one day she'd contact me again and I could go on trying to make things right. That day happened today. She's been living in San Bernardino with her aunt and she saw me on the news."

"So she just wants her money."

"I don't know what she wants, to be honest. But I can't lie and say I'm not glad she's here. Being around you and Ava has made me realize how much more there is in me to give."

That sick feeling is back. "What do you mean?"

"I mean, helping you..." he trails off.

I can feel my chin tremble. "Wait. Hold on." I take in a shaky breath. "Is that why you wanted me and Ava around? Is that why you took such an interest in me, in her, helping us every way you could? To appease your fucking *guilt*?"

He looks like I've just slapped him across the face. "No, it's not like that."

"It is," I say, feeling absolutely humiliated. "I was just a charity case. We both were. You never cared, you just wanted to get rid of your sins, you just wanted to feel better about yourself. No wonder you never loved me! It was never about that!"

It's all coming together in one shattering moment.

I feel like my heart has been condemned.

"No!" he cries out, grabbing my arm and pulling me to him. His eyes are panicked, wild. "That's not it all, it's not. It's not! Nicola. I...I...you..."

"See, you can't even say it!" I yell at him, getting in his face. "That's because you don't feel it and you never will. You only *want* to love me because you think it would make it all so much easier."

"No, please, you are the world to me. You are my whole world," he pleads.

I rip out of his hold. "Well, apparently your whole world has way more people in it than I anticipated."

"Don't do this," he says. "Don't walk away from me, from us. We're so good together, so fucking good."

I fire back at him. "It was all a damn lie! There was nothing real or good about it!" I start heading back into the bar.

"Please!" he yells louder. "There was never a lie, there was only the truth. What we have is the truth. I can't do this without you." His face seems to shatter before my eyes. "I thought maybe you could understand," he adds that in a small voice.

I pause at the door, feeling bitterness snake up my throat. "The only thing I understand is what it's like to be in her shoes and what it's like to be charity. And that's enough understanding for me." I open the door and pause, realizing I'm about to do the hardest, most painful thing.

But the right thing.

"I'm sorry, Bram." Hot tears prick at my eyes and I try to steady my voice. "This is going to break Ava's heart. But we're moving out tomorrow. So we won't be your charity anymore."

I step inside the bar and lock the door without looking back.

Chapter Nineteen

NICOLA

Ava won't stop crying.

I should have lied. I should have told her we were just going away for a short time. I should have told her we would see Bram again.

But I couldn't. The lie would hurt me to say, to even thinking about, and over time it would ruin her.

It was best for us both to be ruined up front.

After I returned home from the Lion, my heart was a bleeding mess in my hands - condemned, unsafe, unstable. The sight of my own apartment – of Bram's charity – was enough to make me sick, so I immediately began packing.

I packed all through the night, with music blaring. I never answered the calls or the knocks at my door. If Bram was yelling at me, I didn't hear it. If he was reunited with the woman and his son – his *son* – I didn't know it. I went on like a demon, until dawn broke the cityscape and my entire apartment was packed in every spare box, suitcase and garbage bag I had.

There were a lot of garbage bags.

What I really wanted to do was find a place to move into while Ava was gone. I was delusional. I don't know why I thought that would happen, why I had the idea that maybe my mother could drop her off in a whole new life. She would never have to see our old place again.

But I had everything packed, no place to go and no car to get me there even if I did.

I called my mom. I explained what happened.

I did it without crying. I thought I was so brave.

My mother came over and the minute I saw Ava's face, I realized I wasn't brave at all.

I was a mess.

She looked around the apartment in confusion. She didn't understand and no matter how I tried to explain it, there was no right answer to what was happening.

I didn't want to blame it all on Bram. I didn't want her to hate him even though I was starting to believe that I did.

Ava doesn't hate. She doesn't have it in her. She just gets broken, like a porcelain doll.

To make matters worse, all the emotions she was feeling, the rejection, the discomfort and the pain of losing the things she loved, made her feel dizzy.

Sick.

She threw up and her blood glucose levels were all over the place.

I'd never felt so alone, even with my mother there, trying to get the proper food into her, water, insulin, balance. I knew Bram was next door. I could hear him, but I would never ask for his help again.

Luckily, just as we were about to take her to the hospital, she pulled out of it.

Then the tears came.

They haven't stopped.

I'm at my mother's house, sitting on her sofa with my legs curled up under me, sipping tea. It's picture perfect but I'm a raging torrent inside.

Ava is beside me sniffling, wiping her nose on her arm, on me.

I can only hold her. I can only tell her it will be all right, even if I don't believe it. It feels so futile, so useless, yet I keep saying it anyway.

Kayla has offered her apartment to the both of us. So has my mother. But I still have a job – and a promotion – so I'm going to stay with Kayla in the city. Ava and I will be squished into Kayla's den, but it's just temporary and I think Kayla needs some help with her rising rent costs herself. Linden and Steph offered their place too, but I can't look at Linden right now. He reminds me too much of his brother. He has offered to move my furniture out of the apartment and put it right into storage until we find a place of our own and get started. That generous act, well, that reminds me of his brother also.

Ava shifts in my arms and looks up at me with big wet eyes and there's so much hope in them that it makes me want to cry. Because I pray that the hope isn't misleading.

She lost Bram who had become her father figure whether I wanted it that way or not.

I lost my heart.

I loved Bram.

I *loved* him.

His smile, his jokes, his generosity. His lips, his eyes, his jaw. His attitude, his good nature, his humor. His ease, his height, his body. His ambition. His adoration. His devotion.

He looked at me like I was magic.

I started to believe it.

We were magic together.

And I still loved him.

After everything, how can I not?

How can I stop?

But this love is what's making me collapse inside.

Second by empty second.

Brick by heavy brick.

Chapter Twenty

BRAM
Six Weeks Later

"You know, I don't think I ever told you how sorry I am."

I hear Taylor's voice from across the table but I'm not really listening. There's a song playing in this San Bernardino strip-mall café, the volume too low and it's bugging me that I can recognize the beat but I can't hear the lyrics.

"Bram," she says softly and finally I look at her.

"Hmmm?"

"I'm sorry about the way things happened with Nicola," she says and that name feels like a fist in my heart. "I shouldn't have shown up at your door like that. I didn't think that…"

"You didn't think that I'd have anyone meaningful in my life," I finish absently. I twirl the watch around my wrist and give a melancholy shrug. "I don't blame you. And please, there's no need for you to be sorry. I'm sure I had it coming. Karma has a sharp eye, you know."

She nods. "I know. But it's been so many years and…I really didn't have the right to show up like I did."

I sigh. She says this but I know she thinks its justified and she's probably right. When someone has been wronged– when someone else has fucked up so much that their debt will never end – there's really nothing they can do that's ever uncalled for, ever too much.

I don't blame Taylor whatsoever. She was watching the news and suddenly there I was, the baby daddy she tried so hard to forget. She doesn't tell me this, but I bet she wanted to throw rocks at her TV, perhaps burn it. She at least screamed and cursed it, I know that.

Then motherly instinct took over and she piled Matthew into the car and drove up to San Francisco to see the man she tried to pretend never existed.

I know she only came for the money, though she tells me that wasn't the case. She said it was about seeing me through new eyes. I was successful and ambitious and, more than that, I was virtuous now. I was the opposite of the man she hated. I had proven that I could get my life on track and actually make a difference in other people's lives, not just my own.

And maybe that's true. But at the moment, I'm not making that much difference. I still have the same tenants in my building, the same ones who can't afford to live anywhere else, the ones that need me. I've got all but two…the most important ones.

Nicola moved out the next day, true to her word. I tried to stop her. I tried everything. She wouldn't have any of it. I'd never seen her so headstrong, so vicious, and I know I deserved it but it hurt more than anything else. She was protecting Ava more than she was protecting herself and when I caught a glimpse of that little girl crying in the halls, well…I lost it that day.

I lost plenty that day.

And the loss is still with me. It's building, not easing. Every morning, I wake up to an empty bed and it's like another fucking black brick is cemented into my chest. Nicola has absolutely no idea what she meant to me – what she still means to me – and what hurts the most is that she'll never see my pain.

I need her to see it, to feel it, to know it.

I've lost the magic in my life.

"You're a good man, Bram," Taylor says.

I let out a dry laugh and raise my brow at her. "Are you sure there isn't a splash of booze in your coffee?"

She gives me a quick smile. "You're a good man *now*. And maybe you were back then, deep down. I certainly thought so. You know I was madly in love with you, Bram. Madly. That's why it hurt so much."

I nod. "As I said. Karma." I pause. "I loved you too, you know."

She shakes her head. "No. That wasn't love Bram. You don't…do things like that to someone you love. I have no doubt you felt what you thought was love, but when you have love, you don't throw it away. You don't give up on it. You don't run, even when it scares you. And if you do, then it wasn't love."

I chew on my lip for a moment. "I don't think it's that simple."

"It is that simple. Human beings are complicated. Love is simple."

"Well," I say, having a hard time arguing with that. I sip my tea, which is growing cold. "Whatever it was that I felt for you, I thought it was love. And I believed it was for the longest time."

"Until you met her."

I meet her eyes but I can't hide the wince. "Yeah. Until her."

"So now you know. What you had for me and what you have for her, they aren't the same."

I can't help but notice her use of the present tense.

She gives me a knowing smile. "No use in pretending you're not still madly in love with her, Bram."

"Well," I start, not sure if I should tell her that I didn't even know I had been in love with Nicola until now.

But she's right.

Because all along, I was in love with her. It was too simple to know. I was expecting something more drawn-out and complicated than it already was. When really, she had my heart for a while.

Just that realization on its own is enough to knock me off my chair.

And to think, when she told me she loved me, I could have told her in return. I could have said anything at all instead of what I did. I didn't have to already break her heart before I broke it again.

"Listen," Taylor says to me. "When I saw you on the news, I didn't go up there to mess up your life. I didn't want you to tell me you still loved me, because I know we have both moved on. And you've been more than gracious to put the two of us up for this last month. It all couldn't have been better timing, with me being between jobs and Matthew really needing a father figure right now. All I wanted from you was for him to know you and for you to know him and so far, that's what he's gotten. He now knows the man behind the socks." She smiles to herself and twirls the coffee cup around in her hands. "The last thing I want is to ruin what you had. If you love her still, you need to go after her. You need to tell her and you need to fight for her."

I swallow misery down my throat. "It's a bit too late for that."

She blinks at me surprised. "It's never too late," she says adamantly. "What did I just say about love? It's simple. It doesn't just go away. If she was in love with you before, and judging by the heartache on that poor girl's face, she was in deep, then she's still in love with you now. Believe me, please, I've been there. Anger doesn't erase love. Pain doesn't erase love. Crying doesn't erase love. Only time does. Lots and lots and lots of time." She flicks her finger at me. "And take it from me, time has barely moved on for the both of you. It's been just over a month. She's going to love you for a lot longer than that. I hate to admit this, but until three years ago, if you had showed up at my door again with one more attempt to win me over, it would have worked."

"And our lives would be completely different," I note, leaning back in my chair. The volume of the song goes up and I recognize Garbage's "The Trick is to Keep Breathing," and I think Shirley Manson's right about a lot of things.

"Different, yes," Taylor says. "But you know what, I don't regret a thing."

I look at her sharply. "What was that?"

"I said I don't regret it. I don't believe in regrets anyway. It's no way to go through life. Whatever happens, happens and it shapes us all to the here and now, where we are supposed to be."

Nicola's motto. It's all too much.

Taylor reaches over and touches my hand. "We were never supposed to be together, Bram. And Matthew wasn't supposed to know his father until now. Because we've been okay, him and I. We're a team. Because of you, the checks, he's never wanted for everything. And it's made me stronger. It's made me realize what I want. Sure, no one asks to be a single mom but it's not the end of the world either. It's just life. You deal with it and keep moving."

"And love?"

She gives me a coquettish smile. "There is a man you know. Irving. He's in the military so I don't see him that often and we're only really friends anyway. But he's fond of Matthew and Matthew is fond of him. And I know it's love. Small love on its way to big love. I just haven't found the nerve to tell him yet. But I will, the moment he gets back."

I manage a smile. "That's great. Good to hear."

She does a little dance in her seat and the way she blushes reminds me of Nicola. "So you see, there's hope for me. And there's a lot of hope for you, Bram."

I suck in her words like oxygen. Hope has seemed like a very dangerous word lately.

"Well," she says, pushing back her coffee. "I should get going back to the house."

I know this is goodbye for now. After Taylor and Matthew arrived on my doorstep, I made sure they were able to stay in the city for as long as they wanted. Then a week ago, they went back down to San Bernardino and I went along for the ride to see where Matthew lives, to be more involved.

I've been staying at a local hotel but now it's time for me to fly back into SF. I've got my cousin coming in from Edinburgh tonight, which means I'll be distracted for the next while, something I sorely need.

"Are you sure you're okay with taking a cab to the airport?" she asks. "I can drive you."

I pat the suitcase beside me. "I'm fine, go rescue Matthew from his aunt." I get out of my chair and though my first instinct is to shake her hand, I end up pulling her into a bear hug. "Thank you for being so forgiving."

She hugs me back, patting me lightly. "Thank you for being so easy to forgive," she says. "Once a charmer, always a charmer." We both pull away and she puts her hands on either side of my face and stares intently at me. "I live with no regrets. You need to too. Go and make sure you don't have any."

"I will," I assure her. As she walks to the door, I yell, "And tell that wee boy that the next time the Dodgers play the Giants, I'll be calling him up, gloating."

She rolls her eyes and keeps walking. Naturally, I don't have much interest in baseball, but Matthew is obsessed with the LA Dodgers and I'm trying to relate to him on as many levels as I can. It's definitely not easy to go from being such a distant figure to someone real in Matthew's life. It's a learning curve for both him and for me. We don't yet have a relationship with each other and I doubt it will ever get to the level where he'll start calling me dad, but you never know. I'll certainly be working on it whenever I can.

But Taylor has made it very clear that they have their own life and though she wants me to be a part of it, I'm to have my own life too.

If only my life had Nicola in it.

I exhale, those bricks shifting around in my chest but never moving. I finish my tea, then pick up my suitcase and head back home.

. . .

The next few days fly by for once, instead of the slow, painful grind. There's nothing like heartache to make every day last a million years, to make every breath feel like your last. But having your cousin, whom you haven't seen in ages, bunk with you makes the clock tick on. I would have put him up in Nicola and Ava's old apartment but I can't quite seem to move on from that. It's empty and I want it to stay that way, just in case they ever come back.

To say I'm delusional is an understatement.

Needless to say, Lachlan McGregor is quite the roommate. The man really opens up when he's drunk, otherwise he's extremely serious and rarely smiles. Normally that would be okay because, let's face it, I can't deal with any more drama. But I'm also the type who cracks jokes to win people over and with Lach it feels like I'm talking to a brick wall. It doesn't help that he kind of resembles one.

Back at his home in Edinburgh, Lach is a rugby player, a wing, for the city's main team but a recent tear to his Achilles tendon has put him on their backburner for the time being. I had known for some time that Lach was pretty loaded, not just from the sport but because he's actually an extremely smart man whose been making a lot of key investments over the years. If anyone is going to disprove the stereotype that all rugby players are dumb gits, well, it's Lach.

Though we chat on FB on occasion, commenting on pictures or whatever else ("oh, you won the game again, way to go you dumb ape" – even though he's smart, I don't want him to think I know that) our relationship never really went beyond that. You know how it is with cousins, especially when you come from a fucked up family.

However, with the news feature on me and then a write-up opinion piece in the *San Francisco Chronicle* that fought for my funding, my whole low-income housing project has stalled. I'm out of a lot of money, paying my mortgage with my savings and no money coming in. If this all keeps up, I'll lose my project and my dream and be in the hole for it. After losing Nicola and Ava, I refuse to let that happen.

So, I swallowed my goddamn pride and called him up. It's not easy asking your cousin, who is far more successful than you and three years younger to boot, for help. But I did it. Because, fuck it, I'm not going to fail again.

To my surprise, Lachlan was bored waiting on the sidelines, and even though he should be returning to the sport by the time the new season starts, he said he would at least come over for most of the summer. Though I grilled him on my idea beforehand, now that he's been here we've really put our heads together trying to come up with the best way to move forward. If things go well and if he can find a backer on his own, he says he'd be willing to join me, make a non-profit corporation and get this thing off the ground.

"Justine!" I suddenly say with a snap of my fingers.

Lach looks up from his beer, his face tired from our day of monotonous brainstorming. "What?"

I grab my beer off the kitchen counter and sit down across from him in my living room. "Justine is a woman I took to the opera once."

"The opera." He snorts, giving a rare smile. So glad it was at my expense.

"Yes, the opera. She comes from money. A lot of it. In fact, it was my father who set us up. He still believes that you're supposed to date money to get ahead, and from what I understood, her family has a lot of money and power. She's a gorgeous gal and you're not too ugly a man, so maybe you can wine and dine her and see if we can get an investment out of her."

He considers that. "What kind of money and power?"

I shrug and take a sip of my beer. "I have no idea. I didn't ask."

"Aye, I see. Too busy shagging her."

"Actually, no," I point out and there's that bloody pressure in my heart. "No, I wasn't interested in her."

"She's gorgeous and has money and you weren't interested?" he asks. "What makes you think I will be?"

"Because," I tell him. I exhale loudly. "I was with Nicola at the time."

"Ah," he says, knowing far too much about her already. I haven't really shut up about her to be honest. Perhaps that's why he always looks like he wants to kill himself.

"Actually," I go on, "we weren't dating at that time but…but that's when she really started to get under my skin, you know. The whole time I was with Justine, I was just thinking about Nicola. Looking back, I can see that I was already a goner. Just too stubborn at the time to see it."

"What's your excuse now?"

"What?"

"You won't stop talking about this bloody bird. If you're not talking about the building it's her and I'm sorry, but in my professional opinion, you need to either move the hell on or get off your stubborn arse and go do something about it. Stop being such a pansy."

"Your professional opinion?" I repeat.

He gives me a look. "Hey, I'm in rugby, right? And aside from some of these scars," he touches a few faded ones on his cheekbone, "I ain't bad to look at. Which means, I get more pussy than you probably do."

The old me would have challenged that but having a pissing contest with my cousin doesn't seem right.

Not right now, anyway.

I'll come back to this one later.

"And," he adds, "with all the pussy comes all the problems. Go sort your shit out soon or I'm going to start using your head as a rugby ball. I need the bloody practice."

I frown at him. "So uncouth." But I don't push it. We may be the same height, and I may almost have the same amount of muscle as he has, but he doesn't seem to give a rat's arse about messing up his face, whereas I do.

The only thing holding me back from what he suggests, from what Taylor suggested, is the same old story. My goddamn pride. My goddamn fear.

What if I go after Nicola and she turns away? She may not want to see me again. She may never trust me again. Even though right now I have nothing left but this dull, hollow ache inside, like some vital part of me has been removed. I also have the unknown on my side and that dangerous hint of hope. In the here and now, I can bitch and moan like a little girl as long as I never do anything about it. I can just imagine that maybe one day, in due time, it will all work out.

But I don't want to listen to *my* motto. Not this time. I'm not leaving this to sort itself out in due time, to take that chance that things will work out.

Nicola is worth so much more than chance.

I need to have no regrets.

Chapter Twenty-One

NICOLA

You know that part of the movie when the hero gets dragged through the mud, or kicked off the team, or captured by the crime syndicate, and all hope is lost and yet you know, no matter what, somehow it's all going to come together and the hero is going to get his big fat happy ending. And while he's being tortured or the town turns against him or his wife walks out on him, you feel for him but you're kind of spurred forward by the knowledge that everything *will* work out in the end. It just has to.

Well, I wish I could say the same could be applied to my own life. Because I feel like I've fallen off a cliff, been kicked through the mud and been tortured and there's no sense of hope or a happy ending in sight.

Of course, all these blows I'm taking, well, they're right in my heart. But that's where they count, that's where they hurt the most. And it's kind of ridiculous, here I am, nearly two months later and I'm still this raw, gaping open wound when it comes to Bram. The rest of my life has some ups and downs. I live with Kayla still while I'm constantly searching for an affordable apartment. It's actually not so bad, and while I know Kayla really appreciates the rent I pay, I know I'm also cramping her style. I mean, Kayla likes to have her fun and more and more she stays out at whatever dude she's seeing's place.

So I know that having me and a five-year-old girl in her place isn't exactly ideal but she knows I'm working on it. My job at the Lion has been going well enough. I mean, it's a lot of work that I'm usually not interested in, and James can be a real bitch of a boss sometimes. But it gives me money and my savings account has grown and grown. Even if everything inside me still feels like it's constantly collapsing and rebuilding itself, I've got some form of security for the both of us.

I've also been concentrating on my designing more and more. I'll spend hours at the sewing machine in the mornings and at night. Being creative is great fuel and I have to admit, it feels good to be pleasantly distracted. Sometimes it's the only way to keep my mind from thinking about Bram.

Which it does. All the time. And I'm ashamed to admit it, even to myself. I don't talk about him with Steph or Kayla and when I do see Linden, I notice he's careful not to bring him up either. There have been a few close calls though. Once I heard he was coming to the Lion with Linden, so I went and hid in James's office for an hour, pretending to work on something. All very mature, I know, but at the moment I care so much about keeping my heart alive that I'm shielding it from everything in sight.

I just want to stop feeling this deep, cold hole inside me when I wake up and realize I'm alone. I want to stop remembering what it's like to have Bram hold me in his arms when I'm sad or run his hands over my body when I'm not. I want to pretend I never had that connection with a man who made me feel wild and free and full of life. I want so much that I can't have.

And so, I trudge onward, that hero in the story, even though I haven't done anything brave. I'm just another broken-souled person on this planet, waiting for time to pass. I don't feel that undercurrent of "everything will be all right." I don't see how I can possibly have a Happily Ever After, that would mean things have to go back to the way they were and how can I ever forget the pain that follows me everywhere?

"Cheer up, buttercup," Steph says to me. I can't help but wince at the word. It reminds me too much of that damn yellow couch.

We're sitting in a booth at the Lion. Ava is across from us and coloring away in a coloring book. Lisa called in sick and I had to work, so I had no choice but to bring Ava in. Luckily James is pretty good about that and she usually just hangs out in the back office with me. Steph is on her lunch break and wanted to have a drink. Lately I'd been leaning on my friend a lot, so I figured I owed her one.

"Sorry," I apologize to her.

"Don't be sorry," she says, peeling the label off her beer. "I just hate seeing you look so sad. You know, now. And all the time."

"I'm fine," I tell her, and watch as she takes the label all the way off then starts picking at the sticky bits that remain. "You and Linden having problems?"

She stops and looks up at me. "Huh?"

"Sexual frustration," I say, nodding at the bottle. "It's why you're peeling off the label."

"Oh," she says. She pushes her beer away, looking at it in surprise. "No. No, Linden is Linden, you know? If there's one thing he's good at, it's – "

I raise my hand. "Please. Just stop."

She shrugs and then picks up her coaster, starts twirling it around. And around. And around.

"Are you okay?" I ask her, noticing her foot is tapping on the floor as well.

"Hmmm?" She looks at me. She says it rather absently but it's a little *too* absently.

"You're acting like a nervous wreck."

"Mommy," Ava says in a lilting voice. "I drew you a bugosaur."

She proudly displays her coloring book. She hasn't even colored in the pictures that she's supposed to, she's just drawn green and brown blobs in all the white space. Blobs with legs. Bugosaurs, I guess.

"Thank you, sweetie," I tell her and she goes back at it, tongue hanging out of the side of her mouth.

"Nicola," Steph says uneasily.

I give her a look. "What is it?"

"Are you still in love with Bram?"

Where the hell did that come from? I can feel my face go white as I wonder if I was speaking all my thoughts out loud earlier. "What?" I can't help but gasp. I look over at Ava and she's watching me, frowning and pouting a little at the mere mention of his name.

"Do you love him?"

I blink at her. My heart thuds against my ribs, as if to remind me that it's still beating.

"Oh, Steph," I start to say, searching for words, for a way to deflect. "It's not that simple."

"It *is* that simple," she says, her eyes boring holes into mine. "It's the simplest of questions. You either love him. Or you don't. There are no maybes in love."

Whoa. Steph is being deep. I don't even know what that means. I don't want to get deep. I don't want to dive down there and pull out what remains of him from far inside me.

"I..."

She's staring at me. Ava is staring at me.

And I can't lie.

I sigh, slowly, softly. "Yes. I love him."

Just saying those words makes my heart seem to exhale.

"Good," Steph says, smiling smugly to herself.

"Good?" My eyes nearly bug out. "Why is that good? It's bad. It's terrible. I don't want to love him. I want to be free of all that and move on."

She wags her brows at me, that stupid smirk still on her face. "Love is good, my friend, love is good."

"What is wrong with you?" I punch her lightly on the arm. "Why did you ask me that?"

She takes a long swig of her beer and says, "Do you know what the worst way to start a sentence is?"

"I farted!" Ava yells with a big smile. "That's the worst way."

Steph nods her approval at Ava and then looks back to me. "Do you know what the *second* worst way is?"

"What?"

"Please don't hate me," she answers and for a moment her smile fades and she flinches, as if I'm about to punch her in the face next. "And seriously, Nicola, please don't hate me."

She looks over at the door to the Lion and my eyes follow. There, outside in the sunshine, is the familiar silhouette of a man. He opens the door and steps inside.

I feel like I'm sinking and rising at the same time.

I feel like I *definitely* hate Stephanie right now.

It's Bram and he's walking toward us and I'm gripping the edge of the table so hard, I may actually break it in two.

She leans into me, whispers in my ear, "I'm sorry. He had to see you and I knew if I told you, you wouldn't meet with him." Then she quickly gets out of the booth, exchanges a quick look with Bram as she walks past him and out the door.

"Nicola," Bram says, his throaty accent jarring me to the core. He stands in a sharp navy suit just a few feet away from the table, hands at his side. His face, that beautiful, handsome face, is the most serious I've ever seen on him.

"Bram?" Ava says softly and I look to her, her eyes wide with wonderment. "Bram?" she repeats louder.

"Hey, little one," he says, grinning at her and she immediately stands up in her seat, flapping her arms up and down. It would be the cutest thing I have ever seen, if it weren't for the circumstances. I may have just said that I was still in love with Bram, but that didn't mean I wanted to see him. It didn't mean that it would change the past. You can love someone and not do anything about it.

But Ava doesn't care. She runs to the end of the booth and practically throws herself at him. He envelopes her into a big hug, picking her up off the ground and I'm torn between being angry and wanting to break down and cry. There are too many big things inside me, vying for me to make a choice, to pay them all attention and in the end I'm just a giant mess.

Bram carefully places her back on the ground but Ava keeps jumping around, going crazy. She's smiling so big, her eyes are so wide, her breath so sharp and shallow.

Her breath shouldn't be like that.

While Bram is now staring at me, I'm staring at Ava in concern, watching her carefully, trying to listen.

"Bram-a-lama..." she starts to sing but she stops and tries to take a deep breath. Her face is going white before my eyes and she rocks on her feet back and forth.

"Oh, shit," I cry out, getting out of the booth just as she tips toward the ground. Bram is there, catching her in time and I fall down to my knees beside her as he holds her up.

"What's wrong?" he asks.

I grab her hand and squeeze it. It's clammy. Her eyes are unfocused, glazed, and that familiar fruit odor permeates from her breath.

"Oh, fuck, no not now," I say as she starts to lose consciousness right there in front of me. "Ava!" I yell at her and her eyes briefly flutter open before closing.

Bram gingerly lowers her to the ground while I crawl over her, tapping on her face. He brings out his phone. "I'm calling the ambulance." I hear him place the call and I'm not about to argue over this one.

"I think it's DKA. Diabetic shock."

"That same thing she had before?" he asks, voice high.

I nod and then he relays the information to the agent. Ava's been great lately, so good. The diet, the readings, everything has been working out well. But the last time she got like this was when Bram left and now that he's here, the emotions are just too much.

"I think it can be brought on by stress and emotional upheaval," I tell him without looking at him. I'm trying my hardest to keep her awake and keep myself calm. I've learned a lot. I can do this. I can get her through this.

But I can't do it alone right now. I finally meet Bram's eyes and see that he looks on the verge of breaking himself. "I need you to get my bag, the large purple one in the booth, and bring it here," I tell him.

He nods and swiftly does as I ask. Now people are gathered around us and James is asking if I need anything and I don't know what to say, I just know what to do. I inject her with the insulin, right into her stomach and she doesn't even flinch.

"That will work, right?" he asks me.

"I hope so," I tell him, not wanting to think about what would happen if it didn't. The last time, she didn't lose consciousness she didn't have that fruit breath. Last time the shot brought her around but this time…this time I'm so afraid it won't.

Thankfully it's not long before the ambulance roars up to the doors, even though to me it felt like hours, and they get Ava on a stretcher and into the ambulance. The EMTs are asking me questions and I'm rattling off everything about her disease and our routine, like it's textbook formula.

But when I try to make my way into the back of the ambulance, they tell me I can't be there with her. It's then that I break down, that I lose it. That I scream and I cry, while they tell me it's their policy not to when the sirens are going.

Bram holds me back, his hands on both my arms, keeping me from lashing out at them in anger. I feel crazed and feral, the worry and panic and unfairness of it all ripping me at the seams. Finally, the ambulance pulls away and I feel like all my hope goes with it.

I lean into Bram and try to catch my breath, to gain back my control. I wish he wasn't the one holding me and at the same time I'm glad he's here.

The only person who really seemed to care about the both of us so much.

You were a charity case, a wicked voice says to me inside my head and I ignore it because what had happened between us has no bearing now, not while my baby girl is on the verge of dying. Nothing else matters anymore.

Bram puts me in his car and then we speed off after the ambulance and to the hospital, the same one as last time. With any luck, I'll have the same doctor and that thought, this little bit of familiarity, brings me a tiny shred of calm.

This time there is no waiting in the emergency room. Bram and I are ushered down the hall toward the room Ava is in, and when a nurse asks if we are her parents, I feel myself nodding. Bram seemed ready to leave but the truth is too sticky to explain and at this moment I need someone like him here to hold my own hand when I need to be holding Ava's.

It's the same doctor as before but the news isn't the same. He says her insulin levels are so off the charts that it's becoming difficult to keep them where they need to be. His words dig deep and now I'm really afraid there won't be a happy ending. There will be no out. It will be one of those ironic ones, the type in a film noir where the mother loses the daughter but gains a husband. But the loss she feels is one that can never, ever, *ever* be replaced.

The doctor wants privacy and has brought in someone else, so Bram and I wait out in the hall, stuck in uncomfortable chairs and I'm rocking in it back and forth, my brain wanting to latch onto the horrid impossible. I keep imagining what it would feel like if they came out with bad news and it's akin to free-falling into Hell. It's so brutal and unbearable that I get dizzy even thinking about it.

Bram rubs my back as I curl up into a ball and try to breathe and stay in the moment and stop panicking. It's so damn hard. But his presence, his comfort, is relentless.

And all this time, he doesn't say anything. He doesn't apologize, he doesn't try to win me over – he doesn't even tell me that everything's going to be all right. Because he knows, as much as I do, that it's not all right. She's in there and it's not all right and no amount of saying it is ever going to make it true.

All Bram does is be there. It's simple.

He's just there.

And it's all I will need to get through.

I just hope that Ava, wherever she is in her head, her mind locked down by her betraying body, can feel him too.

...

"Nicola." Bram's voice breaks through the haze. "I got you a coffee."

I open my eyes and see him holding out a chipped Styrofoam cup filled with inky brown liquid.

"It tastes like bloody petrol," he says apologetically. "But it will help."

I straighten up in my seat and gingerly take it from him, shooting him a quick smile of thanks. I look over at Ava who is lying in the hospital bed, IVs everywhere and eyes closed. She looks more angelic than ever.

"How is she?"

He sits down next to me with a tired sigh. "She hasn't woken up. I think she had a funny dream because she was smiling at one point. The nurses say it's best to let her sleep. Her little system has undergone so much."

That it has. It was about 1am when the doctors were finally able to pull Ava out of her quasi-coma. She wasn't entirely with it at the time, but she recognized me and Bram and thank God she was too doped up she couldn't get emotional over him again.

After that, I pretty much stood vigil at her side, making up stories and telling them to her as she slept. Finally, I must have fallen asleep in the chair, utterly exhausted.

All the while, Bram was here, just like that first time, when I didn't know him at all.

He was there for us then.

He's there for us now.

But still, there's just so much time, space and distance between us, all that messy past to hold us down, that I'm not really sure how to make things right again.

I just think that I want to.

"Bram," I say softly.

He rubs his hand over his face and looks at me. His white dress shirt has the sleeves rolled up, a spot of coffee near the buttons. His hair is disheveled. His eyes are wide but red, his skin tired and grey. He looks like he hasn't gotten any sleep at all and I know he hasn't because of her.

And maybe me.

"Yeah," he says.

I take in a breath for courage. "I know this probably isn't the right time to be bringing this up but…I'm still mad at you."

A small, sad smile flashes on his face. "I know. And you have every right to be mad with me for as long as you want to."

"But I don't want to," I say and look at my hands because it's easier. "Being mad takes so much out of me. It's crippling…I don't want to regret you. That's not how I want to live, with regrets, even if it pains me."

"I don't want you to regret me either," he says and he puts his hand on my arm. I can feel his eyes on me, searching my face, searching for answers that I may not know myself. "Sweetheart. I'm sorry. Unbelievably sorry. I know there is nothing I can say or do to make you believe it, but just hear me out. Just know that it's true. I never meant to keep Taylor and Matthew from you, I wanted to tell you…I was just a coward and so bloody afraid that you'd leave me. No one wants to admit to someone that they were once a terrible person who did terrible things. I was afraid that if I showed that truth to you, it would scare you away for good. That you would forget about the person I became, the person I am."

I nod, wondering what I would have done if he had told me on his own time. It's impossible to know. I might have been okay with it. I might not have been. We might have been strong enough to handle it. Or maybe not.

I think back to what he had said when I told him I loved him. How everything happens in due time. But I think it's more about the *right* time.

"Just please listen to me when I say that you were never ever a charity case, okay?"

Ugh. That part still burns.

"Please," he repeats and I can feel his conviction. "Everything I did for you and Ava is because I wanted to. Because I liked you…a lot. Both of you. I just wanted to be with you. Maybe subconsciously I was trying to make amends for the things I've done or maybe it was the matter of properly helping someone when I finally had the means to do it. I just wanted to make you smile. That's it. That's really all there ever was. I wanted to make you smile because it seemed like such a hard thing to do. And if I could take care of you both, two girls who deserved it more than anyone I knew, then I would do that too."

"You took very good care of us," I tell him, sounding small.

"And I hope I made you smile."

Of course I have to smile at that. "You did that too. Always."

A fuzzy, warm kind of silence settles between us and I can't stop comparing the then and the now and how so much has changed, and so little at the same time.

"Nicola," he whispers and his voice melts my bones. I can't help but meet his eyes and in them I see everything

I've always wanted to see and not because I want to, because it's there.

"I love you," he says and at that moment I know it's true.

Because I can feel it. Because my heart is trying to fly. And I want to let go. Because I know it's going to boomerang right back to him.

"I am just simply in love with you," he says, his fingers stroking my jawline, down to my chin. "And there's not much more that I can say than that. I hope the words are enough because I know them here." He puts his hand at his chest. "And I had to know that first."

My eyes water just when I think I can't possibly have any tears left. My heart swells and swells and swells, threatening to spill over, to drown me, to wash me away.

I welcome it. Because having a heart full of his love, and my love for him, is the best feeling in the world.

"I still love you," I manage to tell him, my voice breaking. "I couldn't stop even if I tried. And I tried. I kept wanting to forget you but you were always still in me, no matter what I did." I swallow hard and he leans forward, kissing me as the tears slide down my cheeks.

I'd dreamed about these lips again and again. Even when I didn't want to, even when it hurt more than it did me good. I'd dreamed about them.

Now, they were here, kissing me, shedding my skin, making me wild and free.

Making love to my soul.

Suddenly the bed creaks, stirring me out of Bram's warm embrace and we break apart to see Ava staring at us in confusion. For a moment, I think she's going to lose her mind again, though who knows which way this time.

But she just smiles, brighter than the sun that's streaming in through her window.

"Are you two boyfriend and girlfriend now?" she asks, her voice a bit groggy but upbeat.

Bram squeezes my arm. "Would you like that?" he asks her.

She nods slowly. "Yes. Because you'll take me to Disneyland again."

I laugh and look at Bram. "Well, it looks like you owe this kid another trip."

"I owe this kid another trip," he jerks his thumb at himself. His smile turns wistful as he stares at me. "We're going to be okay," he says to me. "I promise. Me, you, her. We'll be great."

"Great," Ava says softly.

I kiss Bram on the forehead and get up, walking over to Ava.

"How are you feeling?" I ask her, putting my hand over her impossibly small one.

"Tired," she says. "Sleepy."

"No pain? You know where you are?"

She nods once. "Hospital. Something went wrong with my special disease, didn't it?"

I squeeze her hand. "It did. You got a bit excited when you saw Bram again. Sometimes if you get too excited, it becomes too much. But the doctors were able to help you, and from now on, I have to watch you a little closer, maybe try some new ouchies. But you'll be okay."

"I'll be great," she says sleepily. "Just like you and Bram."

She closes her eyes and drifts off again.

Bram comes up behind me, putting his strong, supportive arm around my waist and the two of us watch Ava as she dreams.

Chapter Twenty-Two

NICOLA

The next few days speed on like a rocket. Whereas everything in my life seemed to slog by in slow motion before, now it was blasting forward. There's been some bumps along the way but that's to be expected when everything around you does a 180, even if it's for the better.

The better, of course, is having Bram back in our lives. The worse is that it's taken a little bit for Ava to pull herself out of her whole episode. It's been three days and she spent a full one at the hospital, recovering. Luckily, James was proactive and he kicked in my health insurance the moment I got promoted, so there were no financial scares this time around.

I'm still at Kayla's, which is fine. Ava and I are used to it. Being back with Bram is so new and fresh still, and things have changed in the last two months that it's taking a while for us to get used to each other again. In fact, I haven't even slept with him after he told me he loved me. I know that's a bit shocking, but it hasn't felt right. Not yet, anyway.

Honestly, I haven't really been alone with Bram. Other than being at the hospital together, I'm still working my ass off at the Lion, refusing to relax even if he's back in my life.

This evening though, is quiet. It's a Saturday night but the city is going through a rare heatwave, complete with actual sunshine, so I guess everyone is hogging up all the prime patio space on the streets and by the bay. A stuffy Irish pub is the last place people want to be.

"Hey, gorgeous," I hear, that beautiful Scottish brogue breaking me out of my thoughts.

I straighten up from organizing the beer in the fridge and look over at the bar to see Bram strolling in toward me. He's wearing a suit – of course – but it's a light stone color and there's no tie, just his white dress shirt unbuttoned a few, showing off that sexy throat and summer tan. In his hands is a bouquet of pink and blue roses.

"Are those for me?" I ask, totally charmed by the flowers and the man holding them.

"Of course," he says, standing on the other side of the bar and handing them to me. "I realize that all this time, I never had a chance to properly wine and dine you. You know, like a gentleman would. All my wooing was through my pants."

I flush at that and grin. "Well, I can't say I objected to Bram McGregor's particular style of wooing."

"Even so," he goes on, "since we're all about starting over in one way or another, I'd like to ask you out on a date."

"Right now?"

He nods. "Aye. I called Kayla and she's agreed to keep watching Ava as long as I treat you right. Actually, she was a lot more, erm, brutal than that."

Kayla, God bless her.

"So, are you ready? Seems kind of dead in here." He eyes the place, biting his lip, as if this whole date thing has him a bit nervous. How cute.

I look over at James who's been pretending not to listen but actually has. "James?" I ask.

He waves at me dismissively. "Go."

So I do. Of course the only problem with going from bar to date is the fact that I don't have any nice clothes with me.

I grab my purse, hoping that at least my makeup and hair are holding up after the shift, and hook my arm around Bram's.

"I hope you're not taking me somewhere fancy because I don't have any nice clothes on me."

"Clothes?" he says, raising his brow and doing his best Doc Brown impression. "Where we're going we don't need *clothes*."

I giggle. "All right, weirdo. Naked restaurant it is."

"You'll see," is all he says, voice husky, and suddenly all I want is to never mind the date and just screw his brains out. It's been far, far too long and he feels far, far too good.

He takes me out into the hot, stuffy night and into his waiting Mercedes. We drive through the city and I get the impression we're just kind of meandering. I can't complain though. With the windows down, the breeze in my hair and Bram's warm hand on my thigh, it's a perfect night with only good things coming our way, I can tell.

"How is Matthew doing?" I ask him. I don't mean to bring him up but Bram's only talked about him in passing here and there. I know that Matthew and his mom live down in SoCal and they have their own little life going on. So far things seem wonderfully uncomplicated but still, I want Bram to know that it's okay to talk about him. I don't mind.

"He's fine," he says, his eyes gleaming under the passing streetlights as we begin to zig-zag down the famous Lombard Street, the most crooked street in the world. Normally going down the street makes me dizzy but tonight I feel nothing but alive.

Bram goes on, "I don't talk to him that often, you know. It's still a bit strange for both of us. Especially since we both knew about the other but we don't have that relationship whatsoever. He thinks I'm just some friend of his mom, even though he knows that I'm his father. I guess the word just doesn't apply other than in technical terms. But I'm all right with that…these things take time and I have no need to intrude on their little unit, you know?"

I can't help but smile softly. "I think you intruding on me and Ava's little unit was the best thing that could have happened to us."

He takes his eyes off the road to look at me. "Do you really mean that?"

"Of course," I tell him. "You changed our lives. And yeah, maybe it was a bit, turbulent, for a while there. But I think it sorted itself out."

He sighs, his hands gripping and ungripping the wheel. "You know, I just keep wanting to apologize. Every single day."

"Don't. You've said enough."

"I know," he says emphatically. "But it feels like it's not enough. You're too good for me, Nicola."

"No," I tell him. "I'm not. And you're not too good for me. I think we're good together and that's enough. It's more than enough."

Bram doesn't say anything to that and we drive through a beautiful, comfortable silence. We head across the Golden Gate Bridge and the city sparkles in the side-mirrors, a ghost in the night. I'm finally about to ask where we're actually going but he pulls the car off to the side and we climb the steep hills to a viewpoint overlooking the city.

There are a couple of cars there, tourists or locals or romantics taking in the sight of the glowing bridge. But we drive further down the lot and park at the end so we're completely alone.

"This doesn't look like dinner," I tell him.

He's looking at me like he's going to devour me and then I know what's really on the menu.

He jerks his head at the backseat and I crane my neck to look as he flicks on the interior light.

There's a picnic basket back there. I hadn't noticed it earlier. He leans back, twisting in his seat, and that wonderfully manly, fresh smell of his makes me tingly all over. I don't dare tell him that I used to sleep with an old shirt of his just to keep smelling him as I fell asleep at night, pretending he was there.

"Ta-da," he says, lifting up the basket. I see a bottle of red wine and a bunch of appetizers in colorful containers – antipasto, olives, bread, cheese, fruit, Greek salad, quinoa. It all looks absolutely fabulous. "I thought we could have our first date here. Can't get a better view than this."

We take out a blanket he has in the trunk and lay it on the grass at the foot of the car. He plays Lovage from his portable iPhone speakers and lights the scene with a few electric candles. We spread out the food and wine and we have ourselves a beautiful feast. It's just us and the city at our feet. I didn't think it was possible to fall in love with Bram McGregor all over again, but it is.

It so fucking *is*.

And after we're done and the white chocolate covered raspberries are licked off each other's fingers, we start, well, we start licking more than that. And I discover my love for him goes further and further.

We make love on that blanket, like the exhibitionists we are. The other patrons of the parking lot are too far away to see, and they couldn't anyway from their angle, but it wouldn't matter anyway. Beneath this rare open night sky and these blinding stars that the fog so often hides, we are deeper into each other than we ever have been before. When he pushes inside me, I feel so complete that it brings tears to my eyes and when I come, softly, whimpering into his sweat-soaked neck, those tears unleash.

"Why are you crying, sweetheart?" he whispers, voice slow and sated.

"Because I love you," I tell him. "And I can't imagine anything better."

He brushes my tears away and doesn't pull out, even though we've both come. He stays in me until he can't anymore.

Later, when we pull up to Kayla's apartment, he puts the car in park and then twists in his seat to face me.

"Nicola," he says, sounding grave.

I swallow, suddenly on alert. "What?"

He takes my hands in his and squeezes them. He clears his throat and looks down at my hands. "I'm going to ask you something. And then I'm going to ask Ava. And if you both say yes, then I might just be the luckiest fucker in the entire world." He pauses, his eyes flitting to mine. "Will you both move in with me?"

"Are you kidding?" I say, wanting to laugh. "Of course we'll move in with you."

"Not in my apartment building, I mean in the actual apartment. You'd be sharing it with me."

"Well, you'd be sharing it with me. And a five-year-old."

"But that's a yes?"

I break out into a stupid grin. "That's a yes."

He kisses me, fast and deep and beautifully. Then we make our way upstairs to my soon-to-be-ex apartment.

By luck – or bad babysitting skills – Ava is still awake, playing a game with Kayla.

"Bram!" she says surprised, and runs over to him. He picks her up and gives her a big bear hug.

"What are you doing up, little one? It's past your bedtime." He eyes Kayla. "Have you been giving Aunt Kayla trouble?"

I smile at the way he's such a natural around her. He puts her back down on the ground and she looks at him shyly.

"I couldn't sleep," she says.

"She wouldn't sleep," Kayla fills in.

Bram grins at them both and then crouches down to Ava's level. "Listen, Ava. I have an important big girl question for you. Are you ready for it?"

She nods, mouth grim and looking overly serious. "I'm ready."

"How would you like to move in with me? Your mom will be there too."

Her eyes widen and she breaks into a smile. She glances up my way.

"Is this true?"

"Yes, angel. If you say that we can, we can both live with Bram."

"What do you say?" Bram asks.

Ava actually looks like she's going to cry. She throws her little arms around Bram's neck and says, muffled, "Yes."

My heart, my soul, my ovaries are all simultaneously combusting.

This man.

This damn man.

I hear a sniffle from beside me and Kayla is actually crying. *Kayla* who *never* cries.

"Kayla," I say, in mock surprise. "You're not soulless after all."

She glares at me and angrily wipes a tear away. "I'm just happy that you guys are finally leaving." But then she huffs off to the kitchen yelling, "This calls for champagne!" over her shoulder.

It calls for a lot of things.

But most of all, it calls for me to count my blessings. Because standing here, surrounded by the people I love most, I realize I have a ton of them.

"Bram," Ava says, pulling on his sleeve. "When we move in, can I have a trampoline?"

I roll my eyes. She's been asking for one for as long as she's learned how to pronounce it properly.

"We'll see," Bram says good-naturedly.

"Can I have a pony too? Mommy won't let me have a pony."

He looks at me and smiles. "We'll have to see about that one, too. I think your mum is going to be calling a lot of the shots."

She pauses, thinking.

Then. "Bram, can I have a bugosaur?"

"I don't even know what that is."

I laugh. "Ava, if you want, you can have a bugosaur."

"Yay!" she cries out and then runs to our bedroom. Thank God for fictional creatures.

Kayla brings over the champagne and we each take a flute. We raise them in the air for a toast.

"To new beginnings," Kayla says. "And getting my apartment back."

"To love," I say. "And not giving up on it."

"To Nicola's arse," Bram says, "and the fact that I'll see more of it."

I roll my eyes but I clink to that anyway.

We finish our drinks and then it's time for Bram to go home. I stand outside in the hall with him, exchanging one long, sweet kiss, his hands wrapped around my waist, my fingers in his thick, soft hair.

"Tomorrow," he says, murmuring into my neck, "you'll come live with me."

"Tomorrow, I'll be all yours."

And the day after that.

And the day after that.

I'll be his forever.

Epilogue

NICOLA

Six Months Later

"Bram-a-lama-ding-dong!" Ava yells at the top of her lungs.

Matthew can't help but join in. "Bram-a-lama-ding-dong!"

The two of them run ahead while Taylor yells at them to "come back, where do you think you are, Disneyland?"

Because of course, yes, we are in Disneyland. We try and go every time we make the trip down to visit Taylor, Irving and Matthew.

"Don't you find it wrong that the kids keep using the word *dong*?" Bram whispers to me, as we make our way through the crowds.

I giggle. "You're a pervert."

"I'm serious. And you're on Team Perv too, missy."

It's Christmas time and Disneyland is in full swing with the decorations and festivities and the SoCal sunshine is such a welcome respite to all of San Francisco's grey. The more we visit Matthew and crew, the more I get attached to the area. I may not want to live in San Bernardino, but anywhere on the coast would be just fine, and no more expensive than SF.

But Bram's making some real progress with his building, so we're probably staying put in the city for the time being. Thanks to the backing of Lachlan, his rugby-playing cousin and wannabe tycoon, and his temporary wooing of a local heiress, they were able to start up a non-profit and have money rolling in to not only pay off the mortgage and provide housing to those in need, but also the potential to open another development.

Now, Lachlan is back in Scotland and he took Kayla back with him. It's a long and crazy story of how they got together— and one I didn't see coming—but it seems that Kayla finally met her match in that macho Scot. I just keep thinking she'll arrive back home in tears, wanting to talk to me and Steph about her drama but so far so good.

Obviously I moved out of Kayla's apartment, so at least I know she wasn't fleeing the country on account of me. Ava and I are happily living with Bram while my old place is rented out at a low-rate to someone who really needs it.

And now, now things are finally back on track. They feel right. It's all coming together. As cheesy as this is to say, and yeah, maybe it's a bit presumptuous too, we're starting to feel like a family. When I'm not at home, Bram usually is, so we take turns caring for Ava. She hasn't had an incident since and has been really good. I know her disease is something we'll always have to watch out for and monitor, at least until she gets old enough to do it herself.

I've gone back to just working nights at the Lion. I did the assistant manager thing for long enough but the more I worked, the less time I had to take my designs to the next level. Bram saw my frustration and said that if I made it my goal to concentrate 100% on my clothing line, that I could quit the bar and he'd take care of me. Naturally my pride didn't like that very much, so we compromised. I still work there as a bartender but I only do nights three times a week. The rest of the time, I'm working on my career.

I think my next leap is happening soon. It involves me renting a space in a warehouse for a week, but Stephanie guaranteed that if I could get a line of t-shirts out, she'd carry them in her online store and help me find other distributors as well.

It's all baby steps for us, but it's happening.

In due time, as Bram would say.

Bram would also say, it's Bramtastic.

"You guys are the slowest couple I've ever met," Taylor yells at us, waving for us to get our legs moving and hurry up. We're walking down the fake Hollywood street in California Adventure and Ava and Matthew have spotted Mike and Sully from Disney's *Monster's Inc.* walking around. Though there are two years between Ava and Matthew, they get along great and their one love in common is dinosaurs (well, actually now it's monsters, which is why they're going apeshit for the poor hot people trapped in the costumes).

We all take pictures and Irving, Taylor's new boyfriend, gets a good one of this crazy, mixed family. While the kids still fawn over the characters like they're celebrities, fun-loving screams draw my attention to the rest of the park.

Every time we come here we always end up on the kiddie rides and we never seem to have the time or the opportunity to go on the big kid ones. You know, the ones that are actually fun.

"You know what?" I say to Bram. "I'm not leaving this park until—"

"We shag behind the Hollywood backlot," he quickly suggests, and I know he's completely serious.

"No," I tell him, elbowing him in the side. "For the last time, IKEA sex was the limit for me. At least we traumatized an old couple, I'm not going to do that to children." He seems to pout. I roll my eyes. "What I was going to say was, I'm not leaving this park until I go on a ride that will have me screaming my face off."

He tilts his head and gives me that infamous smirk. "I know just the ride."

"Bram, if you say it's your cock, I'm going to murder you," I hiss at him, glad we're out of ear reach from the kids. And Taylor and Irving too. I'm sure they don't want to hear any of our cock talk either.

Bram is still smirking at me so I fill in. "I mean it. An actual ride that you do with people. Like the Tower of Terror. Or California Screaming."

"I reckon California Screaming," he says. "Because of the word *screaming*."

"Then it's on." I squeeze his hand and then wave at the gang. "Hey everyone, I thought I would let you all know that Bram and I are going on the rollercoaster and you can't do a thing about it."

Matthew stomps his foot. "I want to go on the rollercoaster!"

He's tall like his dad probably was at his age, so there's a chance he actually might be able to ride the coaster. But not this time. This time it's just for us.

"Oh, Matthew," Taylor admonishes him. "Let them have their fun."

So the six of us wind our way through Cars Land and the fake San Francisco until we're at the perpetually cheery Paradise Pier. We stand there for a bit, watching the coaster cars zoom past on the epic California Screaming, a ride that seems to do what the name suggests – make you scream.

"You sure about this?" Bram asks before we get into the line-up.

"Don't tell me you're a pussy," I tease him.

He pulls me to him, burying his warm lips into my neck. "Speaking of pussy, how about we send Ava off with Matthew and Taylor after we get back to the hotel?"

"Oh, it would be so obvious why."

He shrugs, not caring. "So? I think it's too late for us to pretend we don't have sex." We both look over at Ava and Matthew who are chasing each other on the faux boardwalk. He's right about that.

So we get in line for the ride, passing the time by playing games on our iPhones and finding out who can tell the stupidest jokes (Bram wins at that, obviously). It's nice though, just to be with him and him alone. Even though we're surrounded by people – and both insanely jealous of the couple in front of us who had the smarts to bring two margaritas along for the wait – it feels like we're in our own little world. I'm reminded of just why I love this sexy Scot so much.

Finally it's time to get in. I'm giddy and Bram looks a tad unnerved, which I find adorable. The bars lower automatically from above us, locking us in place so we can't fall out.

Happy, tinkling music comes on from the speakers and we slowly move forward, rounding the corner until we come to our holding spot where we wait with building anticipation until we will be shot forward and straight up the first hill.

"Mommy!" I look up to see Ava waving at me. Everyone has gathered along the railing above the tracks, ready for us to take off.

"Have fun!" yells Matthew.

My heart speeds up and I'm suddenly nervous. Just that sweet, intense anticipation. Kind of like sex. I grip the bar lowered across me as the chirpy countdown goes on, starting at *three*.

"No regrets, right?" Bram asks me with a disarming grin.

Two.

"No regrets." I smile right back at him. "Not in this life."

One.

We take off into the future.

Acknowledgements

As usual, quite a few people to thank. I wrote this book after a lengthy and much-needed break. Unfortunately by the time I went back into the swing of things, my husband and I just moved into our new house. First-time homeowners, yay! But moving and writing are hard to do at the same time. Actually anything plus writing is hard to do and the same could be said for moving. Somehow it got done though, it always does.

But I think it went so easily because of Bram "the man" McGregor. He was such a joy to write that I rarely felt myself stressing over this book, even when I was down to the wire, even when I didn't have an office to write in because it was piled high with boxes that I just couldn't deal with because all my energy had to go into writing. Bram helped me by being so Bramtastic! (yeah I know, stop with the Bram puns).

Of course Bram wasn't the only one who helped. Ali "Claimed Bram" Hymer was a great help, especially in making sure the "mom" scenes were working. Dyann "Hot Nurse" Tufts for ensuring all my medical jargon and diabetes specifics were correct. Sandra "#1 Pervert" Cortez for her input and enthusiasm for car sex. Laura "Eaten by Bears" Helseth for her eagle eyes. Latyoa "Word" Smith (get it… wordsmith) for being a great editor and for having faith in me way back when Sins & Needles came out – it was her love of Ellie Watt and the crew (hell, her love of Dex and Perry even before that) that brought me into the Hachette family and my first publishing deal and I'm so thankful she's still such a great supporter and a fan.

Props also go to everyone on InstaBram – I mean, Instagram, for your teasers and raunchiness and genuine love of books and book boyfriends. My Instagram account feels like family – no wonder I'm on there all the damn time (@authorhalle). All the ladies at #TeamPerv (hasthtag dicks) and dem Whores (who are also pervs, just more subdued) and all the hard-working bloggers for reading and reviewing ARCS and just being so damn fabulous. Dani Sanchez for being the best Girl Friday.

Here's a shoutout to everyone in their thirties and beyond who feel they're expected to grow up – don't. Don't worry if you still feel like you're not where you're "supposed" to be and you don't have a total handle on life. Being an adult is hard for everyone, you might as well have some fun while you're at it. Embrace your inner child, take chances and live with no regrets!

Last but not least, Mr. MacKenzie and Mr. Bruce. I'm always on your team, thanks for being on mine.

Want to contact me? I read every email (all the *nice* ones that my assistant forwards to me, anyway) and try my best to respond: authorkarinahalle@gmail.com

I'm also on Facebook

Twitter: @metalblonde

And I am addicted to Instagram (seriously, I post a lot of pics!): @authorhalle

Keep reading for an excerpt from **Racing the Sun – available in July from Atria Books**

BLURB: It's time for twenty-four-year-old Amber MacLean to face the music. After a frivolous six months of backpacking through New Zealand, Australia, and Southeast Asia, she finds herself broke on the Mediterranean without enough money for a plane ticket home to California. There are worse places to be stuck than the gorgeous coastline of southern Italy, but the only job she manages to secure involves teaching English to two of the brattiest children she's ever met.

It doesn't help that the children are under the care of their brooding older brother, Italian ex-motorcycle racer Desiderio Larosa. Darkly handsome and oh-so-mysterious, Derio tests Amber's patience and will at every turn—not to mention her hormones.

But when her position as teacher turns into one as full-time nanny at the crumbling old villa, Amber finds herself growing closer to the enigmatic recluse and soon has to choose between the safety of her life back in the States and the uncertainty of Derio's closely guarded heart.

Racing the Sun

After I put the kids to bed, I gather some of the leftovers from dinner onto a plate, pour a glass of water, and put it on a tray. I carry it over to the office and knock loudly.

"Derio, I have dinner here for you," I say quickly before he can tell me to get lost. "You should really eat something. The kids actually liked it so I think you should witness the fact that I finally made something appetizing. It might never happen again."

I wait a few seconds and then put the tray on the ground outside the door. I'm about to walk away when—lo and behold—it actually opens and he peers at me with a cocked brow.

"*Buonasera*," he says, his voice sounding extra throaty tonight, which equals extra sexy—and he's speaking in Italian to boot.

"*Buonasera*," I tell him, trying to peek inside. "You're not in your underwear again, are you?"

He gives me a lopsided smile. "I can be. Would you like to come in?"

"Are we going to drink scotch again? Because something tells me you've probably had enough."

"Come." He steps back, disappearing into the office. "Bring the food."

I give him a look that says I'm not his servant 24/7 but bring the tray in anyway and set it on the desk. He goes to the door and closes it. "Would you like a drink?"

I should say no. I sigh. "Yes."

"*Buono*," he says. He goes and pours me a glass. He hands it to me, his eyes focused on mine the whole time, as if holding me in place. Because he's drunk I can't read them for the life of me. He seems to be in a playful mood again but I'm not putting stock in anything Derio-related anymore.

I stare down at the glass. "Did you drug this?"

He smiles. "No."

I squint at him. "Why are you smiling then?"

"I like to smile at you," he says.

I let out a dry laugh. "Right. No, Signor Larosa, you like to frown at me. Glower at me. Glare at me. Or just stare blankly at me like I'm not even there. But smiling at me? Not so much."

The smile slides right off his face. I raise my glass at him. "See, right there. Back to Mr. Angry Face."

"You really don't think much of me, do you?" he asks. His voice is strained and a little rough around the edges.

I take a small sip and suck on my top lip for a moment as it burns. "Actually, I think a lot of you."

"All bad."

"Didn't you say the bad things were the good things?" I ask him.

"Are you comparing me to a bad habit?"

I cock my head, considering that. "Maybe I am. But I happen to like a lot of my bad habits."

"Like the drinking."

"Yes."

"The eating."

"Yes."

"The sex."

A small shiver runs through me as my lips twist into a smile. Even the word sex sounds amazing coming from his mouth. "Especially the sex. It's the best bad habit of all."

He doesn't smile at that—no surprise—but the intensity in his gaze deepens. His eyes burn me, and his look becomes smoldering. He's making me feel like I'm standing in his office completely naked, not wearing the same billowy tank top and skinny jeans I was wearing earlier.

"Stay right there," he commands me in a hushed tone.

My heart does a few solid thuds in my throat. I swallow uneasily. "Okay."

I know I'm staring at him with wide Bambi eyes, I can't help it. I follow his every movement as he comes around the desk and walks toward me.

He stops in front of me, so tall and large. I can see his pulse tick along his throat and the dark danger in his eyes as they peer at me through black lashes.

I grip the glass of scotch hard, afraid of what's going to happen next.

Because something has to happen; something *is* happening.

I've never been looked at this way before—stripped bare by a carnal gaze—and it would be a shame to let it go to waste.

He places both hands on either side of my face and I feel so small, so conquered, so…coveted. His skin is hot and rough to the touch and alights my entire body until I'm buzzing with fiery anticipation.

"I need to kiss you," he says, and it's the smartest thing he's said all day. "Please."

I try and say "okay" but it catches in my throat. I saw this coming—a man can't stare at a woman like that without kissing her—but it still unwinds me like a spool of thread.

He's still staring at me, his brow furrowing, casting shadows down his perfect face. His lips are just out of reach. "I need to know if I can feel anything. I want to feel something."

There's a quiet desperation in his voice. It makes me ache for him.

Then he leans in and kisses me. His lips are soft, perhaps a little unsure as they press against mine, but then the pressure increases, our mouths yielding in unison and it feels like drinking and breathing and living. He tastes like the honey tones of scotch and of faded smoke and mint. It's an elixir that flows down my throat and right between my legs, and his probing tongue stirs it further.

My tongue teases his back as it slides into my mouth, stoking the wildfires. Our kiss deepens and his hands find their way into my hair. He lets out a low moan that reverberates through me and I gasp in response, the glass almost slipping from my hands. I want to pull him into me, I want more of this, all the time. My free hand slips around his back and presses into his firm, hard muscles. I'm so incredibly turned on that I'm seconds from just throwing the scotch across the room and dropping to my knees. I want to take him in my mouth and make him moan again,

I want to make him feel something. I want to make him feel me. I want to know what he looks like when he comes, if it brings him some kind of peace.

I want so much more than the hunger and desire he's already giving me, our lips, tongue, mouth heating up, our kiss fueling our needs and our needs threatening to take over. I wonder if he's afraid of this kiss because to me it feels a bit like drowning. But we're not drowning alone. We're clinging onto each other like a life raft.

I'm so insatiable now, so greedy, that I almost whimper when he pulls away. He holds me, fisting my hair, and presses his forehead against mine, eyes pinched shut and breathing hard. I gulp in the air, unsure if we're going to stop or if I need to refuel to go further. I could go all night and every night after that.

My lips tingle now and a few beats pass.

"Did you feel anything?" I ask softly, hopefully.

He shakes his head ever so slightly, his forehead damp against mine. "No," he murmurs. "I felt everything."

Look for Racing the Sun on bookshelves on July 28th 2015. I wrote this book inspired by my favorite book of all time – Jane Eyre – and it's set in Italy, where I actually went in October to research, so I can tell you…this book is hot, romantic and legit. Can't wait for you all to read it!

Printed in Great Britain
by Amazon